HEART
QUEST.

*More to Love*

HeartQuest brings you romantic fiction
with a foundation of biblical truth.
Adventure, mystery, intrigue, and suspense
mingle in these heartwarming stories of
men and women of faith striving to build
a love that will last a lifetime.

May HeartQuest books sweep you
into the arms of God, who longs for you
and pursues you always.

CAMP HOPE

# Shadowed Secrets

## LOIS RICHER

*Romance fiction from*
Tyndale House Publishers, Inc., Wheaton, Illinois

**www.heartquest.com**

Visit Tyndale's exciting Web site at www.tyndale.com

*TYNDALE* is a registered trademark of Tyndale House Publishers, Inc.

Tyndale's quill logo is a trademark of Tyndale House Publishers, Inc.

*HeartQuest* is a registered trademark of Tyndale House Publishers, Inc.

Check out the latest about HeartQuest books at www.heartquest.com

Edited by Lorie Popp

Designed by Ron Kaufmann

Published in association with the literary agency of Janet Kobobel Grant, Books & Such, 4788 Carissa Ave., Santa Rosa, CA 95405.

Scripture quotations are taken from the *Holy Bible*, New Living Translation, copyright © 1996. Used by permission of Tyndale House Publishers, Inc., Wheaton, Illinois 60189. All rights reserved.

Scripture quotations are taken from *The Living Bible* copyright © 1971. Used by permission of Tyndale House Publishers, Inc., Wheaton, Illinois 60189. All rights reserved.

Scripture quotations are taken from the *Holy Bible*, New International Version®. NIV®. Copyright © 1973, 1978, 1984 by International Bible Society. Used by permission of Zondervan Publishing House. All rights reserved.

**Library of Congress Cataloging-in-Publication Data**

Richer, Lois.
   Shadowed secrets / Lois Richer.
     p. cm. — (Camp Hope ; #3)
     ISBN 9-8423-6438-2 (sc)
     1. Fugitives from justice—Fiction.   2. Intelligence officers—Fiction.   3. Fathers and daughters—Fiction.
4. Canada, Northern—Fiction.   5. Ex-convicts—Fiction.   I. Title.
   PR9199.4.R53S53 2005
   813′.6—dc22                              2004026560

Printed in the United States of America

09  08  07  06  05
9  8  7  6  5  4  3  2  1

*This book is dedicated to the Father,*
*who knows our deepest secrets*
*and loves us anyway.*

# ACKNOWLEDGMENTS

Books are a community effort. My community includes a host of wonderful people. Thanks to the folks at Tyndale—Anne Goldsmith, Lorie Popp, and all the others who work so hard. You are a blessing. To my agent extraordinaire, Janet Kobobel Grant—thanks for being my encourager and an eternal optimist.

Hugs to my friend and best supporter Aven Paetkau—we're two oddballs in the soup of life.

A hearty thank you to Torch Trail Bible Camp for allowing me to poke my nose in.

Grateful appreciation to our local detachment of the RCMP for always being willing to answer just one more question.

And to Barry—thanks for letting me dream.

# PROLOGUE

*20 years ago*

"Betsey wants to give you a hug, Mama."

Angie lifted her beloved doll and gently placed it beside her mother in the big saggy bed. "Isn't Betsey pretty?" she whispered, careful to keep her voice very quiet.

"She's lovely, dear." Mama's white fingers touched the wrinkled dress at the back, fiddled with the spun gold hair, then settled the doll next to her on the pillow. "Sweetheart, you know I'm very sick, don't you?"

"Uh-huh."

"Remember when we talked about heaven? How God doesn't let anybody in heaven get sick?"

Angie nodded, her mind drawing pictures of the golden streets Mama had talked about.

"I think God is going to take me to heaven pretty soon, honey."

"You mean you're not going to get better?" A tear slipped from Angie's eye and slithered down her cheek. She dashed it away. Daddy said only babies cried. "You won't be my mommy anymore?"

"I'll always be your mommy, Angie. Always. But I'm too sick to look after you. Daddy's going to do that."

"Daddy gets mad at me."

"It's because of his face. The burns hurt him a lot, sweetie. Sometimes they make him say things he doesn't mean, but I know he loves you. He'll look after you."

"Are you sure, Mama?"

"Very sure. Daddy loves you." Her mother closed her eyes, rested for a few minutes.

Mama was always right. But this time Angie wondered if she was too sick to understand. Angie didn't think Daddy loved her. He yelled at her because she couldn't do things, because she didn't know things.

"You're very busy making a house with your blocks, aren't you?"

"Yes, Mama." A very nice house, a happy house where the daddy wasn't mad and the mommy wasn't sick.

"I know it will be lovely. Would it be all right if Betsey kept me company while you finish building that house?"

Angie thought about it. Betsey was her very favorite doll in the whole world. But Mama wouldn't hurt her. Mama had made Betsey for her birthday.

"Okay. Betsey can sleep with you. But don't let Daddy see her. Daddy doesn't like Betsey. He says playing with dollies is for babies."

"I think a doll like Betsey is for anyone who needs a hug now and then. I'd like a hug from both of you." Mama smoothed over Angie's topsy-turvy curls. "Never forget that I love you. With all my heart. I've prayed that God will show you how much He loves you too. He'll always love you." Mama's voice got quiet, and her eyelids closed. "No matter what," she whispered. Then her eyelids drooped and she went to sleep.

"Yes, Mama." Angie tiptoed from the room and went back to her blocks.

She ate two apples for supper that night and got ready for bed all by herself. She sat beside Mama for a long time, until the house got cold and dark. But Mama didn't wake up. When it was all dark outside, Angie heard her daddy drive into the yard.

"Good night, Mama." She leaned over, kissed the pale white cheek, then lifted Betsey from the bed. "I love you."

Her mother's eyelids fluttered. "I love you too, darling. More than anything."

The whisper came so quietly that Angie had to lean near to hear it.

"God loves you, Angie. He'll watch over you. You take care of Betsey, my darling. And love Daddy. Good-bye."

The back door opened.

Angie kissed her Mama's soft cheek once more, then scurried down the steps and into her own room. After she tucked Betsey into her hiding place she climbed into bed. She closed her eyes and made herself breathe very slowly when Daddy looked inside. She kept breathing slowly long after he left, until she fell asleep.

There was a noise during the night, a bad sound that awakened and scared Angie. After a long time, she grabbed Betsey and climbed up the stairs to talk to Mama. But her father was in that room. She heard several voices, and Daddy was arguing with someone. He sounded very angry.

Angie didn't like it when Daddy got angry. She hid in her secret place and stayed there until the house was quiet again. After a long time people went downstairs; there was no more arguing. Angie slipped out of the hiding place and crept to her own bedroom. Snuggled up in the big bed, she pulled the pillow over her ears and asked Mama's God to please help.

But God didn't help because in the morning Daddy told her that Mama was gone and she wasn't ever coming back.

# CHAPTER ONE

*October*
*Present Day*

Y ou're not listening to me," Angie Grant said. "I can't come back, not ever. Getting me into the Mounties was the best thing you could have done for me, but if I'd known the RCMP would transfer me back to my hometown, I wouldn't have joined."

"You weren't going to be stationed here forever," Rick Mercer insisted.

"It seemed like it." She twiddled the phone cord around her finger, watched it curl away.

"Angie—"

"You like it there. You've got a promotion and you're happy. I understand that and I'm glad. But it's not the same for me. Every nook, every corner, every neighbor, every back road has a memory for me that I don't want to revisit. I've moved on."

"You're right. I do like it here."

Her skin rippled at the low growl of his voice. She'd missed that quiet assurance, the soft thread of caring that permeated his speech.

"I wouldn't say I'm happy though, Ang. I miss you too much. I miss our Sunday afternoon football sessions, the Friday night barbeques, and your laugh." When she didn't respond, his sigh drained into silence. Then his tone dropped to that gentle brush of concern she'd longed to hear again. "He's not here anymore. I know it's hard, Angie, but you have to forgive—"

"Hard?" she scoffed, irritated beyond measure that Rick had to bring it up now. "Hard? Mowing the lawn when it's a hundred and ten degrees and you haven't eaten for three days is hard. Trying to stave off creditors so you'll have some place to sleep tonight is hard. Forgiveness? That's impossible."

"But your mother's house and land—"

"Can rot and blow away into oblivion as far as I'm concerned. I won't be there to care." Angie gulped down the memories and wondered who she was trying to convince. "I've moved on, Rick. I'm not who I was, thank God. That weak, sniveling victim finally wised up and learned how to look after herself. Get on with your life, just as I'm getting on with mine. Don't wait for me. Don't look for me. Don't hope I'll come back. I won't."

The chasm of silence forced her to realize how harsh she'd been. Rick was the only one who'd ever cared, and now she'd hurt him. Tears dripped onto the receiver. She wiped them away.

"I wish it could be different. I wish I could repay you for what you did, for helping me, for freeing me. But I can't come back any more than I can maintain some kind of relationship. I can't love anyone. *He* made sure of that. Anyway, I'm not sure I even believe in love."

Rick couldn't have heard that hiccup in her voice, could he? Angie swallowed, checking her watch to ensure her call couldn't be traced. Time to cut it short and get on with her job.

"It's better to face the truth. I love what I do. CSIS is far beyond anything I ever expected. Security and intelligence work is full of change, never boring. Finally I've found something I'm good at. I feel alive."

"Where are you now?"

"Can't tell you that. Sorry. It's classified." She glanced out the window, saw a car pull into the driveway next door. "Something's going on. I have to go."

She froze, fingers gripping the phone, every nerve on high alert as a man walked to the front door of the safe house and pushed it open. That was odd. The orders were to keep all the doors locked—always. She waited for the rush of security.

Nothing.

Five agents inside that house and none of them had picked up on this guy? A squeak outside sent every instinct prickling.

"Take care of yourself, Rick." The whisper slipped out just before she hung up. "Good-bye."

*Thud, thud.* Who was banging on her front door? Then she heard a gunshot from next door.

Angie switched off the light, moved to the window, and grabbed her binoculars. In the darkness she could make out two men she recognized from mug shots approaching the house. The third was an unknown. All three had guns. Though she panned every window, she saw none of the agents she was supposed to work with. Angie picked up the phone, dialed a number, and said one word: "Breached."

Another sound, this time at her own back door.

Angie reached under her pant leg, closed her fingertips around the Luger, pulled it up, and aimed. "Freeze!"

"Angel?" The door swung open to reveal a six-year-old with platinum curls framing a face mostly occupied by huge chocolate eyes. Chubby arms clutched a wiggling springer spaniel to her chest.

Angie swung the gun down, hiding it behind her back. Joe was lead agent on Kelly Blair. It didn't make sense that he'd let the kid walk over here.

Unless something was wrong.

"There are some bad men in my house and my daddy is asleep," the little girl whispered. She glanced over one shoulder, shivered, then trained her gaze on Angie once more.

"Sweetheart—"

"Are you my guardian angel?"

Angel? Her? Angie almost laughed, but those eyes snagged her heart and tugged just as someone struck her front door with a resounding thud.

She made up her mind in that instant. "That's exactly what I am, Kelly. Your guardian angel in person. My name is Angie. And now it's time for us to fly out of here."

She seized the dog in one hand, her bag and the child's hand in the other, then headed out the breezeway toward the garage. It took two minutes to belt Kelly in, squeeze the dog beside her, push the key into the ignition. Thirty seconds stretched to eternity as the garage door slid open.

Angie gunned the engine, pulled onto the street, and raced into the night, knowing another agent would show up at the house to get the details. All she had to figure out now was where to hide. Three safe houses in three days, all of them discovered—hiding wasn't going to be easy. Presumably Joe and Zach were out of the picture. So it was up to Angie. This time she'd tell no one where they were going.

Except—she didn't know herself.

Rick's reminder returned to haunt her. The house was still there, empty and silent. Full of memories.

No! She couldn't go back. Never back to that hell. Shame, degradation, despair—all of it waited there to drag her down into a bottomless abyss where life was endured, not lived.

Thanks to Rick she was free of it. And she intended to stay that way. In the meantime she had to find another home for the child. Just until someone else took over.

Angie drove into the night. In spite of her resolve, the memories rushed back to haunt her. Her neck tautened; her fingers gripped the steering wheel as the cloak of dark shadows from the past waited to pounce.

Not this time. She pushed them away, caught the sheen of a single headlight in her rearview mirror, and knew she was being followed. "Time to go." Pressing the accelerator, she took the corner too fast and fought to recover control.

"Angel?"

It took a minute to realize Kelly's moniker was going to stick. "Yes?" She'd thought the tyke asleep, hoped she'd miss out on this part of the night.

"Are we going to crash?"

"No way, sweetheart. We're going to be just fine." Angie didn't have time to check how her response went down. She was too busy threading her way through the city.

"I think I should pray. Daddy says whenever you're afraid, you should pray." From the backseat the soft whisper of the Lord's Prayer began.

Angie sped around a traffic circle, cutting off other cars, ignoring rights-of-way, but she could not lose the biker. Through some perverse twist of city planning, she finally ended up in a cul-de-sac, with nowhere to go. She cut her lights and engine . . . waiting.

Seconds later the Harley roared up behind. Angie twisted the key, but her engine stalled. She tried again and again, her eyes on the rearview mirror.

A foot hit the pavement.

She had to go—now! The engine finally roared to life. But it was too late.

A car pulled up in front of her, blocking her exit.

She'd failed. Again. Angie slapped her hands against the steering wheel. "I'm sorry, sweetheart. I tried."

"It's okay. God will help us. I know He will."

"You hold on to that thought." Angie pulled out her gun as the shadowed figure approached. *Please don't let a stray bullet hit Kelly.*

Her door was yanked open.

"I'm praying, Angel!"

"Good, sweetie." Angie offered the words without hope. She didn't have any illusions about God.

He was never there when she needed Him.

"Aw, come on! It's not even nine o'clock yet."

Sergeant Rick Mercer pulled the pillow over his head, trying to pretend he couldn't hear the shrill summons of his bedside phone. To no avail.

"This better be good," he growled into the receiver.

"Happy New Year to you too, Rick."

The laughing voice made him sit up straight, brought the clarity of the morning into startling focus, even though he'd been on duty at 3 a.m. closing down an out-of-control New Year's party.

"Angie? Is that you?"

"Who else? I suppose you worked a double shift last night." It wasn't a question. "Still playing the Good Samaritan?"

"Just doing my job."

"Yeah. Sure. Goody Two-shoes in a uniform."

He ignored the teasing gibe, content to revel in the sweet resonance of her voice. But after a minute his brain kicked in. Something was wrong or she wouldn't have called. "Where are you, Ang?"

"You know I can't say. I need a favor."

"Name it." Angie Grant was asking *him* for help? Things must be really bad.

"It's just . . . I got to thinking about the house. You were right to remind me. Can you check it out and make sure everything's okay? I thought about renting it out, but I haven't had time."

He frowned. Angie hated her former home, and he didn't blame her. Her father, Syd Grant, was a crook. The fact that he was now in jail probably hadn't helped Angie forget the stigma his actions had attached to her. But none of that explained why she was suddenly so worried about a place she once couldn't wait to get away from.

"I'm sure Camp Hope would love to rent it from time to time," Rick said. "They've been looking for housing for the camp speakers who bring their families. Something a little isolated from regular activities so they'll have privacy but near enough to still be involved. Since your land abuts theirs, your place would be perfect."

"Whatever. I just want to make sure nobody breaks in and falls through the floor or hurts themselves on something and sues me. You know?"

He didn't. But if it meant keeping her on the phone, listening to her low soft voice a little longer, he'd agree to almost anything.

"I'll send you some money. You should get it soon. Use it for whatever repairs you find. I'll send more when I can."

"Uh . . . okay." He paused, waited. "Angie?"

"Yeah?"

"When are you going to come home for a visit?"

Silence hung between them.

When she spoke, her voice barely carried across the line. "I don't know. I miss you, but going back to that house—" She fell silent.

Angie had called Rick exactly twice since she'd left a year ago, just before Christmas. This was the only time she'd even hinted that she missed him.

Rick swallowed the huge lump in his throat and prayed for her silently. "I wish I were there, so I could help you. Are you okay, Ang? Is anything wrong?"

She laughed, but it wasn't her usual chuckle. "Wrong? You could say that. But don't worry. I'll figure it out." Her voice changed to a soft soothing tone and moved away from the phone. "It's okay, sweetheart. I'll clean that up right away. Don't worry. Nothing's ruined."

She was with someone? Jealousy burst in his heart hotter than the New Year's fireworks those kids had set off in the park last night. "Angie?"

"I have to go. It was good speaking with you again, Rick. Take care of yourself. Oh, and Happy New Year."

"Happy New Year to—" The phone clicked in his ear. She was gone. "You too," he muttered, his heart squeezing tight with regret. He replaced the phone, then lay back down, wondering where she was, what she was doing. Funny how one year without her seemed like ten.

*Well, Lord, that's an interesting way to start this morning. I wonder what You've got in store for the rest of the year.*

Rick rolled over, shut his eyes. But despite his efforts, sleep eluded him. Instead he pictured auburn hair flashing in the sunshine, tumbled curls half hiding hazel eyes that could melt like mint choco-late chips or spit sparks of green and gold, depending on her mood.

Angie was still searching for excitement to help her forget the past. It was time he accepted that it would take her a while. Her bitterness against God and her father wouldn't dissipate in one short year—not without a miracle. That didn't stop Rick from praying for her before he rose.

The odd note he'd caught in her voice still gnawed at him—until he realized what he was doing and called himself an idiot. She was strong, tough, resilient. Probably just needed a friend to talk to—other than the one she was with.

Okay. If a friend was what Angie needed, that's what he'd be. As always.

Once he'd showered, shaved, and dressed, Rick considered the day before him while he made himself breakfast. The first day of a new year and he was off duty. He'd stop in and see his friends at Camp Hope later, but first maybe he'd run out to Angie's old place to be sure everything was all right.

He made a face. Always the responsible one. He could almost hear Angie's mocking chuckle above the gurgle of the coffeepot. Goody Two-shoes in a uniform, she'd called him. He liked that she thought it of him.

The road into the Grant place was almost buried. Fortunately his four-wheel drive had no problem handling the drifts that blew over the tree-lined road, but the Grant driveway was totally socked in. It needed a good cleaning.

Rick found a decrepit snow blower in a teetering granary that was so flimsy it would never need air-conditioning. After fiddling with the machine for an hour, it finally coughed to life. Eventually it also consented to chew up the snow and blow it away.

He had no idea of time's passage. Rick only knew he was ready for a break as he shoved the recalcitrant red beast back into the granary.

"I thought I heard a lot of racket coming from here. What are you doing up so early?"

Rick whirled around, grinned at his best friend, Kent Anderson, who was also the director of Camp Hope.

"Early? Ha! To a layabout like you, maybe." He slapped Kent on the shoulder. "Happy New Year! I was gonna stop by later to see you. Figured you'd be sleeping in after the church social last night, so I came over here. Angie called this morning and asked me to check out the place."

Kent stared at him in disbelief. "Angie Grant called you?"

"Yeah." Rick could hardly believe it himself. "Wouldn't tell me where she was, but between you and me, she sounded odd—like she was homesick. I was kind of hoping she might come back for a visit so I cleaned up the drive a bit."

"Homesick? Rick, Rick." Kent sighed mournfully, shook his head. "Angie hates this house and you know it. From what you saw that day you arrested Syd, I guess she probably had good reason, but I'm pretty sure she's not going to come back. Especially not to remember old times. All she ever wanted was to get away." He reached out to tap Rick on the shoulder. "I've never known you to avoid the truth, buddy."

"I'm not avoiding anything. I'm just keeping things up, like she asked. This way it looks like someone lives here, and you won't be calling me to come and kick out vandals before they head over to Camp Hope." He turned away, knowing Kent would see past his facade. "Guess I'll check inside."

Rick walked up the steps, pausing by a newel post to unscrew a loose finial. The key lay inside a carved space. He removed it and slipped it into the lock, twisted the knob, then opened the door. The rays of the morning sun lit the interior, making lights unnecessary.

He took off his boots, waited while Kent did the same. "Think she'd mind if we made some coffee?"

"No, but Georgia will. She's kind of lonely now that Christa and Jon are in Chicago."

"Your sister and her new husband seem pretty happy together."

"They are. She's got her crafts company up and running, and Jon is—"

"Into computers," Rick finished for him, grinning. "I'll stop by for supper, and Georgia can feed me. That should cheer her up."

"Cheers me up too. You can help me eat leftovers. We've enough for an army." Kent pointed to the living room. "Angie left the drapes open?"

"Why not? Nobody out there to see." Rick ran the water a few minutes until the orange rust color disappeared, then poured a decanter full into the coffeemaker. "The whole place feels like she just stepped out. Even the coffee canister is half full."

"Which tells you something about how fast she took off."

Rick ignored the remark and the hint behind it. He wasn't going to tell Kent that he sometimes drove out here when it seemed as if his prayers would never be answered, that Angie would never come home. He'd never come inside, though. It was enough to sit in the yard and remember her.

Once the brew cycle was going, the aroma of freshly perked coffee filled the weary old house.

"Place needs some work," Kent muttered, scuffing his socked toe against the rough floorboards. "Old Syd should have used up some of his energy sanding this. Hardwood's all the rage these days."

"It is?" Rick stared at the floor, his mind sifting details. "What else do you think needs doing?"

"Be nice to get some paint on those walls, something less . . . uh . . . red."

"Yeah, they're pretty bad. Angie once told me she mixed a bunch of partial cans together when her dad wouldn't buy any new stuff. What else?" Rick asked.

Kent sat down on a kitchen chair. It creaked, groaned, then collapsed. He picked himself up off the floor, glared at Rick's shaking shoulders, then dusted off his jeans. "I'd say the furniture needs a little work."

Rick could no longer suppress his laughter so he turned away to pour some coffee into the plain white mugs from the cupboard. He remembered the day Angie had bought the set of mugs with money from her first paycheck as a member of the local Royal Canadian Mounted Police detachment.

"I will never depend on someone else to take care of me again," she'd declared.

Funny how her words still hurt. Rick would never wish her the misery she'd once hinted that she'd suffered here, but when would she learn that nobody got through life on their own, or if they did, they were miserable?

"This room is fantastic. Or it could be." Kent's voice echoed from the living room. "Facing south like this, it gets great light."

Rick followed, then handed him a mug. "Sure warms up with that sun," he muttered, quickly shedding his jacket.

"I'd put in patio doors, make a deck out there. Nobody for at least five miles in that direction, and there's a break of trees between that gives protection without blocking the sun—the ultimate in privacy. Could be spectacular with an awning, lots of flowers." Kent looked at him. "You know what I mean?"

Rick didn't answer. His brain was too busy conjuring up images of what this home could be and how he could accomplish it. Maybe if Angie came back and saw how different the house looked. Maybe if she could forget whatever bad memories . . .

"Well, the conversation's been great, but I have to go." A smile spread across Kent's face. "You coming over and staying for dinner or not?"

Rick glanced at his watch, surprised to see twenty minutes had flown by. "Sure. If your wife doesn't mind."

"She doesn't."

"Thought I'd do a couple of things around here this afternoon. Then I'll head over. That okay?"

They set a time and Kent left, trekking across the land on a brand-new pair of snowshoes his sister, Christa, had given him for Christmas. Across the yard and through the trees, Camp Hope was less than a quarter mile away.

Rick turned off the coffeemaker, rinsed out the mugs and decanter, wiped down the counter. He was almost out the door when he decided to check out the furnace. This was January and they were bound to get a cold snap. If the old monster wasn't running properly, water lines could freeze and break.

The unit was stuck in a dark and dank corner of the basement. Rick moved some sagging boxes that sat a little too near. A pack of furnace filters leaned against the wall, so he dragged out the old filter and shoved in a new one. The water heater was on pilot; that was okay.

A sound upstairs grabbed his attention, and he immediately remembered Angie's comment about vandals. On New Year's Day?

Rick climbed the stairs using the very outside of the step to avoid creaks. Nudging the door open a crack he saw a man standing in the kitchen doorway, looking around. Rick did not recognize him. He stepped up the last step, slammed the door shut.

The man whirled.

"Can I help you?" Rick said.

"I don't know. I knocked but no one answered. I saw a vehicle, so I figured someone must be here." The man's massive shoulders lifted in a shrug. "Thought maybe you were hurt, needed help."

"Thanks, but I'm fine."

"Yeah. Well, that's good."

Rick kept a bead on him, raised one eyebrow.

"I was looking for Angie Grant. Someone in town told me she lived here."

"Used to," Rick told him, wishing he hadn't left his gun in the glove compartment. For some reason he felt he needed it. "I'm renting the place now."

It was a decision he made as the words left his mouth, but when he said it, Rick realized how right it felt. New Year's Day was a time for resolutions. It was time he stopped waiting, got out of his stuffy impersonal apartment, and made a home for himself. Maybe even get a dog. Angie's place would be perfect. He'd pay her rent, do some repairs, and perhaps one day—

"Since when?" the man demanded with a curl to his lip. "I never heard about any renter."

"Why would you?" Rick responded. "It's a private deal. Who are you, anyway?"

A gun was in Rick's face before he could react.

"Somebody she shouldn't have messed with." The cold steel of the barrel pressed against his temple. "You see her, you tell her Max was here."

"I won't see her. Not for a while at least." Rick held his breath, let his nervousness show. "She said she's working a case."

"You talked to her?"

"This morning." Well, that wasn't a lie.

"She say where?" The barrel pressed a little harder.

"Uh, east. Yeah, east. Prince Edward Island. But she wouldn't say which town. Something about security." Rick thought a moment. "She couldn't talk for long, you know. Somebody was with her, and I guess they wanted to go."

"Thanks." The gun slipped away from his temple.

A second later the gun butt slammed into Rick's skull.

His knees buckled and he felt himself heading for the floor, unable to stop his descent as stars whirled into an eddy inside his brain.

# CHAPTER TWO

This is a pretty place, Angel. Look at those trees. It looks like God spilled sugar on them."

Angie smiled at the description, squeezed the hand so confidently clutching hers. "Yes, it's very pretty." She checked the round face. "How are you doing, Kelly? Can you manage to walk a little farther?"

"Oh yes. My new coat is very warm. Thank you." She grinned. "I look like the snow."

No point in explaining that the white jacket had been a deliberate choice to help her blend in. Just as there had been no point in telling Kelly Blair exactly where they were. Angie's job was to protect the child, and that's what she intended to do. No matter what.

"This is a place where God lives, isn't it, Angel?"

Angie glanced around, frowned. "What do you mean?"

"That sign—it said, 'Welcome to Camp Hope—Where nothing is im-impossible with God.' He must live here." Kelly's bell-like laugh echoed through the woods, causing Angie to wince.

"I didn't know you could read so well. You're pretty smart. But remember, we have to be very quiet."

"Because of the bad man." She nodded, her face crestfallen. "I'm sorry."

"It's okay. Let's just keep going."

"Okay. But look. See that big Christmas tree? It's standing there like a tin soldier, guarding us. There are lots of them here. God's soldiers."

Angie didn't have time to look. They were leaving the road that led to Camp Hope and cutting across country. Anyone who looked hard enough would be able to track them in the clean, fresh snow. Kent Anderson was an avid outdoorsman. Tracking them would be a cinch for him. Angie kept going back and forth, across the snow-mobile trails, over the cross-country ski paths, stepping inside recent marks left by a snowshoer, trying to hide their footprints.

It grew more difficult for Kelly to follow in her steps as the drifts got higher. Eventually Angie put the little girl in front and covered the tiny tracks with her own sneakers. When the child faltered, Angie carried her. It was slow going, especially with the constant checks she had to do.

With every step the memories loomed in her mind like a tidal wave waiting to crash and destroy her.

*I guess that's one thing I can thank you for, Dad. You made me tough.* Angie stuffed the past back where it belonged and focused on finding the house.

Suddenly there it was. Five hundred feet dead ahead.

"Thank you, Rick," she murmured, a tiny smile toying with her lips as she scanned the plowed drive. She'd known he'd rush over to check the house, had even counted on it. Guilt suffused her.

Like father, like daughter. She'd stooped so low she was even willing to use the one person who'd cared about her when no one else had. "I'm sorry."

"Who are you talking to, Angel?"

"Nobody, honey. Just thinking out loud. We're supposed to stay at this house tonight, but it looks like someone's here." Angie studied the shiny black truck parked near the back door. "I'm going to go inside and check, but I want you to hide here, right beside this big tree where the snow's really high until I tell you it's safe. Okay?"

Kelly nodded. "Okay. I'll pray. Daddy always says that when there's nothing else to do, you should pray."

"Yeah. You go ahead and pray." Not that God cared one whit about Angie Grant, but it helped the kid get through the times she missed her dad—her dead dad. Angie was going to have to tell her that, as soon as she had confirmation. "Keep the puppy in your backpack. He can't bark, not even once."

"Spot doesn't bark," Kelly told her with a frown. "He knows better."

"Good. Now stay right here till I come get you. You know what to do if you see anyone coming?"

"Hide in the snow and be very quiet. I promise."

Kelly's sweet smile stabbed right to Angie's heart, adding to her determination. No way was anyone getting to this child without going through her. But it would help if she knew whose truck sat in her yard. Last she knew, Rick drove a dilapidated old Buick. This wasn't it. She tried the passenger door, but it was locked; same thing on the other side.

Glad for the gloom provided by an early winter nightfall, Angie worked her way around the perimeter of the yard, attentive to any movement either inside or out. All was quiet, save for the wind that now whipped off the roof and pushed white whorls of snow across the land.

She moved up the back steps, checked that Kelly was still invisible, then tried the doorknob. The door swung open. As quietly as possible, she slipped inside, pasted herself against the wall as she crept through the porch and into the small kitchen. Funny to think of this place as the horrible home from her nightmares. It looked different in the dusk. Smaller.

Her foot hit something, causing a dull groan. Angie squinted, saw a dark shadow on the floor shift cautiously.

"If you're going to kill me, could you do it quickly? Otherwise my head is going to split wide open and I'll die in agony."

"Rick?" Angie felt in a drawer, found a flashlight, and flicked the beam over him. Blood dripped from his temple when he peered up into her eyes. "What in the world—?"

That familiar grin spread across his face. "Hey, Ang. How are you?"

"I'm fine, but you look a little worse for wear. What are you doing here?"

"Having a dream, I think." He eased himself into a sitting position. "A very nice dream. You can visit my dreams anytime. Just don't let him hit me again. It hurts."

"Somebody slugged you? We've got to get out of here." She made it to the door before his words sunk in.

"I don't think he'll be back for a while, Ang. He went on a trip. To Prince Edward Island, I'm guessing. To look for you."

"You're not making sense, Rick." He was trying to stand, so she helped him up and into a chair. After all, she couldn't just leave him, though every tick of the clock made her more nervous. Kelly was out there alone. But Angie had to be sure the house was empty before she brought the little girl in. She checked the exterior again, saw Kelly's backpack, barely making out the tiny variation in white that was the back of Kelly's coat.

"Sit still for a minute till your brain catches up." Her flashlight caught the snapped spindles of the old chair. "Is that what he brained you with?"

Rick began to shake his head but stopped immediately, placing one hand against the wound.

Angie ran some cold water on a tea towel, then pressed it against his temple.

"Didn't I tell you? It was a gun. Kent broke the chair. Should be fixed."

"Kent was here too?" She groaned. "What did you do, have a party?"

"No party." He grinned at her like a dog with a juicy bone in sight. "Boy, it's good to see you, Ang. You look great."

"Thanks." She pressed her hand against his shoulder, touched by his honest affection. "It's good to see you too, Rick. Now stay here while I scout out the place. I don't want any more unwelcome visitors."

Angie peeked out the window. Kelly hadn't moved. After she'd checked every room, Angie slipped outside, told Kelly to stay put a little longer, then paced the perimeter twice more. She found nothing. Several forays into the surrounding woods finally satisfied her that no one had followed them. Given the strength of the wind and the snowflakes starting to fall, her tracks should soon be obliterated.

She collected Kelly and led her inside. Once she'd closed the blinds, she flicked on the kitchen light. "Are you frozen, honey?" She set the wriggling puppy on the floor, then drew off Kelly's fur-lined mittens and chafed the tiny fingers.

"I'm not cold. Neither is Spot. Who is that man, Angel? He has a hurt."

"That's a friend of mine. His name is Rick, and he's a very good policeman who came to help us. Rick, this is Kelly."

"Hello, Kelly." Angie knew Rick's brain was clearing fast by the way he scanned the child's face, then glanced at her, one eyebrow raised. "Angel?"

"'Cause she's my guardian angel," the cheerful voice piped up.

"Of course." He smiled and winked at Kelly as a fiery heat suffused Angie's cheeks. "Angel. I think it suits her."

"My daddy says God sends angels to help us."

"Your daddy is a very smart man. And that's a great-looking dog. I don't know why you called him Spot, though."

"He has a lot of spots." Kelly frowned. "Don't you see them?"

"Spots? Oh yeah. Now that you mention it, I guess I do." He smiled at her, then twisted his head. "So what are you doing here, Ang?"

Rick's cop senses were on full alert now, the unasked questions filling his soft brown eyes. He wasn't going to let her simply walk away, but she couldn't explain. Not yet.

Angie shook her head, glanced at Kelly. "I'm going to make us something to eat. Can you take Spot in that bedroom and see if you can find some toys to play with? There used to be some old dolls in a cupboard by the window. You can play with those if you like."

Her dolls that her father had almost destroyed and she'd painstakingly put back together over and over again.

"I like dolls." Kelly removed her boots, handed Angie her coat, then walked toward the bedroom.

Angie yanked open the pantry cupboard and began pulling out cans of soup and a canned ham.

"You going to tell me what's going on?" Rick asked as he watched her.

She hesitated.

"Angie?"

"I'm in trouble."

Rick sat there, patiently waiting for her to organize her thoughts before she explained. At least Rick hadn't changed. How wonderful it was to know that someone would listen when she spoke. That he wouldn't prejudge or demand answers, that he wouldn't condemn her.

She hoped.

"Kelly witnessed a murder. She's supposed to testify at Carver Simpson's trial next month."

His eyes widened. "*The* Carver Simpson?"

"That'd be the one. I was junior agent on the case. Actually I was talking to you last October when someone breached security, broke into the safe house, and, I assume, killed her father, though I haven't confirmed that. Kelly came waltzing through my back door claiming 'the bad man' was at her house and her daddy was asleep. I still don't know what happened to the guys who were guarding her, and I didn't have time to ask."

She sucked in a breath, trying to bolster the courage that had grown shaky. "We've been on the run ever since."

"But where's your backup? your relief? Surely your handler at CSIS wouldn't leave you on your own, strung out like this."

"You wouldn't think so, would you?" Angie flicked on the stove burner under the pot, then sat down across from him. It felt good to talk to someone about it. "I've called in three times using the security protocol they gave me. I get a nameless voice that gives me directions on where to meet but no information. Each time someone was waiting for us at the meeting spot, but they were not there as friends. The first time we almost didn't get away after they started shooting. The second time I was a little more wary and waited at a vantage point. Two very hostile men in combat fatigues showed up with guns. The third time, I set up a decoy. They pushed the car off a bridge."

She swallowed the tears and frustration that welled, looked Rick straight in the eye. "Someone inside CSIS is working for Simpson. That's the only conclusion I can come to."

Rick whistled softly. "You've landed in it this time, Ang. Carver Simpson is no minor player. He's well connected, with money and power."

"Yes, and somehow he's got an inside track. It has to be him. Who else is there? You haven't heard anything at work, have you?" She sighed when he shook his head. She fiddled with a loose thread on her sweater. "I didn't know where else to go and who to trust, and I'm running out of cash. I can't use my credit cards because the CSIS tracks them."

He nodded, frowning.

"A few days ago I remembered what they taught us at the academy—hide in plain sight. I didn't think anyone would look for me here. Seems I was wrong, since they popped you." She studied the rising lump on his temple and shook her head. "I'm sorry. I should never have involved you."

"You knew I'd come out here to check the place out?" His clear steady gaze demanded the truth.

"I know how you think. You're the responsible one, the guy who goes the extra mile." She nodded. "So, yeah, I figured you'd show up and that if anyone was out here, you'd scare them off. Then Kelly and I could hide out for a night or two, long enough to get some sleep and figure out what to do next. Can you describe the guy who hit you?"

He told her as much as he'd seen.

"Max Vogler. Carver's second in command. He's nasty. You're lucky he left you alive."

"Not lucky," he corrected her. "God protected me."

She opened her mouth to argue, then shrugged. Maybe he was right; maybe God had gone to bat for him. But He wouldn't for her.

"God cares for His children, Angie. He loves us."

"Whatever. Anyway, if good old Max is around, I have to go. He kills for fun." For the first time in her life the thought of leaving this place saddened her. Funny what being a fugitive could do.

"I'm not sure you do have to leave. The guy thinks I've rented the place. I told him I'd talked to you this morning and that you were on Prince Edward Island. I think he bought it."

"Why would you want to rent this place?" Angie demanded. "It's run-down, old, ugly—and fifteen minutes from your work."

"I'm a ten-minute stroll through the forest to my friends at Camp Hope, surrounded by beautiful countryside, and close to work," he countered, grinning. "What's not to like?"

Angie glanced around, shuddered. "Let me count the ways. Drafts, leaky windows, probably field mice, rusty water, no doubt the roof's rotten, and worst of all, it's isolated."

He nodded. "Exactly what I'm looking for. A fixer-upper far from the madding crowds."

She had to laugh at his optimism. Rick wasn't one to linger on the dark side. Somehow he always managed to find a silver lining in everything. In a minute he'd be claiming God had sent him here today.

"Far as I'm concerned, you're welcome to rent this dump. Though I suspect that after the first month, you'll want me to pay you."

"Nope." He rose, smiled down at her. "This place has a lot of possibilities. Because of the past, you won't or can't see them. But I can."

"Be my guest. But for tonight, I'll have to be yours. I don't think Kelly can go any farther."

She walked to the bedroom door and pushed it open. As she'd expected, Kelly lay on the bed, fast asleep.

"Poor little thing. She keeps her chin up and does everything I ask of her, but it can't be easy on her to be dragged around like this. I wish—" She swallowed the words. What good would wishing do? Kelly was alive. It was Angie's job to keep her that way. She sagged against the doorframe.

"Have you eaten anything today?" Rick stood behind her, his breath brushing against her ear.

She shook her head. "Ran out of money. Besides, I wanted to get out here, and I didn't dare stop in town in case someone recognized me. I had a sandwich and fruit for Kelly."

"But nothing for yourself." His voice held none of the censure she'd expected after tricking him. "Come on, Angie. You need to get some of that soup inside you; then you can rest too." He flopped an arm around her shoulder and drew her away from the sleeping child.

Angie told herself to move away, to be independent. She didn't need some man to take care of her—she never had. Her dad had made sure of that. But she was so tired of running and always checking over her shoulder. Working for CSIS had been her escape from here, a chance to be free of the past, to let her wings expand and to experience life. It had turned into something far different.

"Here. Sit down." He held out a chair for her. "I'll turn the water heater up, and you can have a shower after supper."

No doubt Rick wondered why the house hadn't been closed up properly. CSIS had given her a week before she had to report, long enough to do the necessary things. Instead she'd thrown out the perishables, locked the door, and walked away from everything that reminded her of her painful past.

Now she was back. That alone would probably give her nightmares.

Except that with Rick here, the house didn't seem quite as bad. The water pipes still rattled, the furnace still groaned and moaned, the memories still lay shrouded in the corners and tucked under the floorboards, but the solidness of his wide shoulders and that tall lean body diminished their power.

"You're staring at me, Ang. Something wrong?"

She blinked.

His eyes crinkled with teasing. "Is it my haircut?"

Angie focused on the short black strands sticking up from his head like porcupine quills. "You cut it yourself again, didn't you?"

"Just a bit here and there." He turned back to the pot on the stove, stirred it. "Had to. I was in the Christmas parade. When it sticks out the edges of my cap, I look like I'm sprouting wings."

"This is an improvement?" She rolled her eyes. "It looks like you got caught by a maniac lawn mower."

"Well, it's a good thing you're back, then. You can give me a trim."

"Maybe." Her fingertips tingled at the memories of a few halcyon days they'd shared before she'd left everything behind.

"You haven't said much about CSIS. Is it what you expected?"

"It's okay. Different kind of work than we used to do. More intense." Angie felt his stare and knew he'd picked up on what she hadn't said.

"Did you find the excitement you were looking for?" His quiet question hid a deeper unspoken inquiry.

"Excitement?" Angie laughed, knowing he'd hear her bitterness but not caring. "I've been on the run with a little kid for over two months because somebody betrayed me. Now I have no money, no contacts, and I've run out of hiding places. I guess you could say my job is exciting."

Rick favored her with one long, intense look, then flicked off the burner. "Soup's ready."

"Are you staying for supper?" she asked, reaching for bowls.

A funny look washed over his face. "I forgot—Kent invited me for supper." He checked his watch. "I should have been there by now."

"So go. We'll be fine." She ladled out a bowl of soup for herself, pretending a nonchalance she did not feel.

"I can go another time. But I wish the phone was hooked up. I feel bad for letting Georgia down. Kent says she's a little lonely now that everyone's left."

"Who's everyone?" she asked, sipping the soup as she thought back to the hours she'd spent at Camp Hope. "Christa?"

He nodded. "She and Jon moved to Chicago. You wouldn't believe the change in her."

"I'm sorry I missed their wedding, but I couldn't get any leave at that time. Who else was there?"

"Doug Henderson."

"Georgia's lawyer friend from Calgary?" She frowned. "Why would he come out here for Christmas?"

"Lonely, I guess. He and Abby Van Meter talked a lot. Georgia and Kent invited some of the detachment staff out too."

"Have there been a lot of changes at RCMP?" she asked diffidently, wondering who shared Rick's time now.

"Some. Arden's still there. We have two vacancies, one of which is a staff sergeant. I haven't heard yet when they'll finally fill the other position. Yours."

Angie ignored that.

Rick went on to explain the various moves and retirements of RCMP members she'd known during the time she'd been on the force.

"The same but different," she mused, glancing around. Funny how quickly the shadows appeared. "You better get going to Camp Hope."

He stared at her for several moments, then shook his head. "I don't think I'll go."

"But you have to! Otherwise they'll come over here to check up on you. I don't want a lot of people coming and going while we're here. In fact, I don't want anyone here. I just want a place to hole up for a couple of days. After we leave you can have all the guests you want."

*Leave and go where?*

"Guests? Oh yeah. Like I'm a party guy." Rick seldom showed his feelings, but his hurt was obvious now. "You still don't know me very well, do you, Angie?"

He was angry with her. Strangely enough, that was easier to deal with than his gentle concern.

"I know you. I know you'd like to be with Kent and Georgia right now, so why not go? I'll be fine. I can take care of us. I've been doing it for a while now."

He opened his mouth as if he wanted to say something and just as quickly closed it. Angie knew the look, knew he was controlling his temper. His decency prohibited him from telling her off, though he was clearly tempted.

"Oh, Rick, your life would be so much easier if you didn't hang on to these principles of yours." She smiled sadly. "I know I'm a pain, but I'm not your problem. Go have supper with your friends. Enjoy the evening. Please?"

He frowned. "You want me to go?"

"Yes. And I'd prefer it if you didn't come back tonight. I don't want to draw any more attention to this place."

"What if one of Carver's men shows up? How will you get away? I didn't notice a car in the yard."

"I didn't bring one." She met his gaze and held it. "I'll be fine. I've made plans. I'm an agent with the security and intelligence service. I know what I'm doing."

After a moment, he rose, then pulled on his coat, his boots, and his gloves. "Okay. But I'll be back tomorrow after work, and you can't talk me out of it. I meant it about renting too. First thing I'm going to do is paint. This place needs a face-lift to get rid of the past." He glanced around. "You must have a way to contact people."

"I have a cell."

"It works out here?"

"It'll work." Angie stood, walked to the door. "If I don't see you again, I want to say thanks for helping us. It's good to see a friendly face for a change."

"You don't have to leave yet. No one's following you. You'll be safe."

"Yeah." She wasn't convinced.

"Well—good night, Ang."

"Good-bye, Rick."

She knew he didn't miss the significance of that, but he didn't comment on it either. He lifted a hand, traced the stubborn line of her jaw with one finger, smiled that wistful crook of his lips, then turned and walked out.

Angie stood at the window, watching until his SUV disappeared into the night. She turned out the main light, switched on the small fluorescent on the stove. From outside, with the blinds down, it would look like a night-light.

In a matter of minutes she'd finished the soup, cleaned up the dishes, and arranged the kitchen as it looked when she'd arrived. At least that kept back the memories.

The furnace cut in, sending a blast of heat into the room. She should have felt warm, but all at once chills ran up her spine. The old house yawned around her like a specter from the past, waiting.

Angie tossed away her silly emotional reaction, chalking it up to tiredness. After checking on Kelly once more, she put the dolls away, retrieved her backpack from where she'd hung it, and pulled out her cell. She needed to know if the trial date had been changed and when Kelly's testimony would be needed. But first she needed to take some precautions.

Once everything was ready, she checked her e-mail. Nothing. Nor was there anything noteworthy on the news site she accessed— still not one mention of Kelly's father, his death, or remaining child. That troubled her.

Angie cut the connection, waited five minutes, then redialed. She jumped through all the security hoops her bosses had in place, finally gaining admittance to her voice mail.

"Return to Ottawa, Agent Grant. Failure to do so will force us to issue a warrant for your arrest. Bring the package."

Arrest for what?

Suddenly aware she'd stayed on too long, Angie clicked off, noticed how oppressive the silence of the house had become. In the past few months she'd honed her senses so that the least niggle of uncertainty brought a reaction.

At the moment she had more than a niggle. Something wasn't right. A muffled noise from outside decided her. She grabbed the sleeping puppy, her backpack, their jackets and other belongings, slipped into Kelly's room, and woke the child.

"We have to hide," she whispered.

Kelly nodded.

Angie knew every inch of this bedroom, had spent hours in here, hiding, weeping, planning. Years ago she'd used the secret place for those interminable hours when her father had held his parties. It was the only option now.

Ears pricked for every sound, Angie pushed Kelly and Spot under the bed, straightened the covers, then joined them. She slid open the panel and pointed for the child and puppy to go inside; she followed, leaving just enough space to hear whoever had just entered the kitchen. She didn't wait long.

"I tell you there's no one here. That cop left a while ago, but he'll be back. Apparently he's renting the place."

"He's welcome to it. Syd must have hated this dump. Too near those Holy Rollers at that camp." A snide laugh. "Guilty conscience maybe?"

Every nerve in Angie's body seized. Since her father was in jail, there was no reason his friends would come here now.

"I told the boss she wouldn't come back here. Apparently the kid detested the place almost as much as Syd did."

"The boss thought she would come here because Syd once told him the place was her mother's legacy. Some legacy."

The sneering voice reminded Angie of those times her father had hosted his weekend get-togethers. Chills rippled up and down her back at the burst of memories, but she thrust them away to concentrate on the conversation.

The sudden silence seemed unnatural. Was that because she'd confused past with present? This house was getting to her. She saw

Kelly reach toward the knob and gently slide the panel. Angie stopped her, shook her head. She wasn't sure why. A hunch.

"You hear something?" one of the men asked.

The other laughed. "You're just nervous. Old houses are always full of sounds."

"Why not burn it down? That would solve all our problems."

Angie heard a click.

"Don't be stupid! Last thing we need is every nosey cop and every volunteer fireman in the county showing up. Arson means investigators. That's not in our best interest."

She heard them going through the house, opening and closing doors.

"This is nuts. I told the boss she wouldn't come back. If the cop's living here, why would your runaway want to hide here? She doesn't know about—"

"No, she doesn't know." The voice came very near. Angie stared at the hard rounded end of a military boot. "She'll come back. It's the only place left." The boots turned, walked away, paused at the door.

"No sign of the book we're looking for. Hardly a book in the place. Let's go. This cop you hit said she was on PEI?"

"Yeah. Maybe our intel was wrong."

"The boss doesn't pay for mistakes. It was supposed to be quick and easy. Find what we want and leave. A cop in the mix is the last thing we need."

Silence.

"The problem is Syd, not the cop. None of this should be necessary."

"Relax, Max. Boss man said Syd did all right by him all these years. It's only recently that he's developed his conscience. He'll get over it." A long pregnant pause; then the heel clicked against the floor. "Let's go. Syd'll be out soon. Then we'll settle this once and for all."

Angie lay there with Kelly pressed against her heart, trying to understand what was going on. But nothing made sense.

She suspected that someone at CSIS had betrayed her and Kelly's whereabouts to one of Carver Simpson's henchmen, but these people hadn't mentioned Kelly. They talked about Syd, about the past. About his getting out.

But her father was in jail for bank robbery and hadn't served even half of his time. Rick had told her that he'd make sure Syd didn't get early parole.

Angie pressed her fingertips against her eyes. She'd come here for a breathing space, to figure out why she was deceived every time she arranged a meet with the people who were supposed to be helping her. What she'd learned tonight didn't clear up anything. Her brain whirled with questions, but just one made her head ache.

How did Syd come into it?

Angie had intended to leave early in the morning, to get away before Rick returned. Now it looked like she'd need his help.

"Are they gone?" Kelly's whisper-soft voice breathed the words into her ear.

Angie checked her watch. Ten minutes since she'd heard them speak. "Stay here. I'm going to check."

She eased herself out of the hiding spot and out from under the bed, listened, then carefully slipped out the open bedroom door. The house was empty. She could feel it, but she did a sweep of each room just in case. Nothing.

After locking the back door, Angie slipped a chair under the knob. Not that the chair would be any protection against someone intent on entering. But it would make a noise, give her a chance to react. *That's all I need, a chance.* She checked to make sure her cell was still hidden. She could leave no sign.

She fed Kelly some supper, cleaned up by the faint light of a flashlight, then lost a game of Go Fish while they waited. No one returned. She relaxed, glanced at the child, and felt a rush of pity. Poor kid.

"Wanna have a shower, Kel?"

"Okay."

"Come on, then." Angie took Kelly upstairs to the room her father had once occupied. Just being in here gave her the creeps, but at least the en suite bathroom had no windows for light to shine through and thick black-out drapes that were supposed to have eased her father's headaches.

"Can I have a bath instead, Angel?"

"Sure."

The little girl grinned, began shedding her clothes beside the puppy's spread-eagled body.

As Angie helped her, she explained the rules. "If someone comes, you hide where I showed you until I tell you it's okay. Got it?"

"Yes. Can I have hot water this time?"

"All you want. Rick turned it on before he left."

An hour later they were both tucked in bed, but Angie couldn't sleep. Too many memories kept fluttering through her mind.

*"God loves you so much, Angie."*

*"Then why doesn't He help Daddy?"*

*"He does, my sweetheart. Every day He's right here with us, holding us in the middle of His love. If you're scared or afraid, all you have to do is talk to Him. He loves us more than we can imagine. Remember that, Angie."*

*"Yes, Mama."*

But love hadn't healed her mother. It sure hadn't done anything for Syd.

*"Can't you understand? I don't have any money for pictures! We're broke. There are bills to pay. It's expensive to have a kid. I haven't got money to waste on graduation pictures and dresses."*

Angie shook her head. Why keep going over it when nothing could change the past? Let it go.

*"Forget it, kid. You hear me? Unless you're going to tell me where that book is, we're both going to die in this place."*

That had been the night before the bank robbery. Inevitably Syd had clutched his head after one of these rages and either hidden in his room or left the farm. The scary silence when he'd gone had been almost worse than his verbal abuse.

She would not go there again!

Angie rose and went to the kitchen, rubbing her arms as she waited for the kettle to boil. The mint leaves she'd grown herself still sat in the cupboard in the old-fashioned tin. Rose hips, hibiscus, a bit of granulated sugar, lemon zest—the rest of her ingredients were all there. Once she had a cup brewed, she carried it into the living room and sank into the old sofa, staring out the big picture window as she sipped.

Ten thousand glittering crystal stars lit the southern sky, their radiant facets sparkling off snowdrifts illuminated by silver moon glow. She picked out several constellations carefully displayed against the black velvet sky as a fine jeweler would exhibit his work.

Rick would say it was the handiwork of God.

She believed that too. But her God was different than his. Her God punished people who made mistakes, and coming back here only reminded her that she'd made the worst.

She longed for forgiveness, but that couldn't be.

There was no forgiveness for what she'd done.

None.

# CHAPTER THREE

Rick signed the last page on the stack of paperwork and handed it to the secretary. "That ought to do it, Shauna." He stood, locked his desk. "I'm beat. Please tell me there's nothing else." The day after New Year's always wore him out.

"Nothing we can't handle. I hope that new member they promised us three months ago shows up pretty soon. Tomorrow morning, bright and early, would be nice. You guys are drowning, and you're going to take me down too."

"Tell me about it. If somebody doesn't show up soon, I'll be too crippled from filling out all these forms to lay out the welcome mat. I sure wish they'd send us a boss while they're at it. These extra details are giving me nightmares."

"Maybe they'll choose you," Shauna said. "You've been doing it so long, you should be on the short list of candidates."

If only that would happen. Rick had been promoted last year, but it seemed he'd been working toward the higher rank of staff sergeant forever. Rick tamped down his longing and faced reality.

"I'd probably have to move to get a promotion like that, and I don't want to move." Not yet, anyway. Especially not when Angie had finally come home.

Another half hour passed before Rick finally left his apartment wearing his down jacket, oldest jeans, and a threadbare flannel shirt he refused to toss despite its holes. The wind had picked up, and the sky had turned that dull leaden color that meant more snow.

First stop, the grocery store. His heart found a new rhythm.

If Angie was still there she might appreciate something other than soup and toast. He pulled into the parking lot, went inside and grabbed a cart, and worked his way down the frozen-food aisle.

"Hey, Rick. You run out over Christmas?" Fred Jones, handyman at Camp Hope, pulled his cart alongside and grinned at the stack of boxes Rick had accumulated. "Looks like you're feeding an army."

"Have to stock up for this blizzard they've predicted. I'm renting the Grant place. Thought I'd take some eats out there in case I get stranded or start working on something and don't want to quit."

"Renting, huh? That explains the car I saw there last night."

Rick's heart stopped, then picked up double time. "A car?"

"Yeah. Big black thing. I noticed it around seven. I was doing rounds and saw someone had cut the fence on the south pasture. Two someones, according to the footprints. Kinda hoped we were finished with trespassers for a while." Fred scratched his head. "You didn't ask anyone to go out there?"

"Well, I've been asking for bids on different stuff. I guess it could have been a painter or something." He'd only started asking this morning.

"No painter I ever knew drove a car like that or showed up on New Year's Day." Fred chuckled. "Maybe you should get a security system for the place so you can work those unending shifts and come home to no surprises."

"Good idea. I'll check into it."

"Well, gotta go. Ralna needed her pills refilled before we take off to see our new grandchild. I figured I'd stop by and pick up a few things to munch on during the drive." He motioned to his cart, which held a huge bag of chips, two chocolate bars, and a box of doughnuts. "Don't know how I'm going to sneak all this into the car."

"Ralna's on another diet," Rick guessed, unable to suppress his grin.

Fred nodded. "Claims Georgia's Christmas baking did it. This morning she asked me if I thought she was fat."

"You'd love that woman no matter what she looked like." Rick gulped at the affection shining in Fred's eyes.

"Yep, I would. But I'm not stupid. I'm not about to step into quicksand by answering that question. No, sir."

"So what did you say?" Rick asked curiously.

"Nothing. Not verbally anyhow." Fred winked, grinned. "Let me know if you want help with your new place."

Rick chuckled all the way to the checkout counter. Fred and Ralna were like a pair of kids, even after thirty years of marriage. Rick wanted that kind of love for himself.

Once he had the bags loaded in his vehicle, he walked into the hardware store and emerged an hour later with the newest security devices the store could provide, four gallons of cream-colored paint, and a bag of dog food.

He was about to start the truck when he remembered he hadn't seen Angie carrying any suitcases. She and the little girl would need clothes. Rick headed for the one store where he might find what they'd need, but by the time he got back into his vehicle, he was sweating bullets.

Buying clothes for females—child or adult—was no easy job, especially when the clerks in Kicker's Department Store had given him the third degree about who the clothes were for. If Angie didn't like the things he'd bought, she could throw them out or use them for paint rags, but he wasn't going through the doors of that particular establishment again for a very long time.

As he rolled out of town, Rick's stomach grumbled a reminder that it hadn't been fed since he'd swallowed a bowl of cornflakes for breakfast. He stopped at the Chicken Coop, and they had a nice little take-out package ready in less than five minutes. He licked his lips as the odor wafted through the interior on his drive toward the farm.

It was almost dark when he arrived. There were no lights on in the house. His heart fell. She'd gone, left without a word. "So what am I going to do with fifteen pieces of chicken?" he muttered, opening the rear door of the house.

"Share, I hope." Angie's voice held the promise of a giggle. "Need some help?"

Rick ordered his heartbeat to slow down before he faced her. "Sure." He glanced down at the smiling child. "You too?"

"Yes, please."

"Okay." He handed off two bags of clothes. "Here you go."

It took him three trips, but when groceries, gifts, and paint were all inside, Rick made one more trip back to the truck for his service revolver. No point in taking chances.

Angie shoved the last of the frozen food into the freezer while Kelly set the table, her eyes on the chicken bucket.

"What is all this stuff?" Angie's gaze settled on all the packages.

"I figured you two might need a few things, so I went shopping. Go ahead; open them," he urged, avoiding Angie's quizzical look. "This one's for you, Kelly."

"A present?" Kelly flopped on the floor. "Are we having Christmas?"

"Sort of." He couldn't look away from her shining eyes as she pulled out the T-shirts and jeans he'd purchased. At the very bottom she found books, a puzzle, a CD player and two CDs, a doll, and a necklace.

"Oh, thank you, Mr. Rick," she cried, jumping up and tossing her arms around his neck and hugging him. "Thank you very much. My daddy told me he'd buy me a necklace when I got to be a big girl. This is almost like the one we looked at in a book. It had lots of pictures."

He hugged her back, overly conscious of his rough hands against her soft silky hair where it tumbled down her back. This funny wobble in his stomach—was that what a father felt when he hugged his child?

Rick cleared his throat. "You're welcome, sweetheart. That last gift is for Spot. He can chew on it."

She giggled at the pup's rumble as he attacked the rawhide, tugged on the bone until he tripped over his own feet.

After a moment she glanced up. "Spot said thank you. What did you get, Angel?"

Angie dug in a bag, pulled out the flannel pajamas the saleswoman had assured Rick were perfect for cold winter nights on the prairie. She met his eyes and grinned at his red cheeks.

"Your face is the same color," she teased, then dived into the next package. "Rick, this is too much. You must have spent a fortune." She held up a black cashmere sweater. "This is gorgeous."

"It was half price, so don't get all crazy on me." He wasn't going to tell her that he'd imagined her skin glowing against the dark knit, or daydreamed about her hazel eyes peeking out from between those fire gold lashes. "They all assumed I was doing my Christmas shopping late, and I didn't tell them otherwise. There's more."

Angie *oohed* and *ahhed* over two pairs of jeans and a gray pullover, then made a face at the bright blue T-shirt's inscription: *An understanding friend is better than a therapist—and cheaper too.*

"I'm very understanding, Angie." He let his eyes do the talking.

"Cut it out. A relationship isn't in my future. I haven't got what it takes." She pulled open yet another package and gasped. "Hiking boots," she whispered, staring up at him. "How did you know?"

"I'm trained to follow every clue," he told her smugly. "Besides, those sneaker tracks are a dead giveaway."

"Yeah. I didn't have a chance to change. Thank you, Rick. I don't know how I'll ever repay you."

"I don't want repayment. I just want you to be safe. And happy." He held her gaze, knowing she would probably turn away.

But Angie faced him, her jaw set in a stiff line, her voice bitter. "It's a nice thought, but I don't think someone like me can aspire to happiness."

"Aim higher," he murmured, swallowing the words he wanted to say. *Give her a chance to relax, regroup. Then maybe*— He looked away only when Kelly's voice rang around the room.

"Can we please eat? I'm hungry."

They ate by the light of two stumpy, half-used candles because Kelly insisted it was their Christmas dinner. To Rick the greasy chicken was ambrosia that beat out any gourmet meal simply because he shared it with Angie.

When the meal was over, he helped her toss out the paper plates and carried the garbage bag outside to the rusty Dumpster on the way to his truck.

"More stuff?" She raised one eyebrow at the stack of boxes in his arms when he returned. "What is all this?"

"A security system. For now we'll put the boxes under here. I'll set it up as soon as I get time." He put the boxes inside a cupboard and closed the door. "Fred gave me the idea when I met him in the grocery store. By the way, he said he saw a car out here last night and tracks from two trespassers." He barely caught a flicker of fear ripple through her eyes.

Angie turned to Kelly. "Do you want to listen to your CDs before bed?"

"Yes, please."

Once Kelly was ready for bed, Angie set up the little girl with headphones and the new CDs and player in the bedroom.

"I didn't want to talk in front of her," she explained as she set a pot of coffee brewing for him, put the kettle on for her usual cup of tea. "There was someone here last night." She whooshed out a breath of air, then looked at him. "My father's friends." She related what she heard of their conversation. "Weird, isn't it? Syd coming back."

Rick stared at her, then shook his head. "Angie, you've let things get to you. Your father is in jail. He can't hurt you."

"That's where he's supposed to be. But look." She held out a piece of paper she'd found by the back door. The message read: *Syd should be out around the first. He'll fix things at home.*

"Syd isn't getting out, Angie. This must be from someone else or about something else."

"The guys who were here talked about burning the place down."

"Burn—" Rick couldn't finish that sentence. To think of Angie and Kelly imprisoned while flames and smoke smothered them—

"They know Syd pretty well. Probably think he'd try to collect some insurance money." Her voice was acid.

"Maybe they wanted to make it so you couldn't come back." He watched her closely, trying to gauge her thoughts.

"Coming here wasn't my first choice," she admitted. "But I ran out of options. And money." Her chest rose as she gulped in a breath. "I shouldn't have come. Now I've drawn you into this."

"What do you mean?"

"For one thing, our visitors mentioned you. Then I got a voice mail last night that insisted I come back to CSIS in Ottawa. I checked in again this morning. They're accusing me of killing two of Kelly's guards. If I don't go back right away, they'll put out a warrant."

Rick couldn't believe she was serious, but the shocking pallor of her face convinced him. The old protective urge flooded his insides in a rush that made it seem as if she'd never left. He still needed to be there for Angie Grant. But he couldn't sit back and wait this time; he had to help her before things got any further out of hand.

"Stay here. I'm going back to the office to see what I can find out." He grabbed his coat and left the house. Inside his truck, he reached for the radio, thought a moment, then put it back. Some things were better left off the airways.

Rick made it to town in ten minutes in spite of the howling wind that carried snow in a whirling pattern across the road. No one was in the office, which wasn't surprising. It was after eight. The night shift would be out on patrol. He shuffled papers on the night-watch desk, searching for the clipboard with the latest bulletins from CPIC, the Canadian Police Information Centre. He was flipping through it when the printer bleeped and began spewing out a document.

Rick stared at the computer screen, his heartbeat increasing to double time, banging a rhythm into his brain that sent his hands clenching at his sides.

It was there—her picture, her fingerprints, all of it.

*Angela Valentine Grant. Wanted in the kidnapping of a federal witness and the murder of two agents. Armed and dangerous.*

Officers were advised to contact a special number if they spotted her. No mention of her CSIS ties.

Without a second thought, Rick snatched the sheet and stuffed it inside his jacket. He waited until the image had cleared from the computer and the familiar RCMP crest screen saver was in place while he sorted through the possibilities.

But no matter which he chose, the awful truth remained as a stolid lump in his midsection. A warrant couldn't be ignored. He was a cop, head of the detachment, even if that was temporary. There could be no sidestepping his duty. His job was to turn Angie in—and Rick always did his job. For the first time since basic training he wished he'd chosen some other vocation.

He had a lot of questions. The first of which was why Syd Grant was free, if he was. He strode to his desk, picked up the phone, and called the penitentiary.

"Was in solitary but his lawyer got a bunch of visitors in to see him," a guard said. "Big shots from somewhere out east, meetings all day, I heard. In and out, badges flashing. A real parade."

Rick ignored the scathing tone. "Sorry to bug you about this. I'm just doing what they tell me—check on Mr. Grant every six months. Now that I have, I can tell the boss." He paused. "You said these guys were from the East. Where exactly?"

"Hey, they didn't visit me. All I can tell you is that they were big shots."

"How do you know?"

"Heard they got the big conference room for their meeting. The warden only uses that for very special guests."

"I see."

"All the fuss they made, you'd think the guy was some kind of celebrity instead of a thief. Sorry, guess I'm bawling on your shoulder and it's not your fault. Lawyers drive me nuts. According to them, everybody in here is innocent and deserves to be free. Bureaucracy is a pain, isn't it?"

"Ha! You should see the junk we have to fill out to requisition hand soap." Rick traded stories with the guard for a few more minutes, then hung up. *Head honchos from the East.* He pulled out the bulletin, trying to come up with a connection between what he'd just learned and the warrant. The bottom of the page caught his attention: *For further information call . . .*

He was going to call that number, but not from here. They'd be able to trace him, and he wasn't ready to answer any questions. Not yet. Not until he'd put some security in place for Angie and the little girl and Angie's office took over. She was too isolated now.

He could always ask Kent to check on her, but if he let anything slip—

Rick shook his head. For the moment her location was a secret he intended to keep to himself. He needed to figure out what was going on. Except he didn't have long. Duty had always come first; that wouldn't change.

He'd have to bring Angie in tomorrow morning, even though every cell in his body screamed no!

On his way out of the station, Rick noticed a big black car parked across the street. He was reminded of Fred's observation about last night's visitors to the farm. The same car? He decided to see if his hunch was right.

Rick pulled away from the building, accelerating as he zipped onto the highway. The black car followed. At Parsons' corner, he turned in, parked, and killed his motor. The black car slid past in front of him. The military plates surprised him.

He grabbed his radio. "This is Mercer. I'm at Parsons'. Anybody free to stop a black sedan going south? It was speeding. Just take a look and tell me who's inside."

Several moments passed. He saw the patrol car pass.

Two minutes later the report came through. "Criminals contained. The Murdock sisters are on their way home from the seniors' community dinner. I clocked them at the breakneck pace of twenty-five. You copy, Rick?" Lots of laughter.

"Roger that. Thanks." He pulled out of the Parson yard and continued down the gravel road toward Camp Hope, that twitchy feeling still irritating the back of his neck. There'd been only one driver in the car he'd seen, and neither Fiona nor Emily Murdock fit the description.

*Am I going nuts or what?* He turned in at the big sign that proclaimed this Camp Hope—Where nothing is impossible with God. *I sure hope You've got a way out of this, because if anyone finds out Angie's at my place, the place I'm renting from her. . .* He let his prayer die away, knowing God saw the truth in his heart. *Help me help Angie, Lord.*

Rick parked at the south end of the camp by the barn where his vehicle wouldn't be visible. He zipped up his jacket, snatched his gloves, and began working his way through the woods while the wind whipped across his face, stabbing his skin with icy sleet needles. The blizzard, he remembered suddenly. Looked like the meteorologists had gotten it right this time. The sky loomed low and heavy, almost black. It was building into a big one.

The house lay shrouded in shadow, quiet. He let himself in, listened for a minute, heard no sound. Had she left? "Angie?"

No response.

He was about to flick on the light when a soft voice called to him from the bedroom, "Rick, can you come in here?"

He raced into the bedroom, stopped in the doorway. Angie sat on the side of the bed, a letter in her hands. "Angie, what's wrong?" He stood in front of her, unsure of his next move.

She lifted her head, her beautiful face drawn tight in lines of pain.

"I was downstairs when I heard a noise. I found this on the porch," she whispered, stretching her arm out toward him. "It's from my father."

Rick took the sheet of paper, glanced down, and felt his whole body chill.

Angie,

You've put yourself in grave danger. Get out of there. Run as far away as you can. I can't protect you anymore. I wish I could.

S.

# CHAPTER FOUR

A harsh bark of laughter burst from Angie's aching heart.

"When did he ever protect me?" she demanded, forcing the words from between her gritted teeth. "The only person I was ever in danger from was him—and his horrible friends."

"Where's Kelly?" Rick asked.

"Sleeping. Don't worry. I made sure she was safe." She stared at the note, trying to make sense of it. "Where did it come from? How did it get here? Who knows I'm here?"

"I don't know."

A ratty chair stood beside the bed. Rick sat down and immediately Angie felt better, as if she were no longer alone in facing whatever lay ahead.

"Perhaps one of the men you heard before returned," he offered.

"No." She shook her head. "I've been keeping a very careful watch. I saw no one."

"It's winter. It gets dark early. You couldn't have watched all sides no matter how careful you were."

She glared at him. "I know how to guard someone, Rick. I didn't fall asleep on the job."

She saw his eyes flare with surprise and bit her lip. She was always so defensive with him, always trying to prove she was stronger than the whiny girl he'd helped all those years ago. She'd intended to show him how strong she was.

"I wasn't criticizing, Angie," he apologized. "I just meant—"

She smiled, shook her head. "Forget it. It's me. I'm too tense."

He nodded but said nothing.

"How do you suppose my father came to think I was in danger? He's somehow connected to those two who were here earlier. I guess he's hatched up some new trick and sent people here." Angie glanced around the room. "I can't think why. We've nothing to steal." She frowned. "You know, it's funny—when I was in Ottawa I started thinking about how poor we were when I was a kid. I mentioned it once at CSIS. A friend was surprised. She figured Syd should have received benefits because of his injuries."

"Oh." Rick seemed less than interested in finances. He continued to study the note.

"This afternoon I phoned the government's toll-free number and asked some questions. I don't know why I didn't think of it before." She laid a hand on his arm to draw his attention. "They were very helpful. My father has been receiving benefits for years, though they wouldn't stipulate how much."

"Uh-huh. So?"

"Don't you see?" Angie said. "He must have gotten a paycheck from the government every month. But doesn't that seem strange given how poor we were?"

Rick had always loved a puzzle. "Well, maybe he didn't get that much. Besides, he probably had bills for medication, that kind of thing. His burns looked pretty severe, and medication can really eat up—" He stopped, stared at her shaking head. "What?"

"I was told that the government's disability insurance covers all medical expenses. His check was free and clear." She closed her eyes in remembrance. "Syd didn't fix up the house, and he drove an old beater of a car. Do you remember the rags he wore? what I wore? He certainly never spent money on clothes. With what food he bought I could barely put a meal together. We were always behind on our bills. So where did it go?"

"A bank account?"

"I don't think so." Angie blinked, reconsidered. "If he had money, why did he rob a bank?"

"True." Rick made a face, then waved the letter. "Are you sure this government agency you spoke to had the right person?"

Angie nodded. "According to them, he's still getting a check. In jail. It's cashed every month."

"Then I'm sorry but I have no answers for you. I can tell you one thing though."

"What's that?" She yawned, trying to hide her utter weariness.

"You don't have to worry about Syd. Your father can't hurt you. I checked when I was at the office. He's still in jail."

"Okay." She took a second look at his face. "And?"

"There's a warrant out for your arrest. Kidnapping a federal witness and the murder of two CSIS agents."

She lifted her head and stared straight into his eyes. "I didn't do it, Rick," she whispered, praying she would see the gentle light return to his eyes. "I didn't kill anyone. I took Kelly because those were my orders, but I didn't kill anyone."

He knelt in front of her, grasped her hands in his, and squeezed them. "You don't have to tell me. I know that. I know you. You're not a murderer. You're a cop, and there's nobody more dedicated to her job. I know that you did it for Kelly's sake."

She could see the truth reflected in his steady brown eyes. He was speaking what he believed. He had no doubts. Rick had always been the one honest person in her life.

"Thank you," she said softly, peering at her hands as she blinked away the tears. "Thank you for having faith in me."

"I have faith in someone bigger than both of us, Angie." He tilted her chin up and stared into her eyes. "You can trust God to get you through this. He's bigger than Syd, bigger than the men who are after Kelly, bigger than any problem we have."

"Don't say any more about God, Rick. Please." She dragged her hands from his and placed them behind her on the bed so she could lean back, away from him. "You know I don't believe that."

"But you used to. You were like a beacon for God. What changed?" He rose, stood looking down at her, his eyes brimming with sadness.

"Me." Angie gritted her teeth, swallowing the well of tears that threatened to undo her self-control. "You can hang on to faith for only so long before your fingers get tired and you have to let go and face reality."

"Or until God works it out."

She smiled faintly. "But that's just it, you see. He never did." When Rick opened his mouth to answer, she held up her hand. "I don't want to go over it all again, okay? I'm tired. You'll have to turn me in tomorrow, and I need some time to regroup. Can we just agree to disagree?"

"Sure." He stepped back, set the note on the nightstand, then shoved his hands into his pockets. "But that won't change anything. God will still be right here, waiting for you to turn to Him, to ask for His help."

She turned away, fluffed up the pillow on the bed.

"Good night, Angie."

"Good night, Rick. Thanks for coming back."

"Anytime. I'll keep watch. You get some rest."

A moment later she was alone. Angie lay back on the bed, switched out the light. She rested her head against her pillow and stared into the darkness, her mind replaying Rick's words.

Kelly's puppy padded into the room, jumped onto the bed, and snuggled down beside her. Angie laid one hand over the glossy ears and stroked them as tears rolled down her cheeks.

"It's too bad he doesn't understand that there are some things

God just can't forgive," she whispered. "But I can't tell him. Some secrets are better kept, especially this one."

The wind whistled through the crack in the window as if to remind her that when Rick was gone she'd be all alone. Though it hurt, she accepted that that's the way it would have to stay.

>=◇=<

"Angel, aren't you ever going to get up?" Kelly's plaintive whisper carried to the living room.

Curious, Rick walked to the doorway and pretended he wasn't staring at the fully clothed woman lying on the bed in formfitting jeans and a wrinkled old RCMP academy sweatshirt.

Angie Grant awakening . . . it was a slow but beautiful process. First she blinked her incredibly long lashes at Kelly, her green gold irises finally peeking out from their shades. Then a slow smile spread across her face, carving tiny dimples in the corners of her mouth and showing off her sparkling white teeth. One hand raked through her lustrous auburn hair, tangling in the curls.

"Good morning," she greeted Kelly, accepting the child's tight hug and slurpy kiss as easily as if she'd been born to it. "How are you, sweetie?"

"I'm fine. I'm making breakfast, Angel. Aren't you going to get up?"

"I don't know."

Angie's wink snagged his heart and sent it into overdrive. Rick fought to control his breathing and pretend nothing momentous had just happened.

"I think I'll sleep some more." She closed her eyes and faked an unladylike snore. One eyelid lifted. "Unless . . . what are we having?"

"Pooched eggs an' toast and some peaches out of a can."

"Pooched eggs?" Angie looked from Kelly to Rick. "Something to do with Spot?"

"No, silly." Kelly burst into a fit of giggles, which were exacerbated by Angie's tickling fingers.

Angie would make a wonderful mother. Gentle, tender. She was one of those gifted souls who had the innate ability to see the world through a child's eyes and share that moment. He'd seen her at the camp the year she'd turned eighteen. Some kids had dared her into a game of tag. For those few moments she had become ten again, pigtails flying as she streaked across the camp, laughingly dodging outstretched fingers, yelling just like the rest when someone tapped her and she was It.

Whispers. He looked up.

"He looks kind of cranky," Angie murmured loud enough for him to hear.

"Starvation does that." Just for the moment he'd shrug off their problems and enjoy being with her. Who knew the next time that would happen?

"Starvation?" She giggled. "I don't think you're starving, Rick. What time is it?"

Rick checked his watch. "Eight fifty."

"In the morning?" Angie's face fell as she stared at him. "Aren't you supposed to be at work?" Her eyes asked a different question.

Rick shook his head, walked to the window, pulled the blind up. "I'm on the late shift tonight, but it wouldn't happen anyway, sleepyhead," he said, pointing to the white flurry outside. "We've got us a blizzard."

She groaned. "I knew this place was a bad idea for you. You're missing work, and I bet it's the first time that's happened since you started. It's all my fault."

"You don't control the weather. Don't worry about it." A stab of pain radiated through Rick at what lay ahead. He'd prayed for a miracle, but nothing had changed. He'd still have to turn her in. Not yet maybe, but soon.

He glanced at Kelly. "Honey, I think Angie needs us to leave her alone for a minute while she gets ready for your super-duper breakfast."

"Okay." Kelly bounced on the bed twice, then leaped into his arms.

"Hey!" He grabbed her just in time. "Watch it, kiddo."

"I knew you'd catch me. You're another one of my angels." She brushed her lips against his cheek and then wiggled to get down. "It's time for me to crack the eggs now," she told him as she raced out the door.

"You okay, Ang?" He checked her face carefully, looking for a sign, a reason not to do his job. It wasn't there. Angie looked great, radiant even.

"Yes. I'll be out in a minute." She swung her bare feet off the bed and sat staring at her pale pink toenails for a moment before glancing up at him. "Promise me something, Rick?"

"If I can." He waited, oddly ill at ease under her steady gaze.

"Don't blame yourself. I got into this knowing the cost. You're like me—the job comes first. I know you'd never do anything illegal, and I don't expect you to change your code of honor now. You'll drive me to the office, and I'll turn myself in. That's how it has to be." Her smile wobbled but held. She was trying so hard to be brave.

Rick nodded. "Okay. But we won't be going in for a while. It's pretty wild out there. I'm sure my truck is already buried. For now let's just enjoy Kelly's breakfast."

"Okay."

He wanted to say more but she turned away, picked up a brush, and dragged it through her curls. The determined set of her chin decided him; he had to say it. "You did well by her, Angie. You kept her safe, got her away from that situation and the people who pursued her, and you did it without filling her with fear. Well done, Agent Grant."

"Thank you for saying that," she whispered, staring at him in the mirror. A shiny tear dangled on the edge of her lashes.

Rick knew it was time to get out of here before he dragged her into his arms and started asking her questions she didn't want to answer. "Don't be long," was all he said before he closed the door behind him.

The waiting drained Angie.

If she'd known exactly who or what she was afraid of, if she could have defined it in ten words, the fear would be powerless. But not knowing what would happen next or who would appear and when—that was the hardest. The skitters that climbed onto her back and clung sent an ominous thrum purring in her brain. The sense that she'd missed something notched up, though Angie couldn't say why.

"It's a good thing this doesn't happen too often," Rick muttered. His head was resting back against the chair, his long legs sprawled out in front, but he didn't look relaxed. "Neither one of us is good at being housebound."

Angie knew exactly what he meant. She'd felt jittery, caged, and the feeling had only intensified with the passing hours. Now she walked to the picture window and stared out into the darkness. There was nothing to see.

The questions wouldn't stop. She'd done something wrong. She must have; otherwise they wouldn't have sent out that warrant.

Guilt settled on her spirit as it had back in the days when she'd been a teenager and life had looked impossibly bleak. "It's funny, you know."

"What is?" Rick lifted his head, peered at her through the gloom.

"This. Us. Or rather me." She walked over to the coffee table, picked up the board games they'd played with Kelly all afternoon, and returned them to the cupboard. A few seconds later she caught herself straightening the rest of the room, making sure nothing was out of place in case Syd came home.

She bit her lip and flopped onto the sofa.

"Angie? What's funny?"

"Wrong word. More like sad." She saw confusion fill his eyes. "I had this idea that if I could just get away from here, away from the past, from being *that Grant girl*—I figured if I could go somewhere and start over I'd prove to the world that I had what it took to excel.

Excel? I'm about to be arrested. It was a stupid dream. I should have known better."

Angie stopped because her emotions were too close to the surface. Defeat nagged at her spirit, but that didn't mean she had to drag Rick down.

"I don't think it was stupid. If we didn't have dreams, goals, flights of fancy—how could we build a better world?"

"You think the world was built by dreamers?" Angie tilted her head back and studied the grungy ceiling.

"Of course."

"Dreamers like the Murdock sisters?" she asked, knowing that the entire town thought the two sisters fell on the left side of eccentric.

"Exactly like them." He sat up straight. "People make fun of them, but Fiona and Emily see possibilities and then they set about changing their world to make them happen. It's mostly because of them that the senior center in town is always in use. They had an idea to get shut-ins, disabled people, the handicapped—anyone who was alone—out of their isolation and into a place where they could talk. They kept that dream alive until someone got a fund for the Handivan rolling."

"I didn't know that." Angie thought back to the many times she'd run to the sisters when living at home had become impossible. Their gingerbread Victorian house had always seemed like a magical place, far removed from the mundane grind of her own life.

"Did you know they're thinking of moving into town?"

"You're kidding?" Angie tried to imagine that huge three-story house without the sisters perched on the porch or serving tea in their summerhouse.

"They've decided to buy a place, set it up as a kind of boardinghouse for seniors who can't or don't want to live alone. If you go over to visit them now you'll trip over the piles of boxes that are lying all over. They figure they can sell most of their father's antiques to get a down payment on a place, but they're trusting God for the rest."

That was the difference, Angie told herself. She couldn't trust

God because of what she'd done. Guilt took its place as it always did, burrowing up from the nether regions of her mind. God always balanced things out. Always.

"Good for them." She let the silence stretch until she had to break the tension. "What about you? What are your dreams?"

He blinked at her, sat a little straighter. "Me?"

"Mm-hm. You talked about making staff sergeant. Why?"

"Well . . . ," he started as if he couldn't decide whether or not to tell her. "Did I ever talk about my family?"

"Just enough so I knew you had one. I always got the feeling you were hiding something," she told him candidly.

"Hiding?" He laughed. "No, just a little embarrassed. Ramona, my eldest sister, is a biochemical engineer for a big drug company. Donna, the middle one, is a thoracic surgeon. Tracey is the baby; she's a nuclear physicist."

"Really? Your Christmas dinner discussions must be interesting." He had a strange look on his face that piqued Angie's curiosity. "What?"

"I'm a cop," he told her.

"Yes, Rick, I know that."

"Sort of a step down, don't you think? All those brains and me just a cop?" He laughed again. "I guess I always figured if I could make it to staff sergeant, I'd finally show them."

"Do they care if you don't?"

"I don't know. Probably not," he admitted at last. He glanced up through the long black lashes she'd always considered wasted on a man. "But I do."

"So keep working toward it. You'll do it one day."

"Yeah, one day." He sighed, leaned back, closed his eyes.

A light clicked on inside her head. "But not if you're involved with me," she guessed. "Oh, boy, I really messed up this time, didn't I? It was wrong to come back and involve you in my problems. I apologize. I've placed you in an awkward situation, and that's the last thing I wanted to do."

Angie bit her bottom lip. Promotions were hard enough to come by. One black mark on his record and he could be bypassed for years. Still, maybe taking her in would make up for that.

Or cause more questions.

"I just remembered something," he said. "I need to call the station to tell them I'm stranded."

"There's a snowblower—"

"Angie, have you looked outside—really looked? I could blow some of it away, but it would be pointless."

"That bad?" Angie slid off the couch and walked to the back door. She turned on the outside light, opened the door, and stared.

It was like looking into a snow globe that had just been viciously shaken. Undulating drapes of snow spun relentlessly in a wind that reached inside the house to tug at her hair, her clothes, anything. It whipped through treetops, tore at wavering pines, and spun whorls of white, making it impossible to see more than ten feet ahead.

"Oh, my, I haven't seen a blizzard like this since I was a child and my mother—" She gulped, let it go.

"It's beautiful, isn't it?" He stood behind her, a solid shield that would be so simple to lean on, to shift some of her burden onto.

But Angie couldn't do it. She had no doubt that Rick would be there for her, but she didn't want to give him hope that anything had changed between them, because nothing had. She couldn't care for him, not the way he wanted or needed. Love was something other people shared. It wasn't for her.

Angie shivered. She shut the door, locked it, then flicked off the exterior light.

Rick took his phone from his jacket. Once the tiny antenna was set up in front of the living-room window, he played with it until he found a signal.

If only things had been simpler, if she'd come home for a visit, showed him she was in control of her life, that she was fine on her own. Of course, if that were true she'd never have returned.

"It keeps losing the signal," he muttered as he dialed for the third time.

She sank into a chair and waited, remembering another time. Rick had driven her home from choir practice. Her father stood in the shadows, waiting until he'd left, then flew into a rage. What had it been about that time?

The same as always. The book. He'd been drinking and started harping on that book, the one she didn't have and didn't know anything about.

Outside, the wind roared as it tore around the house, pushing its way in through every nook and cranny it could find. Angie shuddered, then froze as Rick's voice broke the silence.

"Hey, Shauna. Working late again? I'm stranded in the back woods. Doesn't look like I'll be reporting in for a bit."

He moved closer and held the phone so Angie could hear.

"Hey, boss. No problem. The rest of us are taking turns on the shifts." Her voice faded, then came back. "—quiet. We're trying to keep people off the roads. We've got some volunteers checking on the seniors. So far no problems."

"Didn't expect any. We're an organized team." He listened to her chuckle, waited for the intermittent static to clear. "Maybe someone could check on the Murdock sisters too. I sure don't want those two on the road in their feather hats and high heels."

"Roger that. Say, boss, we've got a puzzle—warrant for An— Grant has been—"

The phone crackled. Angie leaned forward, straining to hear the rest of her sentence.

"I can't hear you, Shauna. Say again."

"War—can—. Mistake." Then total silence.

Her body immobile, Angie could only sit welded to her chair and watch Rick who, after clicking off the phone, closed his eyes and bent his head, his internal battle evident.

"You could try again outside. Sometimes that works," she suggested.

"What's the point? We already know what she's going to say," he replied. "I'm so sorry, Ang. I'd give anything to change it, make it go away."

"You can't." She dredged up a smile. "It isn't your fault; I know that."

"But you still feel betrayed?"

"It's hard not to. CSIS has the means at their fingertips to find out who killed those two agents. Why pin it on me—make me their scapegoat?"

"Angie—"

"It feels like déjà vu," she whispered, fighting to retain the control that everyone had always complimented her on. Reality had stripped away her equanimity, left her feeling abandoned and alone.

Betrayed by the very ones she should be able to trust—it just proved you could never really forget the past.

# CHAPTER FIVE

That fatalistic tone—Rick had never heard it in Angie's voice before and that bothered him. The storm was wiping out his last link with civilization. He would have a few hours—maybe another day—with Angie before he'd have to do his job. Now was the time to ask questions.

"Angie, tell me about your father."

Her head jerked up in surprise as she stared at him. "Why?"

"Because I want to help you if I can, and I can't do that without knowing about your relationship with your father. I never understood why you seemed to hate him."

"No, I don't imagine you could." She gnawed on her bottom lip for a moment, but her gaze never left his face.

"Please tell me."

"Tell me what you know first," she whispered as the gold in her eyes changed to a deep impenetrable forest mirroring variegated shades of green.

"Okay." He began to tick off what he knew on his fingers. "Syd Grant regularly attended First Community Church, sat on one or two committees, gave to the church's mission fund."

"Yeah, he was good at giving money I saved."

The starkness of those words shocked him.

Angie smiled at his surprise. "You didn't know that about good old Syd, did you? Did you know he was too tight to buy me a dress for my graduation, that I had to ask the Murdock sisters to help me sew one?" She laughed, the sound a harsh echo in the dimness. "No, I can see you didn't know. I don't suppose anyone ever thought to tell my father that charity begins at home."

He was beginning to get a picture that didn't jibe with what he thought he'd known about the man. Before Syd Grant robbed a bank, he had been a pillar in the community. Or so Rick thought.

"Angie—"

"No—" she held out a hand—"you asked, so now you're going to hear. Syd Grant was never the wonderful Christian you and everyone else believed him to be. He was a mean, hateful man who drank in secret and took his anger out on me. 'Be a good girl, Angie. Love your parents, Angie.' Why should I love him? What did he ever do to deserve my love? He took what I gave, and he hated me for it until I learned to hate him right back."

She gulped, regained control, and looked up. Her jaw thrust out in anger. "My father was the worst kind of father there is. And you know what galls me the most?"

He shook his head, watching pain flood her eyes.

"I lied for him, cheated, almost stole—all to keep his precious image intact, to protect him so no one would know what I knew— that Syd Grant was a figment of everyone else's imagination." She dashed a hand across her face as if to brush away the tears, but there were none.

Bitterness laced her voice as she continued. "He let me do it, relied on my covering for him. Then in front of whoever happened to be present at the time, he berated me. Condemned me for my sins. That 'good Christian man' set a lovely example, don't you think?" She spat the words out as if by doing so she could rid herself of the memory.

Rick didn't know what to say. He had no words to ease her

distress. So he did the only thing he could; he sent a plea for heavenly help. "I'm so sorry, Angie."

"For what? It wasn't your fault."

"But it was. Mine and every other person who calls himself a Christian. We're too ready to believe that a person is okay just because he seems part of our group, calls himself that name. Christians are as fallible as anyone else, maybe even more so. We need to keep checking on each other to make sure we live what we speak. I'm sorry we failed you."

Angie said nothing for a few moments, but her foot kept up a regular rhythm against the ugly carpet. He waited.

"So now you know. I don't love my father, like a good Christian girl should. In fact, I detest him. I never want to see him again. And I certainly don't need his ridiculous notes pretending to care about what happens to me. He hurt me too many times to make up for it now."

The pain behind her words bit deep, gouging a hole of compassion in Rick's heart. But he said nothing when she sprawled on the sofa, turned her back to him.

A moment later she lifted her head to look at him. "I can't talk about this anymore, Rick. We knew two different people, and I only want to forget the Syd Grant I knew."

"I understand."

Her expressive eyes told him he didn't know half of what she'd suffered and for that he felt like a heel. Worse, because Rick felt pretty sure that after he turned her in, Angie would classify him in the same category as Syd.

When she sat in a jail cell, her freedom taken, he'd be as good as dead to her—she'd never forgive him.

⟞⟝◆⟞⟝

"Angie?"

She awoke immediately, bending to reach for her gun.

"Relax." Rick's large warm hand held her still. "Listen."

His face loomed in the darkness, inches away from her own, solemn eyes liquid soft, his aquiline nose and rock-hard jaw telegraphing the integrity tinged with compassion that was so much a part of his nature.

"Hear anything?"

She listened, then shook her head.

"I did." He turned toward the picture window.

Angie followed his glance. Outside, the storm swirled snow around with a dizzying force. "Just the wind," she whispered. "It looks bad."

"It is." He didn't dispute her judgment but didn't move either.

"Is Kelly all right?"

"She's fine. Woke up a little while ago. I read to her from your stash of books. She's quite a child. Her faith in God is unshakable."

"Yes. She's one of the chosen ones, I suppose." As soon as she'd said the words, Angie wished she'd remained silent. She swung her legs off the sofa, hoping to avoid the question she knew would follow.

Rick sat beside her, leaned forward, elbows on his knees. "Chosen ones?"

"That's what I call them. One of the ones God sticks up for, really cares about. They're the kind who know He'll always be there, no matter what." Bitterness burned a hole straight through to her soul, and she thought longingly of the comfort she'd been denied so many years ago. "People like you. And Kelly."

"I don't understand what you mean." He tilted his head. "Can you explain it to me?"

"I don't know." Perhaps it was the drone of the wind outside, the dimness of the room, or the warmth of the furnace spilling out into the air, chasing away the chill. Whatever the reason, Angie found herself speaking of things she'd never told anyone.

"God can only forgive so much," she said. "Once you step over the boundary, you can never get back into His good graces."

"Angie, you haven't done anything that God can't forgive."

"You don't know!" She glared at him, then looked down at her hands, feeling the mantle of guilt settling heavily on her shoulders.

"This trouble, the things that have happened—it's because God doesn't love me. Because He can't."

"No!" Rick shook his head. "That's not true. Don't you remember your Bible? The same question is asked in Romans. It goes something like this: 'Can anything ever keep Christ's love from us? When we have trouble or calamity, when we are hunted down or destroyed, is it because He doesn't love us anymore? And if we are hungry or penniless or in danger or threatened with death, has God deserted us? No. Overwhelming victory is ours through Christ who loved us.'"

"Trouble, calamity, hunted down—sounds like me, doesn't it?" She summoned a smile and wondered if her face would crack with the effort. "A fugitive. I've felt like that for years, just like the fox in those English hunts. There he is living his own life when someone catches him. He thinks it's over until someone puts him in a cage. He's got food and water—no freedom but then he isn't dead either. He begins to accept his new life. He thinks, *Hey, this isn't so bad.* Until the day they let him out of the cage. The dogs chase him for so long that he finally wants just one thing—to give up and let them destroy him."

"Angie, God isn't hunting you!" His eyebrows lifted high with surprise.

"Really?" She sighed, rubbed her eyes with her fists. At this moment giving up seemed awfully tempting. "Forget it, Rick. You don't understand and I can't explain. I'm too tired, I guess."

He was silent for several moments. "You never told me how you got away from your pursuers."

"Didn't I?" She frowned. "Kelly came through my back door and said her daddy wouldn't wake up. I'd seen a few men approach the safe house. They just waltzed in, even though I know the door was always kept locked. In retrospect, I suppose it could have been a setup. Anyway, when someone started banging on *my* front door, I grabbed Kelly, got us in the car, and took off." She paused a moment to look around. "I haven't seen that dog in ages."

"Spot's fine." He looked troubled. "So you just drove away without any problem?"

"Not quite." She shook her head. "I drove all through the city, trying to lose whoever was behind me. But they stayed on my tail. I took a corner, pulled into a cul-de-sac. A Harley roared in behind, and a car pulled in front of us, blocking our exit. When the driver started to get off the bike, I figured we were finished. The man yanked open my car door. I thought he was going to shoot us, but he waved me ahead. I didn't ask questions; I took off. I was almost a block away before I noticed that the biker wasn't following."

"Why wouldn't he follow?" Rick stretched out in the chair.

"I've got a better question. Why didn't the guy on the Harley just shoot the other guy and come after me? Why didn't he shoot at us through the back window? Carver Simpson isn't known for delicacy in these matters. Example—Max. He's a hired gun who has no qualms about taking anyone out. So how come I'm alive?"

"Good question. So you drive away, eventually end up here. But then other people show up, and someone starts talking about Syd." He shook his head. "Okay, I agree; the pieces don't fit. How did you happen to get assigned to Kelly's case, Ang? Were you the only available agent?"

"Good grief, no. There were several who were senior to me, still rookies but with more hours on the clock. One day I got a call, was told to forget the job I was on and go to a certain address. I was given the bare bones of Kelly's story and ordered to act as backup."

"Why were you in two different houses?"

"We weren't at first. Kelly and her dad were kept upstairs; we stayed down, watching windows and stuff like that. I was the gofer—groceries, intel, whatever they wanted. I got to be pretty good at disguises. Then somebody found the first place. And the second. Each house was somehow discovered; each time we got away just in time. Headquarters would alert us, we'd get out, and they'd decide where we should go next."

She sighed, wiggled to get more comfortable while she explained. "The last house we were at was large enough for all of us, but somebody must have decided to broaden the protective net because I was ordered to stay next door. I was by myself when I saw those men walk in. I heard a gunshot just before Kelly came in the back. *Bang!* on my front door. We ran."

And she'd been running ever since.

"So you kept moving from place to place for the past two months?"

Angie nodded and laid her head back against the cushion as weariness engulfed her. It could hardly matter now if she told him. "I hid, got in touch with the office, was told to go to a meeting spot. I told you this part."

"That someone set you up, that they tried to kill you?"

"More than once."

"Yeah, I remember. Huh." He leaned forward, rested his elbows on his knees. "So the bad guys let you get away, but the good guys tried to kill you? It doesn't make sense."

"I know that." The rhythm and tone of the wind had changed. A downspout rattled against the house. What was that high-pitched whine? She listened, every nerve on high alert, then relaxed. Nothing but the wind.

"Why?"

She frowned, lifted one heavy eyelid, and glared at him. "Why what?"

"Why would CSIS want you out of the way? Dead, even? Why would the bad guys let you go?"

She yawned. "Maybe the bad guys are really the good guys, and the good guys are somebody else," she mumbled, the whole picture swirling into an eddy of confusion just like the snow outside. "I don't know. How is my father involved? For every one of your questions I've got three of my own. Nothing makes sense."

"But one thing is certain: your father can't hurt you anymore."

She froze, sat up straight, blinked away the haze. "I heard what those guys said, Rick. Believe me, I didn't dream that part. They said he's coming."

"He's in jail, Ang."

"He's supposed to be."

"He is."

She saw the certainty in his eyes. "And you believe this because . . . ?"

"I checked with the prison. Your father's still there—he even had a bunch of visitors to see him. Which means he couldn't be here." His eyes softened. "You must have misheard."

"I don't think so," she muttered stubbornly. "I heard what I heard. What else could it mean?"

"Yet another question."

She had a ton of them, beginning with why someone in her own outfit would issue a warrant. If they wanted to ask her questions, why not just order her to return? It wasn't as if she'd taken Kelly to frustrate them. She'd left detailed reports of the problems they'd encountered on her handler's voice mail. She'd done the job they paid her to do.

"Angie, I wanted to say—" Rick's voice dropped into the silence. He cocked his head, listened, then moved to one side of the window.

"What is it?" By the time she'd said it, Angie didn't have to ask. She knew the sound of a snowmobile as well as anyone. The question was where had it come from and why was it here in her yard.

She slipped off the sofa and stood beside Rick to gaze at the wide expanse of white that made up the front yard. Soon lights flickered through the snow as the snowmobile circled the house slowly.

"Checking to see if anyone's here," Rick whispered against her ear. He grasped her hand and pulled her with him into the kitchen. They watched together as the door handle turned. The door did not open.

Rick grasped her chin, turned her to face him. Angie read his lips—*double locked*—and nodded.

Footsteps crunched down the stairs outside. A moment later the machine roared and moved around the west side to the front yard.

This time Angie led Rick back to the living room, careful to keep to the shadows, grateful for the cold metal press of her gun against her ankle. The bright yellow light of the snowmobile swung in a circle to focus its beam directly on the living-room window.

"What's he doing?" she whispered.

"Wait."

She stood watching, her stomach settling into a leaden weight that slowly rose to fill her throat with the acrid taste of fear. Dear God, how much longer could this go on? Steel bands tightened around her head, but she kept peering out the window.

Suddenly the motor rose in pitch until it attained the screaming whine of a machine pushed to full throttle. Then a single shot blasted the silence of the night and burst a hole through the center of the window.

In one fluid movement Angie crouched, pulled her gun out, and searched for a target. She was bumped off-side by Rick when he stepped in front of her, shoved open the front door, and clipped off one round before the figure and the snowmobile roared off into the night.

Silence settled as if it had never been broken. The wind edged up a notch.

"Did you hit him?" she asked, holstering her gun.

"Couldn't tell. Stay here." He was out the door before she could protest.

She watched Rick's lean, lanky shadow push through the drifts until it disappeared in the whiteness. When the tiny beam of a flashlight flickered, she caught a glimpse of him hunched over. Then he headed back toward her.

Angie met him at the door. "What did you find?"

"No blood, so I don't think I hit him. Hard to see in all that snow." Rick brushed off the snow, relocked the door. From his back pocket he pulled out a bright orange hunting cap, the bill of which was stained and dingy. "Found this."

Angie couldn't tear her eyes away from the word stitched across the front just above the visor. *Hunter.*

"Do you recognize it?" Rick tossed the cap on the table. "Angie?" He touched her shoulder.

"Don't touch me!" She flinched under his touch and stepped

away from him, dread wrapping its ugly fingers around her neck in a choking grip.

"What's wrong?"

She looked up. His eyes were transfixed on her face, as if he couldn't understand what he was seeing.

"It's my father's cap," she explained in a burst of breath. "Yesterday—no, the day we arrived here—was that yesterday?" She scrubbed at her forehead, unable to separate the days. "I saw it hanging in the porch."

"He's—"

She shook her head. Confused maybe, but one thing stood clear and certain in her mind. "He's out of jail, Rick. He's coming here. He's coming back for me. That last day—he was out of his head. He said I'd die if I didn't give him the book. Don't you see? It's starting all over again. He's coming back here to get something I don't even have!"

——◆——

Give him a kid with a smart mouth, a drunk driver, a doper on crack—Rick could handle any one of those. But he had no idea how to help the ashen-faced woman he saw before him now.

"Syd is in jail, Ang. There's no way he can get free. Maybe that was one of the other men you heard. Maybe someone's trying to play with your mind. Maybe they just want you to think he's coming back to scare you into leaving."

He watched her pull herself together. The mask of dread and fear that had covered her face mere moments ago when he'd touched her now cracked and dissipated.

He laid his palm against her narrow shoulder. "You're safe with me. I'm not going to let anything happen. Good old Rick is still on the case." He wanted to be more than good old Rick, but at the moment he'd settle for never again seeing the look of sheer terror that had rained through her eyes a moment ago.

He walked into the kitchen, flicked on a light.

The green of her irises lightened until gold flecks appeared as she finally responded to him in something close to her usual snappy way. "You're not old." She frowned. Her eyes widened. "What are you doing?"

"Making coffee. I need a cup. Want some?"

"I'm not going to sleep now, that's for sure. Why not?" She sank into one of the kitchen chairs. But after a moment she rose and walked to Kelly's bedroom.

"Everything okay?" he asked when she returned.

"She's on the other side of the house. The shot didn't wake her. Spot's standing guard. Or rather lying guard—with both eyes closed." Angie moved restlessly back and forth, then paced into the living room.

Rick followed her, saw her gazing at the wall where the bullet was lodged. "I'll take that with me to work tomorrow. I can get it analyzed. I wonder what he was using. Might give us a tip to who is out here shooting at houses."

Angie disappeared for a few moments and returned with a pair of tweezers and a plastic bag. She dug around beside the bullet until it was loose, then carefully eased it out and dropped it into the bag. Rick stood in the doorway, watching as she went to the kitchen, dug in a drawer. After she lifted out a magnifying glass, she leaned over the stove to study the bullet under the light from the range hood.

"Rifle," she told him. "Probably telescopic. Don't think it's a hunting rifle. Military assault, I'd guess."

He blinked. "And you know this how?"

"CSIS offers a number of courses for any interested agents. I was quite interested in learning everything I could." A wry smile lifted her lips. "One of those classes taught me how to tell the difference among bullets. Turns out I have an aptitude for bullets. Of course, I'd need a microscope to be more specific about the weapon, but—" she shrugged—"you get the idea."

"Yeah." He waited until the coffee had finished dripping, then poured them each a cup, adding cream to hers.

"Thanks." Angie sat at the table and sipped the steaming brew.

Rick sat down across from her. "Got any other information you'd like to share, Agent Grant?"

"It was a warning shot to tell us they were watching."

"How'd they know we were here?"

"Maybe they didn't, but it doesn't matter either way. They weren't trying to kill us."

He stared at her. "The back door?"

"Maybe he wanted to leave another note."

"He?"

"My father—whoever left the first one." She walked back to the living room and closed the drapes. "I think that bullet was my father's way of telling me he's watching."

"Angie—"

"I don't care if you think I'm paranoid. I know Syd is out of jail." Angie looked at the skepticism on his face. "Forget it." She returned to the table and sipped her coffee, gauging his reaction. "At CSIS they train you to follow your hunches. This one is strong."

Her intractability irritated Rick, but he couldn't argue. He knew the value of a hunch in police work. The wind squealed in through the cracks in the window frame above the sink, reminding him that he was helpless out here without backup. His palms itched. For the first time in all his years with the force, he felt cornered. He was senior officer on staff, temporary head of the detachment, and he was as jumpy as a helpless kitten. He needed something to do to get rid of this case of nerves.

Then Rick remembered. One by one he pulled the boxes from under the cupboard and lined them up on the counters. He'd helped another officer install a security system in his house and had learned a few tricks in the process. With a good idea of where he wanted to place each device, his mind clicked into the familiar rhythm of solving a new problem.

"You're going to do that now?" Dubious didn't begin to describe her tone.

He twisted around to grin at her. "Why not? At the very least it will show whoever decides to visit next that someone expects them." He held up two motion detectors. "I'm going to set the system up. I've got two cameras—one for the back door and one for the front." He picked up a roll of duct tape. "Never can tell when you'll need this stuff. It should seal off that bullet hole in the window until I can get it fixed."

When he returned after taping the window, Angie hadn't moved. She met his stare, her lips tight. "Don't do this for me. I'm not going to be here that long."

Her face was pale but composed. He waited for her to continue, hating the words even before she'd uttered them.

"You cannot ignore that arrest warrant, Rick. It's your job; you have to turn me in. There's no other way—I know that." She rose, looked him straight in the eye. "You love your job. You've worked hard to get where you are. You've pushed yourself up through the ranks with one goal in mind, becoming a staff sergeant. Don't let me ruin that for you and don't feel guilty for doing your job. This is a problem I created all on my own. I'll just have to handle it."

A light tap on the door had them both reaching for their weapons.

"Rick? It's Kent. Is everything all right?" Another tap. "Rick?"

Angie unbolted the door. She glanced over one shoulder at Rick.

"They'll know soon enough anyway." She pulled open the door. "Come on in, Kent."

"Angie?" Kent Anderson said, then looked to his friend for an explanation.

"What are you doing hiking around in a blizzard, Kent?" Rick decided not to explain, simply turned back to the security-system parts while he tried to think of an explanation that sounded plausible.

"I saw your truck behind the barn when I went to check on the horses. I figured you were out here by yourself. I didn't know—" Kent stopped.

Silence. Another long stretch of it. Rick knew Angie was waiting to follow his lead.

"For the moment, Angie's hiding out," he muttered. "I'd appreciate it if you didn't spread that around. She's got a little girl in protective custody. As soon as the storm breaks, she'll move on."

Kent shook his head. "I never imagined you'd come back to this place, Angie." Then his face turned a bright red. "I mean—"

"I know what you mean. I could hardly wait to get away, could I? Actually that's why I came." The wobble in her voice was obvious, though she paused just long enough to quash it. "I figured nobody else would imagine it either."

Kent opened his mouth but Rick interrupted, his narrowed stare intent on the friend who'd never let him down. "I'm a big boy, Kent. I've been looking after myself for a while now. Why don't you tell us why you're really here?"

"We heard something," Kent admitted. "Sounded like a gunshot. I remembered talking about vandals and wondered if I should make sure everything was okay. Then some guy on a snowmobile took off on our side road at about a hundred clicks. If he hits a tree at that speed, he'll be seeing stars. I decided to check things out before I tried to call for help."

"Did you get a look at this person?" Rick knew his tone was curt, but he desperately needed an answer.

"No. I saw the tracks under the trees coming into your yard, though. By the sound of that engine it was a new machine."

"He put a bullet through that living-room window you admired so much." Frustrated, Rick raked a hand through his hair "And then took off."

"What?" Kent's face drained of all color. "Someone is shooting at you?" he asked Angie.

"Not exactly at us. It was more in the nature of a warning shot— from my dad."

"Syd? How? He's in jail." Kent took a second look at her. "Isn't he?"

"Angie believes he's free. She's sure his friends are expecting him to show up here."

"Friends? Those guys in a black car that Fred saw? Never even dawned on me that could be Syd." Kent frowned. "But I don't think you have to worry about him, Angie. Our prison visitation group went there a few weeks ago. I spoke to your father for a few minutes. He seems like a different man. Quieter, more introspective. He didn't say anything about getting out. As a matter of fact, he told me he'd just signed up for a prison Bible study."

"Imagine that." Angie loosened her fingers from the handle of the mug and forced a gritty smile. "Bible study. Repentance, you think?"

"Perhaps. What's wrong with that?" Kent glanced from one to the other, saw them exchange a look, held up a hand. "Never mind. I don't need to know. Just tell me how I can help."

Rick held his gaze, kept his tone friendly but firm, unequivocal. "Thanks, pal, but at the moment there's nothing you can do. It's late and you need to be at home with Georgia, so go. If you still feel inclined tomorrow morning, it'd be nice if you could dig your way over here and help me put in a few of these gizmos. I'm going to make it . . . challenging to get inside this house." He listed the tools he'd need.

"Sure, no problem." Kent appraised the room. "You won't be going anywhere for a couple of days anyway. Our current conditions aren't supposed to blow over for another twenty-four to thirty-six hours."

"All right!" Rick grinned, his spirits soaring at the thought of a few peaceful hours spent with Angie before he had to turn her in.

Kent blinked and half smiled at Angie. "Silly me, I thought sitting out a blizzard in the boonies would be bad news."

"What can I tell you? He's weird," she told him with a shrug.

"You're a good friend, Kent. To both of us. But we're fine. Now go home before Georgia makes herself sick worrying about you. You won't get lost, will you?"

"Me?" Kent snorted his derision.

Rick made a split-second decision. There were no guarantees their visitor wasn't lurking in the woods, waiting. Kent could be a walking target. He wasn't going to let his friend go back alone. At least Angie had her gun. Kent had nothing.

"I'll go with you." Rick pulled his coat on. "There's something in my truck I need."

"You need it now, at this time of night?"

Rick met Kent's questioning stare. "Yes."

"Suit yourself." Kent glanced at Angie. "Would it be okay if I brought Georgia tomorrow? She'd love to see you again."

"Sure. But just you two, okay? I don't want a bunch of people knowing I'm here. I have to watch out for Kelly until I can hand her over to the proper authorities."

"Kelly? That's the little girl you're protecting?"

Angie nodded.

"Okay, just us two. Not that there's anyone else to tell. Fred and Ralna went to see their new grandbaby. I talked to them today—last night," he corrected, glancing at his watch. "They'll stay put until it's safe to travel. Is there anything you need that Georgia could bring?"

"Thanks, but we're pretty well set up, courtesy of Rick."

"There's no one better to depend on." Kent tossed a speculative look at the Mountie. "Except God."

"God." Angie heaved a sigh. "Uh-huh."

Something more than a simple lack of faith lay behind those doubting tones. Rick frowned, opened his mouth to remind her she'd once placed all her hope in God, then paused and took a second look. Her irises had shifted color to that curious green gold shade he remembered so well.

Angie was hiding something.

Now all he had to do was find out what.

# CHAPTER SIX

At the mention of God, Angie's whole demeanor had changed. Her spine straightened, her shoulders went back, and her chin thrust out. She wanted to say something; Rick could see it blazing in her eyes. But after a few timeless moments, she simply turned away.

"See you tomorrow, Kent," was all she offered as she carried her cup into the living room.

Kent waited till she disappeared to glance at Rick. "I feel like I said something wrong," he said sotto voce.

"Don't worry about it." What was wrong with Angie was going to take more than either of them could offer. "She'll be fine." He hoped.

"If you say so. You ready to go?"

"Sure." Rick walked across the kitchen, stuck his head around the corner. "I'll lock the door behind me, Angie. Shouldn't take long to walk him back to camp. Will you be okay?"

"I'll be fine." Angie didn't look up from scrutinizing her cup.

It was as if she'd dismissed him from her mind the moment she'd finished speaking, but Rick knew that wasn't true. She was thinking ahead, trying to come up with some plan that would keep Kelly away from whoever was chasing her. Angie would grit her teeth and face whatever she had to, but she wouldn't let the child get in the middle.

Neither would he.

Outside the wind had picked up. It howled around corners, blasting icy particles into the skin with drill-like precision. At the moment it was hard to see more than a foot ahead.

"Don't you just love the prairies in winter?" Kent muttered, fastening his snowshoes.

"Oh yeah." Rick walked behind him, peering through the snow swirls. They trod single file as far as the camp barn and arrived at Rick's truck that was now almost hidden by snowdrifts. "Can you make it from here?"

"You're the one who's puffing." Kent grinned. "Maybe you should take these." He pointed to his snowshoes.

"That's a surefire way to kill myself." Rick unlocked the truck, tried to use his radio. Nothing but static. "I wish I could get hold of the office, but everything seems to be out."

"It's the wind. When Fred phoned, he said a tower had gone down. Shortly after that our phone went out. That's why I came over instead of calling somebody to check on you. I figured your guys are up to their necks in town. They don't need to come running out here."

"Yeah, you're right. Not a lot they could do anyway." Rick was sorry he wasn't there doing his job, but keeping Angie safe mattered more. Angie won hands down every time.

"Angie seems convinced that Syd is after her. You think there's anything to that?"

"Hard to say." Rick scrubbed at his chin. "You said he was making plans for the future when you saw him?"

Kent nodded. "Reparation. Seemed genuinely sorry he'd hurt someone while robbing that bank."

"Genuine is hard to judge." Rick squinted through the flurries. "Our boy Syd is a deep subject. Nobody could figure out why he suddenly took it in his head to rob that bank or who phoned in the tip that led us to him. Syd wouldn't talk, but I always figured there was something else going on with him. Nothing I could prove but—"

"What?"

"I have this feeling that I'm looking at things the wrong way," Rick admitted. "It's as if something shifted, changed." Angie's castigation of her father rang through his mind. "I always thought I was a good judge of character, but I sure misjudged Syd."

"We all did." Kent's eyes narrowed. "Rick, is something wrong—besides the bullet hole?"

"I don't know. I'm still trying to put all the pieces together. Something about this whole situation nags at me."

"You'll figure it out. You always do."

Rick appreciated the confidence. Just as long as he didn't untangle it too late to help Angie.

"I better go," Kent said. "I'll see you tomorrow. Be careful."

"Always." Rick watched him track through the trees. The camp yard lights were all on. With the buffer of protection the tall trees offered, the wind's force was diminished, making it easier to see across the compound.

Once his friend had disappeared inside his house, Rick returned to the truck, lifted the rifle from behind the seat. He'd kept it there for emergencies. A bullet through the window qualified as an emergency.

That done, he gave the radio one last try. There was a lot of static so he reached out to turn it off, his hand freezing as he heard his name.

"—tell Rick. He's not going to be happy."

"Tell me what?" he yelled into the hand piece.

A burst of static was his only answer.

He wanted to stay there, to keep trying, but the memory of Angie alone in the house filled with painful memories urged him to turn the radio off. He locked the truck, then pushed his way back, facing into the wind, losing his bearings a couple of times in the whiteout conditions. It was a scary feeling to stand in the whorl of snow and have no idea which way to go. Each time he stopped where he was and prayed for guidance. Each time a window of clarity opened just long enough for him to recognize some sign that led him back. It reminded him that he needed to seek heaven's illumination on Angie's problems.

The house was dark. The wind dropped, and a sudden calm lent the world around him an eerie silence. Rick was about to open the back door when he heard the low growl of a snowmobile engine. So their visitor was back. He crouched in a shadow as the headlights circled and focused on the Grants' garage, not twenty feet away.

Like the rest of the property, that building was almost past the repair stage and listed to one side, but that didn't stop the intruder. He dismounted, tugged open the door so his headlight shone in, then disappeared inside.

Rick waited and watched, the rifle across his knees. Better to stay here than face the guy and maybe get bumped off. Dull thuds emanated from the garage, as if some boxes had been knocked over. Two minutes later the intruder appeared carrying a dark square object. It hit something on the machine and gave a tinny clang.

The man climbed on his snowmobile, adjusted the weight of his stolen item across his legs, and rumbled out of the yard.

The door behind Rick squeaked open.

"You saw him?" Angie murmured. "What was he doing?"

"Finding something," he told her, easing her inside and closing the door behind him.

She turned on the range-hood light, peered up at him. "What did he take?"

He met her stare with his own and glimpsed a flicker of fear dancing through her shadowy eyes. "That's the sixty-four-thousand-dollar question, Ang. I have no idea."

⇒◆⇐

"I'm out."

"And do you have what I want?"

"Not yet."

"Then you'd better pay your daughter a visit, hadn't you?" the voice on the other end of the phone snarled.

"Not a whole lot I can do with a blizzard happening, Mikey. Anyway, a couple of days won't make a difference."

"It makes a difference to me. I gave you two weeks. I won't give you more."

Syd chewed his bottom lip at the reminder that the clock was ticking. "Anything new happening?"

"Nothing for you to worry about."

"I heard something in town. A warrant—"

"Let me do the hard thinking, Syd. You just finish your job. That kid of yours is becoming a menace."

"She didn't do anything wrong."

"One of you has something I need. I want it soon. Or else."

The phone clicked in Syd's ear. He put the handset back into place, then let the door of the phone booth whoosh closed behind him. He trudged through the deepening snow to his motel room, alert for any curious observer. No one.

Inside his room he eyed the bottle he'd purchased a few hours earlier. All this time, and the temptation was as great as it had ever been. He stared at the marks on his fingers where they curled around the chiseled glass. The scars were faded and the marks toned in with his undamaged skin, but the pain lingered. She hated him. He could live with that. But she wouldn't take the fall for his mistake. He had to protect her.

"Help me," he whispered. With a wrench of his wrist the cap flew off. He poured the contents down the drain, tossed the empty bottle into the trash. One battle won.

Syd walked to the bed, sank onto the edge. The television was on, but the only face he saw was his wife's.

*"You shouldn't have done it, Syd. No matter what."* Her voice faded into the sound of the wind. *"You should have never done it."*

She was right, but he'd realized it too late.

Angie closed the lid of the dusty box, wishing she could cut off the past as easily. Kent's laughter in the kitchen above, the puppy's woof, and Georgia's soft greeting made her yearn to forget the past, let go of the pain, and share whatever happy times she could find with them. But they wouldn't want her, not when they learned what kind of person she really was.

Anyway, she'd soon be in jail. But she wouldn't give up, not even there. She'd keep fighting because this time she had not done anything wrong.

Angie dusted off her jeans, stretched, then climbed up the basement stairs. Pretending to be strong had eased her through twenty-six years. It would work this time too.

Georgia was seated at the table with Kelly on her knee. "Angie! How are you? You look . . . different. New makeup?"

"Dust," Angie told her. "Someone hasn't been doing their housework."

"Is there anything I could get for you? Something I could do to help?" Sympathy shone from the depths of Georgia's kind eyes.

"Thanks, but I think what I really need right now is a break. Digging through those boxes of Syd's old records was ugly. Hey, Kel." She ruffled the little girl's curls. "You okay?"

"Yes, Angel." Such a solemn face. "I was worried about you."

"You don't have to worry. I'm fine, honey."

"Want some coffee?" Rick grabbed a cup, then waited for her response.

"Thanks." After accepting the cup, Angie sat down across from Georgia. "How have you been?"

"Great. I'm loving this blizzard. We've got about a foot of snow out there and no end in sight."

Angie glanced out the window, blinked at the wall of white. "I thought it would be almost over by now."

"Nope." Kent flopped down beside his wife. "This one's a biggie. Supposed to last at least another day. You're stuck here, Angie."

She felt Rick's eyes on her and turned, met his querying look with a smile. "It's kind of nice to be back with you guys," she said.

"It is?" Kent asked. "But I thought you couldn't wait—"

"Tell Rick about the call, honey," Georgia intervened.

"Huh?" He stared at her.

Angie caught the look that passed between the two and knew Georgia was trying to spare her feelings.

"The call. Oh yeah." Kent snapped his fingers. "We got a phone call this morning from your buddies, Rick. I told them you were stuck out here, and it didn't look like you'd get out any time soon. They said to tell you everything's quiet in the office. Most of the highways are closed. People are staying put."

"That's good. No point in risking your life in this."

"Shauna asked me to tell you to call her as soon as you could. Something about a warrant and a surprise. She wasn't too specific."

Angie felt Rick's concerned gaze rest on her. She glanced at the mirror on the wall, noticing her lack of color. No wonder Rick was staring. She looked horrible.

Rick cleared his throat. "Thanks for telling me. If I can't get my radio or cell to work this afternoon, I'll walk over to your place and borrow your phone."

"You're welcome to, if it's working. Service has been interrupted— more off than on." Kent finished his coffee, then gestured at the pile of boxes littering the floor. "Guess we might as well finish your security system."

"Yeah." Rick moved beside Angie, touched her hand. "Will you be all right?"

"Of course." She kept her voice low, met his scrutiny. "I'm not going to run away. I don't want you to get in trouble because of me. Besides, I need to find out what's going on." She couldn't stand to see sympathy in his eyes, so she kept her gaze on Kelly.

"Angel, this lady brought me something. Can I watch it on the TV?"

"VeggieTales," Georgia explained. "I know the antenna is down so you can't get any reception, but I thought if you had a VCR . . ."

"Of course," Angie said. "I'll set it up for her."

Two minutes later Kelly was happily ensconced in the master bedroom watching the vegetables teach a lesson on forgiveness. As the first words about pardon were spoken, Angie cringed, kissed the top of Kelly's head, and quickly returned to the kitchen. "She's entranced. Thanks for thinking of it."

"No problem." Georgia watched Angie sip her coffee. "Are you really all right?"

"No. But I'll be fine. What's happening at the camp?"

"Well, we'll soon be gearing up for a Valentine's weekend. It's a marriage seminar, and we're almost fully booked. I've got to get to work on centerpieces and stuff. This is when I miss Christa the most. Food I can handle, but coming up with the crafty ideas she did?—" she shook her head—"just not my forte."

"Maybe you can hire her. I understand her crafts company is growing by leaps and bounds."

They chatted easily for a while; then Georgia got up to put the roast she'd brought into the oven. "I hope you don't think I'm taking over. I just thought that with the blizzard and all . . ." She paused.

"Georgia, I appreciate the thought. I'm afraid my cooking skills are fairly limited. My father—" she gulped, regained control—"Syd usually bought hamburger so I learned to make that a thousand different ways, but I don't get very creative beyond spaghetti, chili, stuff like that."

Angie didn't want to talk about Syd or the past, so she rose and headed for the living room. "I've got a couple of puzzles in here somewhere," she called out. "Want to work on one while the boys play with their toys?"

"Sure. Just let me season this meat and I'll be there."

By the time Georgia came into the living room, Angie had all the puzzle pieces turned right side up on the worn coffee table. She sat cross-legged on the floor, assembling the corner of a boat.

"My father used to buy a puzzle every Christmas," Georgia told her as she pulled a chair close and sank into it. "He'd bring it out after dinner, and my mother and I would try so hard to fit more pieces than he did, but we never could. He had a way of looking at the pieces and seeing where they fit that I never mastered."

"What do you mean?"

"Well, this is how I work on a puzzle." Georgia picked up a piece with the dark red of a sail on it and tried to fit it in six or seven places. When it didn't fit, she put it down, found another with more red, and began trying to place it.

"Not very efficient, is it?" she giggled. "My dad would study the picture on the puzzle box for a long time. He'd focus on one specific part and gather all the pieces he thought belonged in it. Then he'd choose a piece, just one, and examine it from every angle."

Georgia picked up one of the pieces and held it out. "This one, for instance. He'd say it had tentacles like a lopsided octopus with pointed jowls. Then he'd look at the pieces he'd gathered and hone in on the ones with the same bumps and points."

"I guess it's a good strategy," Angie responded, watching as Georgia snugged the piece into place.

"When I was ten I asked him why he did it that way. He said it was silly and frustrating to waste time trying to fit one piece into nine hundred and ninety-nine others, but that if he targeted one specific part of the puzzle and got that together, eventually all the parts would join together and it would all make sense." She snapped two sections of blue together and grinned. "You see? I've often thought it was a good way to achieve your goals. Choose one thing and work on it until it's better, then move on to the next. Eventually all the pieces fit together."

"I wish I'd known your father." The words slipped out without thought.

"I wish you had too. He was a wonderful father even though he'd had a terrible childhood. Somehow he learned how to put the past behind him and focus on the future."

"I wish I could."

"Tell me about your father, Angie."

"What's to tell?" A wave of fury engulfed her. Georgia's father had no doubt eased her path into maturity. Syd had made life hell. "I hate him."

"I'm sorry. He must have hurt you a great deal."

"Yes, he did. And I'll never forgive him. Never."

"Does that make you feel better, hating him?"

It wasn't the remark she'd expected. Angie frowned. "What?"

"Does hating your father ease any of your pain?" Georgia sat back, looked her straight in the eye. "Does the pain lessen when you keep going over and over what he did or said, dwelling on the bad memories again every time you remember the past?"

"Yes!"

"Are you sure about that?" Georgia's soft inquiry irritated her.

"You think I'm exaggerating, that it wasn't so bad?" Angie demanded.

"Oh no. I'm sure you suffered terribly. I would never want to diminish what you went through."

"Then you understand what I mean."

"The need to lash out—yes, I understand that very well. But that isn't the point." Georgia leaned forward. "If your father walked through the door right now, what would you do?"

Angie drew back, and the band around her temples cinched tighter. "I don't know."

"What would you like to do? Kill him?"

"No."

"Beat him, send him back to jail for the rest of his life?"

Angie tried to count to ten, but it was no use. "Yes!"

"No question there." Georgia nodded. "You want him to suffer, right?"

"Just like I did. Yes!"

"But how does that make it any better? How does that change what happened to you, make it more bearable?"

"I don't know but it does," Angie insisted stubbornly.

"Really? Maybe it just prolongs the pain. Maybe it's a way of avoiding moving ahead, of trusting others. You tell yourself your father wasn't to be trusted, your own father. So who can be?"

"I don't know. I don't know!" Angie winced at the pain in her jaw and realized she was clenching her teeth. "Maybe I am doing that. All I know is that he hurt me. Over and over again he hurt me with his impossible demands, his constant orders. Nothing I ever did was good enough. Nothing. So don't preach forgiveness to me, Georgia. I will never forgive him."

"I'm sorry." Georgia's eyes were shiny with unshed tears. She fiddled with the puzzle piece in her hand. "I know it sounds like it's too easy for me to say. You probably think I'm parroting what everyone else says."

"Aren't you?" Angie bit her lip. Now she was blaming Georgia.

"I hope not. I've never been very patient with those who try to minimize someone else's problems."

"Then—?" Angie waited.

"After I lost my baby and my husband—" Georgia swallowed— "I hit rock bottom. I was furious with God and everybody else whose normal life went on while mine remained dead. But that anger, that pain is exactly what kept me from moving on to what was left of my life. I had to come to Camp Hope to learn how to let go. If I hadn't—" She shook her head. "It was eating me up, stealing the joy from my life. Anger is an acid. It consumes everything, but it only gives back more pain. My choice was either to stop the cycle or keep my anger and spend the rest of my days in a never-ending haze of hurt."

"You make it sound so easy to forget." Angie touched the sofa, remembering the hours she'd huddled here, alone, afraid her father would never come home.

"No, it's not easy. And I haven't forgotten. But it is part of my past now."

The memories were too many; they tumbled back in spite of Angie's resolve to keep them in check. She jumped up, spilling the pieces all over the floor, her chest tight with tears she refused to shed.

"I'm glad for you, Georgia. Really glad that you and Kent have each other. But it isn't the same. How am I supposed to forgive Syd for what he did to me?" she hissed, clenching her hands in fury. "How do I wipe out eighteen years of my life?"

Georgia stood also, wrapped an arm around her shoulder, and pressed her blonde head next to Angie's. "I can't tell you how," she whispered. "I can only tell you who. The only way I know to find the grace to forgive is by asking the One who dispenses grace to us in abundance. If you ask, He'll answer."

"God, that's your answer?" She stared into Georgia's blue eyes, saw the peace reflected there, and knew Georgia spoke from her heart.

"He's the answer. To everything."

"Then I'm in even worse trouble because God isn't going to help me," Angie told her. "In fact, He's punishing me."

Georgia shook her head. "No, Angie. God has always loved you. Syd is the one who hurt you."

"But—why did he do it? Why?"

"I don't know. Maybe you should ask him the next time you see him."

"Maybe I will." Angie's teeth ground together at the thought of facing the man she was supposed to call father. The fury built inside into a hotter, whiter fire until every nerve, every muscle was taut with it. She drew away from Georgia, bent, and began to pick up the pieces of the broken puzzle.

A *broken puzzle*—her mind mocked the significance of that. Syd had pushed himself back into her life, claiming he was trying to protect her, yet he didn't know what she was running from. How could he? Her father's concern had always been only for himself.

"If Syd doesn't give you the answers you want, who will?"

Angie pretended she hadn't heard Georgia's soft query while she told herself she'd hated him for too long to wipe it away in some act of penitence.

All these years later and nothing had changed.

Syd Grant deserved to pay.

# CHAPTER SEVEN

Rick lounged in the doorway staring at Angie's form huddled under the quilt. She shifted slightly, a moan squeezing from her lips. She stretched, then snuggled back down into her pillow.

She was innocent of any wrongdoing. He knew that as surely as he knew his name, but there was little he could do. A warrant forced him to take her in, to lock her behind bars of steel, to send her to a place where he couldn't protect her.

"Aren't you going to wake Angel up?" Kelly's voice was whisper soft, her warm fingers curled into his.

"Not yet." He eased the door closed. "She's very tired. We'll let her sleep a while longer. Come on, honey." He tugged on Kelly's tiny hand, marveled at its strength. "Let's go find you some breakfast."

"Georgia's making pancakes. I love pancakes."

"Good." He smiled, forced himself to sit at the table and eat what was set before him, though his brain had no idea what his mouth consumed. If only he could find out who had issued that warrant, then maybe he'd have a chance of figuring a way out for Angie.

The conversation rolled around the table, but Rick took no part in it. His soul sagged with responsibility he knew he couldn't shirk. The storm would ease off today or tomorrow; then the plows would come. He would have no excuse for keeping Angie here.

"Can I play with the dollies now, Mr. Rick? I love Angel's dollies." Kelly's sweet face looked up at him.

"Sure."

"Do you know which one is Betsey? Angel loved Betsey best of all the dollies because her mom made it. She told me lots and lots of stories about Betsey and her mom. I want to know which dolly is Betsey."

"I don't know, sweetheart. You'll have to ask her when she wakes up." As Rick watched the little girl skip across the tired linoleum, he caught Kent's wistful smile. "Wish I had that much energy."

"Me too. I'll take a nap later. You should too." Kent nudged Rick in the ribs. "You know we're getting old when night watch wears us out."

"You're older than me, so you're probably wasted. I, on the other hand, am just getting my second wind." Rick winked at Georgia, then turned back to Kent. "You didn't see anything out there, did you?"

Kent shook his head. "All quiet or I'd have awakened you. You know that."

"Yeah, I do. Did I say thanks for staying?"

"You don't have to. We were glad to do it." Kent waited for Georgia's agreement, then asked, "So, buddy, how is this thing going to play out?"

"You mean the warrant?" Rick had explained the situation to them last night while Angie was busy with Kelly. "I'll take her in, lock her up, and try to figure out what went wrong, I guess."

"And Kelly?" Georgia asked.

"I don't know what to do about Kelly. Obviously she'll have to stay somewhere until CSIS sends another agent to watch her. I'll contact social services."

"No!" Georgia touched his shoulder. "Leave her and the puppy with us, please, Rick. We can watch her, protect her. Don't make that sweet child stay in some foster home where she knows no one."

Rick thought he caught a hint of condemnation in her voice. "I don't want to do this, Georgia, but I have to. I'm a cop. I've sworn to uphold the law. I know Angie's not guilty of anything except caring for that little girl with her life, but there's a warrant out for her arrest. I can't ignore it."

"I know. It's horrible for you too." She covered his hand with hers. "But it seems all wrong! I wish there was another way."

"Believe me, so do I," he murmured. He didn't tell her he'd spent the night trying to come up with alternatives, with little success.

"Hey, you two are getting me down. And this blizzard is driving me nuts. I've got to get outside and work off some energy." Kent carried his dishes to the sink, began running hot water. "Rick, if you think all your security doodads are working all right and you don't need me for a bit, I'm going back to camp to feed the horses and clean off some walks." He grinned. "I know I'll have to do it all over again when it stops snowing, but I could use the exercise."

"I'll go back with you, honey, if Rick can manage on his own. I want to change clothes and pick up a few things for Kelly to work on. She's getting a little bored."

Rick stood, ashamed he'd been so immersed in his own problems that he'd completely forgotten their needs. "You guys have been great. The security stuff isn't much help in all this blowing snow. But I don't think we'll get a third visitor with the snow getting so heavy. Go. Do what you need to. We'll be fine."

Before they left, Georgia washed the dishes and Kent dried. Rick knew he would only be in their way so he stayed seated, sipped his coffee, dark thoughts of turning in Angie preying on his spirit.

"We'll be gone a couple of hours. Not more. Then we'll spell you off and you can get outside for a break. It's windy and snowing a ton, but according to Angie's thermometer it isn't that cold." Georgia brushed his shoulder with her hand. "We won't be long."

Though Kelly sat in the next room talking to her dolls, the house seemed empty after they'd gone. Rick went to his room and cleaned his gun, listening for any unusual sound. When that was done, he brought his coat in from the porch, Kelly's as well, to warm them up. Maybe he could take her for a little walk later. She was a sweet kid, did as she was asked, but she must be sick and tired of being cooped up.

He bent down to pick up her boots and saw the corner of a white card. He picked it up. Black letters were printed in the center of the card. *CSIS*. Below that a name, *D. Renner* and a phone number written in a tiny scrawl that did not resemble Angie's handwriting. On the back of the card were the letters *MP*. Military police? Maybe this guy Renner had something to do with that black car.

Rick tucked the card in his pocket, went to check on Angie. Maybe she could clarify it. If she was awake.

He peeked inside the bedroom. Angie wasn't there!

He checked Kelly's room, but Angie wasn't there either. The bathroom—no, the door was open, no one inside. Then where was she?

"Angie?"

He heard the sound of footsteps; then the basement door burst open.

"What were you doing down there?" he demanded, trying to control the rush of fear that left him drained when he caught sight of her flushed face.

"Good morning to you too." Angie grinned, her eyes dancing with barely suppressed excitement. "I was having a dream and when I woke up, I remembered something." She opened her hands, let the papers in them fall to the table. "Look at this."

"Tax returns?"

"*Syd's* tax returns," she clarified. "From years ago."

"Okay." Whatever she was getting at eluded him completely. But Angie didn't notice. She was busy lining up folder after folder in historical order. "Um . . . what's so interesting about a lot of old tax forms?"

"A great deal, Sergeant. Beginning with the amount he showed as income. Where did all this money go?"

"How much money are we talking about?" He sat down beside her and stared at the recorded amounts. A whistle slipped through his lips.

"We were dirt poor. I skimped and saved on everything because he told me we didn't have any money. I never had a birthday party, never invited anyone over, did without new sneakers when mine were falling apart. But according to this, we should have been living quite well."

"Disability, pension. Hmm. Not bad."

"Yes, and that doesn't include my mother's life insurance that was paid in a lump sum and for which he paid no income tax. See?" She pointed to a spot on the old yellowed form.

"Too bad you couldn't get hold of his bank statements. Then you could track the money trail."

"I have them. Doesn't help." She slid a paper from one envelope and unfolded it. "There's no record of Syd's depositing even one of his checks in all the statements I've looked at. He deposited cash, but only tiny amounts, never the amount of the checks he received. He withdrew cash."

"But he had to turn in those checks somewhere in order to get the cash." His interest was growing.

"I know." Angie fidgeted in her chair, her thoughts on something he couldn't see, far in the past. One finger tapped against her cheek. "He could have cashed them anywhere. They were government checks, so no one would worry about them. Besides, he was known around town."

"Uh-huh. And in those days even the banks would cash a check without making you deposit it, so it would have been easy to get cash." Rick scoured the documents she'd assembled. "So Syd reported his income for the tax department, but he made sure there's no paper trail that anyone could follow."

She met his gaze. Nodded.

"Which leaves us with a question. Was he into something illegal?" The moment the words issued from his mouth, Rick wished he'd kept silent.

Angie's face blanched, she swallowed hard, then began reassembling the documents. "Like wh-what?" she whispered when the silence had grown tense enough to crack.

"I'm not sure. Angie, who is D. Renner?"

"David Renner. My boss at CSIS. Why?"

"I found this on the floor." He held out the card. "Does MP stand for military police?"

"I don't know," she murmured, her forehead lowering as she stared at the words. "I was reading over Kelly's file one afternoon. The card was in it. I guess it fell out. I put it in my jacket pocket to return it but never got the chance. It's funny, you know, because I've tried to talk to Renner personally several times lately, but I can never get through. So I ended up leaving a message. He hasn't called me back once."

"And the phone number?"

She took a second look, shook her head. "Don't recognize it. Do you think Kelly's problems are somehow tied to my father?"

"I don't know." He studied her hands that seemed unsteady, the hollows of her cheekbones that hinted at sleepless nights and meals too often missed. Her eyes that filled more often than not with shadows. Could she handle it? He had to try.

"Angie, will you tell me more about your father?"

⟹◆⟸

Angie didn't want to remember the past anymore. These few days in this house of nightmares had brought back more than enough. She wanted to forget and move on. But to what?

"Was Syd always harsh and cruel with you?"

In spite of herself, the pictures tumbled back. "Yes." Then a memory bubbled up. "Well, I guess sometimes he tried to do things with me when I was little. He took me to the circus one day." Like a mirage, a face appeared in her mind. She shrank back from it, gall rising in her throat in a wave of disgust.

"What's wrong?"

"Nothing. Horror stories about my old man always make me nauseous." She fixed a grin in place.

But Rick wasn't buying it. "That wasn't a horror story. You were talking about your father taking you to the circus. What made you flinch?"

"A man." She stared at her hands. She shouldn't have said it, shouldn't have opened that can of worms. But she'd done it, and now it would all come flooding back.

"What man?"

She closed her eyes at the words, unclenched her fingers as the face swam into focus. "Just . . . a man. He kept showing up all through my childhood. I don't know his name. I never did, didn't want to. The moment he arrived my father would think of an excuse for me to leave. When I was young Syd would dump me at the Murdock sisters' place, abandon me, just like he did when he wanted to get away and didn't want me tagging along. Once he even left a message at the school for me to go there instead of home. The sisters would feed me, play with me, sometimes even sew me new clothes. Later on they taught me how to sew so I wouldn't always look like an orphan."

Rick remained silent, but his eyes grew dark with thoughts he didn't share. She avoided his stare, loathe to let him see how fragile her emotions were after so many years.

"How often did this man come around?"

She looked up. "Not a lot. Two or three times a year, I'm guessing. Never announced his visit, not that I heard about, at least. And I'm pretty sure my father was surprised by his appearances. The old man would get this look in his eye." She shuddered, then glared at him, anger burbling inside. "I suppose you think I should have more respect for my father."

"I'm not here to judge you, Angie. I wasn't there, but I know it couldn't have been easy." His hand covered hers, comforting in much the same way as his low quiet tones did. "Just tell me what you want to. I'll listen."

Angie didn't want to tell him about her past, and yet she did. She wanted to expunge herself of the guilt. She wanted to let it all go and she'd tried. But it wouldn't stay buried.

"Are you too tired? Would you rather talk later?"

When would be better—when she was in jail? She'd only dream about it, and that would be worse.

"No, I'm fine. If you have to know this stuff, let's do it now." She sighed. "Well, I was just a kid, so a lot of what I saw and heard was probably blown out of proportion. Take everything I say with a grain of salt. Several grains of salt," she corrected, remembering Georgia's suggestion that she was fostering her bitterness by going over and over the past.

"Okay." He waited.

"As I said, the guy gave me the creeps, but I was young. Maybe I got the feeling from Syd."

"Why do you say that?"

Angie thought about it for a minute. "When this guy came around, I always felt Syd was nervous, wary. Something like that. Too eager to please, if you know what I mean."

"Any idea what made you feel like that?"

She let her mind re-create one of those times. "Syd changed. I don't remember my father so . . . nervous. He was morose and sour, sometimes furious. Always cranky with me. Often he'd disappear. Then when he came back he'd seem more in control for a little while."

"But when this man came around, Syd acted differently?"

She nodded. "He had this fake attitude, like they were celebrating something and it was up to him to create a party mood even though he forced it. He'd load in the booze, and they'd drink it like water. I never knew where his guests came from. They were a disgusting bunch, and they drank themselves into a stupor." She paused to get a grip on her emotions. She hated for Rick to see her so weepy. "From the stories they swapped, I assumed they were buddies from his days in the service."

"Syd was in a war?" He sounded shocked.

Angie smiled. "He was in the armed forces. The Murdock sisters once told me he was part of a small tactical unit that rescued the American hostages in Iran in 1980. Do you remember anything about that?"

"I heard about that rescue but never connected it to Syd, never thought of him as a hero," Rick answered.

"I was pretty young, but the sisters said my mother told them he got a medal. He and some of his team were the last out. There was an explosion. I guess that's how Syd got burned." She made a face. "Not that he ever talked about it with me. What I know I gleaned from the Murdock sisters and those times when Syd was drunk and he babbled."

"He would have been taken out of active duty because of his injuries."

"Yes. The accident must have changed him because he sure didn't seem like the kind of man my mother would choose."

"So maybe this man you saw visiting was one of his team? part of his tactical unit?"

"I guess."

"You don't sound sure."

"I never thought of them as his friends, in spite of my father's chummy pretense. That one fellow was the one he deferred to; the rest were just bystanders. Syd was always on edge around that one guy." She needed to change the subject. "About the other night, the person you saw go into the garage—did he come back?"

"No. Why?"

"Just thinking. I wonder why he went in."

"What's in there?"

"I haven't been inside in ages, but there used to be a lot of junk. A couple of old trunks. My mother's doll patterns. Fiona and Emily told me she had a little doll-making business when she moved here. She sewed fancy dolls that people ordered from some kind of catalog. I don't know much about it except that she made me several dolls, for birthdays and Christmas and stuff. Most of them got wrecked by Syd. Syd had a thing about dolls. He hated them."

"Are you sure you didn't imagine that?" Rick asked.

"Hardly. Every so often he'd be in a tizzy, tearing through the house, messing everything up. Once he even tore one of the heads off. Usually he wasn't that nutso, though. He'd pick open a seam or something, and I'd sew it back up. I hid them eventually. When he went to jail, I got out some of my mom's stuff and tried to fix the worst ones. Those are the dolls Kelly's playing with. I'm not nearly as good as my mother. She could create something from nothing." She let the memory of happier times take over. "In the winter we'd sit in the living room, and she'd stitch while she told me stories about the dolls. She was fun."

"I'm sorry."

"Yeah. So am I." Angie chewed her bottom lip to gain control. "Talking about the garage—I just remembered. There's a bank safe in it."

"Maybe Syd hid his money in there."

"If he did, I never saw it. For as long as I can remember the door has been fixed so it won't close and lock somebody inside. I guess my grandparents didn't share the combination with my mother."

"Your grandparents lived in this house?"

"That's what the Murdock sisters told me. According to them my mom was raised here. I think my grandmother had been dead for a while before my grandfather passed away. Apparently my father was overseas when my mom decided to move back in. Emily said Mama told her that Syd had always wanted to farm, but I don't think that was true. Old Syd knew as much about harvesting a crop as he did about the combination to that safe."

"Huh." Rick looked confused, and she didn't blame him. Nothing in her life made sense, especially where it included Syd.

A new thought burst into her mind. "You think it was Syd on the snowmobile, that he took away a box of money after all these years? Sounds a little weird."

"Yeah, it does. He'd hardly leave cash lying around. Anyway, I found the bank's money the day I arrested him."

"You're right." Angie clamped her lips together and waited for Rick to complete his thoughts.

"I didn't get much of a look at the box, but I remember it clanged against the snowmobile when he loaded it."

She sat up straight. "The only metal box out there that I can think of contained my father's military stuff. I got into it once and he was furious." She jumped to her feet. "I'm going to see if it's still there."

"But there's a blizzard outside."

"I know. I know. But it's only about twenty feet away, and I want to know if that's what he took. If it's gone, there must be something special in it. Something I never noticed."

"Or something that wasn't there before," he speculated.

"Maybe." She grabbed her coat and zipped it up, tugged on a cap and some mitts, then snatched a big flashlight from a nearby drawer.

"Be careful, Angie. You don't know who could be out there."

"Is there something I should know?"

"Not that I know of. But that doesn't mean they aren't there."

She leaned down, showed him her gun strapped to her ankle. "I'm prepared. You just take care of Kelly. And Spot."

"You know it."

The merciless wind tore in when she opened the door. Angie squeezed outside, then slammed it shut. The snow was thick underfoot, making the steps slippery. She used the side of her boot to clear a space. Within seconds it was covered again. She grimaced. *No point in that.*

Before going any farther she scanned the yard, looking for anything out of the ordinary. Not an easy task. She could barely see the trees. Every so often a white space opened up, hinting at the shadows beyond the yard, but that was all. The garage was a dark blob directly across the way.

Angie leaned her head into the wind and pushed forward. It was hard going. The white fog of her breath was ripped away as soon as it emerged, but she kept pressing her body toward the garage. Somehow, somewhere, there was an answer. Maybe it was in there.

She lifted the bar on the door and opened it, then switched on her flashlight. As she swept the beam across the space, her fingers tightened with tension.

Nobody here. Good.

She closed the door, moved to the left, and flicked on the overhead light. It didn't work. Using her flashlight, Angie began to scour the contents. She'd forgotten how much stuff she'd left behind. To the left lay the workbench and an assortment of rusty tools her father had never taken care of. The dust lay undisturbed. No one had used them in ages, probably since her grandfather had lived here.

Ignoring the tools, she walked past the workbench. Chicken wire, baling string, some stakes for the garden, a dilapidated barbeque missing one leg—beyond that she saw nothing but broken and damaged furniture that had been brought out for repair and forgotten about.

At the center of the garage sat three old trunks—one made of metal, two made of wood. They weren't locked, but she didn't need to open them. She knew what was inside. Books. Her grandfather had been an avid reader. Her mother had often spoken about his love of literature and how she'd packed away his friends, thinking to send them to a library. Fearing mice would destroy them, Angie had reminded Syd about it once, but he'd been furious, told her to leave them alone, leave him alone.

The right of the garage was what could only be called a mess. Boxes—some full; some empty; some ripped, torn, or damp. Not one was metal. Angie froze. There—something had been there. She walked over to a clean space on the floor where she remembered Syd's army box had sat. It was gone now, stolen by the person on the snowmobile, she was certain. But knowing that didn't help, because she didn't understand why he'd taken it.

Beyond the boxes was a stack of suitcases. Nothing in those. She'd checked years ago, hoping for some memento of her mother's past. On the far right sat the safe, its door wired open as it had always been. Nothing was inside.

Her spirits dropped. There was nothing here to help her, nothing that would explain anything that was happening in her life now. It was just . . . the past.

"Angela?"

She slowly swiveled on her heel to peer through the shadows at the man she'd hoped never to see again.

"It's me, Angie. Don't you recognize me?"

It was a good question—she almost didn't. His hair was white now, short bristles that stood at attention all over his head. His face, puckered and wrinkled from the scars, was somehow different, less angry. He wore a thick navy parka, snow pants, and heavy boots. The scarred fingers she remembered were covered by leather gloves.

Syd.

"Are you all right?"

She couldn't say a word, so she nodded.

"Good. Now listen to me. It's very important that you do what I say."

Angie boiled. "It always was, wasn't it, *Dad*? Obey you, be your slave." She couldn't stop the anger. "Well, no more. Go back to wherever you came from and leave me alone."

"I can't. You're in danger, Angie. A lot of it."

"Yes, from you. How did you get here, anyway?"

"I walked."

"Sure you did. In a blizzard."

"I've done it before."

"Uh-huh." She glanced around but saw no one else. "I meant, how did you get out of jail?"

"Never mind that. It's not important. What does matter is keeping you safe. I've tried to do my best, but it's no use now. I don't think I can protect you anymore, Angela."

"Protect me *anymore*?" she blazed. "And how, pray tell, did you protect me before, Syd? By shrieking at me, telling me how incompetent and useless I was?" She narrowed her eyes. "Or are you here to take care of me the way you 'took care' of my mother? Is that what this is about?"

She thought of her gun, felt the smooth chill of it against her ankle. If necessary—

"What do you mean? Why do you say it like that? I took care of your mother the best I could." He stepped closer but stopped when she held up her hand. "Angie, explain!"

"You don't order me around anymore. Not ever again."

"I'm not trying to order you to do anything. I'm trying to understand what you're insinuating." He tugged off a glove and scratched the burned lobe of his ear as he always did when he was trying to figure something out. "I loved your mother more than life. I would have done anything for her. Anything."

"Including kill her?" The words slipped out, as if from the depths of her turmoil. But Angie was glad she'd said them, felt relief that what she'd secretly harbored in her soul for so long was finally out in the open. "Is that how you're going to protect me?"

"Kill her? No!" He gaped at her. "You can't really believe I harmed Eve. Never! She was my other half."

"She was alive!" Angie clenched her fingers at her side, daring him to deny it. "She was sick but she was getting better. Until you came back. Two weeks later, a noise in the night and *bam!* My mother is dead."

"I didn't kill her! I didn't. She had cancer, Angie. She'd had it before you were born, and we thought she was in remission. But then it came back. We saw a specialist. She was going to have chemo while I was overseas. The doctors said she'd recover!" His scarred face looked tortured. "When I came back she told me she couldn't endure the chemo. It took too much out of her. She'd quit fighting by then. All she wanted was to spend her last days in her childhood home, here on the farm. I got two weeks with her. Two lousy weeks! Then she was gone."

Angie pressed her forefingers against her temples to stop the pounding. It couldn't be right. He was lying. He had to be. "I was awake the night she died. I heard her fall. You pushed her. You killed her."

"You're wrong, Angela. She pushed me away from her. I'd made a mistake and she was so angry." He raked his hands through his hair, then suddenly looked straight at her. "But I did not kill Eve."

"I don't believe you."

His hands dropped to his sides. "You don't have to. Check with Dr. Magnusson. He's still around. Ask him about it. He'll tell you."

"Angie!"

The yell surprised them both.

"It's Rick."

"Go to the door. Call out so he'll know you're fine." Syd's fingers closed around her arm. "Do it, Angie! And hurry. I haven't got much time to prepare you, and you must be prepared for what's coming."

Torn between longing to run away and never see his face again and hearing more of this fantastic story, Angie debated her next move. She would be taken to jail tomorrow. Locked behind bars, she would have no opportunity to find out anything more. Maybe this one time Syd could help her, if she could trust him.

"Stay here." She walked to the door, pulled it open. "I'm fine, Rick," she called loudly. "I'll be in shortly."

A pause. Then the reply, "Sure?"

It was an old password system they'd developed on a case, a way to make sure the other wasn't in danger.

"Certain sure," she responded.

Angie couldn't see clearly through the blanket of snow, but she thought she heard a bang. The house door? At least she didn't see anyone coming toward her.

She stepped back into the garage and closed the door.

"Look, Angie, it doesn't matter what you think about me. Believe whatever you like. But listen to me because things are going to start happening soon, and I can't stop them. It's not a game any longer, if it ever was. I have to know where the book is."

"Again with the book! When are you going to get it into your head that I have no clue about any book? I don't know what you're talking about. I didn't then, and I don't know now where any book is.

Okay? Are we clear? I never saw a book, other than what was in the house."

"But you *had* to have seen it! I thought you'd remember after all these years. That book is my last hope."

"Well, I don't remember anything about a book." She glared at him, saw the flicker of fear wash over his face. "Maybe it's in there, with my grandfather's books. Maybe it was in your locker box that you took out of here the other night. I don't know and I don't—hey!" She wrenched her arm out of his and stepped back, reaching for her gun at the same moment.

"Someone came here?" Syd's eyes blazed with something, but it wasn't fear of her. "Someone took my stuff?"

"You did."

He shook his head. "Not me. But if they were already here and took something, then things are moving much faster than I'd guessed. You've got to hear me out. As soon as the storm's over they'll be back and you'll need to be ready."

When he stepped toward her, Angie leveled her gun at him. "You're a felon, Syd, and you're supposed to be in jail. No court in the land would convict me for protecting myself."

"I'm not a felon. I'm out legally." He held up both hands, stood silent, and watched her. After a moment, his arms dropped to his sides, his fingers tapped against his thighs, signaling his impatience. "There's no time for this. Just listen to me."

"Why?"

"Because you need to know. Knowing might be the only thing that can keep you from walking into a trap."

"*I'm* in danger?" she asked, incredulous that her father was aware of this. What did he know that he wasn't telling her?

He nodded.

"From whom? Where do you get your information?" She frowned. "I only took Kelly to keep her safe. That's my job."

"It's not about the kid. Not directly anyway. Listen to me." Syd pressed the heels of his hands against his eyes as he took deep breaths.

"There is a book, a small one. Sort of like a notebook. I have to have it."

"Why? What's in it?"

He opened his mouth to say something, then paused. Voices penetrated the flimsy walls. Angie turned, opened the door a crack, and peeked outside. Georgia and Kent were plodding through the snow.

Angie closed and latched the door, then turned toward him. "Don't worry—" She looked around. He was gone. Disappeared into thin air. Actually he'd slipped out the rear door.

She stepped outside to listen. The voices grew faint, died away as the back door of the house slammed. She heard no motor, no sound at all, except for the wind. But there were footprints leading away from the garage. Could Syd really have walked?

A noise at the door alerted her. She swung around, her gun aimed.

Rick stepped inside the barn. "Angie?" His eyes followed her movements as she holstered her weapon. "What are you still doing out here?"

Angie straightened, meeting his puzzled gaze. "Talking to my father." Her knees were shaking so she reached out, appealing for help without words.

Rick was there as he always was, her rock. He wrapped an arm around her waist. "Don't you dare faint," he ordered, supporting her with both arms. "Angie?"

"Yes?" she whispered, laying her head against his chest and breathing deeply of the lime-scented aftershave he always used. She'd been strong for so long. How wonderful to just rest here and know Rick wouldn't let her down.

"What did Syd say?" he asked, one hand smoothing her hair.

"He said I'm in trouble," Angie murmured. Her father was right, she admitted to herself.

She was in big trouble.

Angie looked into the secret place of her heart where she hid her feelings and knew that Rick Mercer was much more than the friend she'd always pretended he was. Rick was the only one she could trust, the only one who would never betray her.

But if he knew—if he ever learned the secret she'd kept hidden for so long—he'd never hold her like this again.

# CHAPTER EIGHT

Leave her alone, Rick."

It took some doing to tear his gaze away from Angie's slight figure snuggling the little girl on the sofa as they read from one of the big books, the old-fashioned lamp spreading a golden glow over both of them.

"I'm not touching her," he told Kent.

"You've had her pinned under that all-seeing stare of yours all afternoon. She's not going anywhere, man. Nobody's going to steal her. You don't have to watch her every moment of the day."

"I know." But Rick couldn't stop staring. A few hours, another day, and she'd be locked up, then hauled away. He didn't know what to make of her meeting with Syd or why he'd suddenly appeared. What Syd suggested confused him, but why would the man lie?

"You care about her a lot, don't you?"

"Yes," Rick admitted, keeping his voice low. There was no point in denying it.

"That was easy. No hesitation?"

"None." Rick looked at his friend, shook his head. "You know better. Angie's been special for a long time."

"I know. But she's got problems, Rick. More than she ever had."

"Don't we all?"

"Of course. But there's a warrant out on her. You're a cop. You'll ruin your reputation and your chances for promotion if you aren't very careful about how you handle this. She could hurt you, buddy. In more ways than one."

"I know."

"Do you? Are you really seeing this situation without bias? Angie's carried her burdens for a long time, and they've affected the way she looks at things, the way she looks at you."

Rick knew that Kent was speaking about her spiritual situation, and he appreciated the comment. Rick was certain that Angie longed to rebuild her faith, though she'd never admit it now. His part should be in helping—not hindering—that process. But he couldn't do that if someone carted her back to Ottawa.

"Rick, are you sure you're not trying to make up for what she's had to deal with? I mean, you were the one who got her out of this house and to the Murdocks' when you arrested Syd. Your help got her into the force; you taught her how to do the job. You even gave her the reference she needed for CSIS."

"All I did was open a door. She walked through herself." He held Kent's stare and waited for the rest of the argument.

"Okay, if you want to put it that way. That was very decent of you. But you can't save her from this. Things have changed. Angie's running from more than her bosses and her father. From what Georgia's told me, Angie's carrying a lot of guilt. You haven't seen her in months, so you don't know what she's been doing or how it's affected her." Kent huffed out his chest, tilted his chin, and sighed. "I know it's not my business, but you're my friend and I don't like what's happening."

"She's not going to shoot me, Kent."

"Maybe I should," he joked. "At least then you'd be forced to sit still long enough to think this through. That torch you're carrying for her is pretty bright. Just make sure it doesn't sway you into doing something you'll be sorry for."

"Don't you trust me?"

"Always. But this is a no-win situation. If she has to leave again, if she decides not to come back—both of which are entirely likely— you're going to be hurt. I don't want to see that."

"Neither do I. But there's not a lot I can do about it. I care about her. I'll do whatever I can to help her through this. I can't do anything else. Angie matters . . . a lot." He cast a sideways glance at Kent, hoping his friend understood that he didn't want to talk about Angie anymore.

"I was afraid of that. But be careful, Rick. Remember who's God and who's not."

Rick frowned. "What does that mean?"

"One thing I learned when Georgia came to Camp Hope. There are things you can control, and there are things that God has to work out and all you can do is sit and wait for Him to unravel the threads. Which I'll admit I'm not very good at, but it emphasizes our need to depend on Him." He got up from the kitchen table, stretched. "Lecture over. All I can do is pray for you both. Right now I feel trapped. I'm not used to being cooped up inside. Want to take a walk?"

"Go for a stroll in a blizzard? Maybe I'm the one who should be worrying." Nevertheless, Rick got up, retrieved his coat, and pulled it on, then walked into the living room. "Excuse me, Angie. Kent and I are going outside for a few minutes. Will you be okay?"

The outside door slammed shut as Kent left.

"Of course. Go with Kent."

"Where's Georgia?"

"Using some of that paint you bought on the master bedroom. She said she can't stand Syd's black and gold another minute. I'm going up to help her. Kelly is going to paint a picture, and hopefully Spot will sleep."

"Sounds fun."

"It will be." She met his gaze, her own resolute.

He wanted to reassure her, to smooth the line from her forehead and tell her nothing bad would happen, that everything would work out. But he couldn't lie. Life held no guarantees, especially now.

Angie sent Kelly upstairs, then stepped forward, covered his hand with hers. "You've been patient, kind, understanding, more than generous. But this is something I have to face on my own."

"So there's nothing I can do?"

She studied him. Finally the vestige of a smile feathered over her lips. "Maybe pray?" she whispered. "I'm not very good at that."

He touched her cheek, loving the satin touch of her skin against his. "What makes you think I ever stopped? Kent and I just had this conversation. I know where my answers come from, Angie. I know who holds tomorrow—the same person who sees those secrets you still cling to."

Surprise flared in her eyes. "How—?"

"I'm a cop. I can tell things." He smiled at her. "People always say that when nothing else works they pray. Wrong way around. Pray first."

"I-I'll try."

"It's a good place to start, Ang." He looked at her a few moments longer, turned, grabbed the rifle he'd brought from his truck, and walked out of the house.

Kent stood at the bottom of the steps, glanced at the rifle. "What's that for?"

"Just in case. You see any shovels?"

Kent reached under the stairs and pulled out two.

"Seems pretty futile, but why not? At least we'll burn some calories before Georgia feeds us again." Rick sized up his longtime friend, patted his shoulder. "All that good cooking—you're going to get fat, my friend. Very, very fat."

"Ha!" Kent gripped a shovel and dug into the snowdrift as if to prove that not an ounce of adipose tissue could ever form on his washboard stomach.

Rick stuck the rifle under the steps, then copied Kent's actions.

Though it was very windy and the snow rendered almost whiteout conditions, it wasn't bitterly cold. The snow was fluffy and light, making it easy to shovel. Together he and Kent cleaned off the steps and a good chunk of sidewalk buried under a drift more than two feet high.

But no matter how hard he worked and despite his willingness to let the wind to tear away all the unanswerable questions that littered his mind, Rick could not get the basic one out of his head: why would someone want to arrest Angie?

"Okay, I'm beat. I want to walk over to that stand of birch and take a bit of the bark for Kelly. She wants to glue it on her picture. Just let me get the rifle." Rick nodded at Kent's look. "I know; I know. I'm overprotective."

They made it past a lilac bush and two scraggly willows before Kent caught Rick's arm, urged him behind a pair of towering spruce.

Rick followed Kent's stare to see two men creeping through the woods beyond, noting the rifles looped across their shoulders. He slid the rifle he'd brought off his own shoulder and handed it to Kent. "Just in case. You're the marksman."

Kent nodded. "Who are they?"

"No friends of mine," he answered, glad that the wind ripped away all sound.

"What happens if they head for the house?"

"We stop them." Rick slid his fingers around the comforting grip of his revolver.

"Notice the outfits? They're dressed alike," Kent pointed out. "Some kind of tactical unit maybe?"

"Syd was in the military," Rick reminded him. "If he made it through this storm to talk to Angie, I'm guessing he had training in some special ops outfit. If these are his buddies, we could be in trouble. This would be a good time to pray."

They stood together, frozen against the massive tree trunks, and barraged heaven for help, until the two men stopped not ten feet in front of them. A sudden lull in the wind carried the intruders' voices toward them.

"There's no one here. This is a wild-goose chase."

Acting on his instincts, Rick stepped out from behind the tree, his fingers wrapped around the gun in his pocket. "I'm here. Something I can do for you boys?" The tension was as thick as the snowstorm. "You do realize you're trespassing? How'd you get here in this blizzard, anyway?"

"We . . . uh . . . we were on our snowmobiles. Ran out of gas."

"I see." Rick glanced around, pretending to be curious. "So they're in the bush? Both of them empty?"

"Uh, no. Just one. Thought maybe we'd ask for a hose to siphon from one tank to the other."

Rick recognized the last speaker as the one who'd hit him in Angie's house, the one who called himself Max. "Do I know you?" he asked, knowing identification would be difficult, especially with the man's ski mask.

"Don't think so." Max turned his back to Rick to confer with the other man.

Rick frowned, then shrugged as if it didn't matter. "Well, I just moved in. There's no way I'd be able to find a hose for you. The place is a shambles. I'm having some work done so everything's a little disorganized, if you know what I mean."

"Sure. Sure. No problem." Nothing but friendliness in that voice. "We'll both ride back on the one machine. Thanks anyway." He turned to leave.

"You're sure you can find your way?" Rick did a three-sixty around the yard. "Easy to get lost unless you've got GPS."

The first man patted his pocket. "Never go anywhere without it."

Something in the way he said it snagged Rick's attention. They weren't amateurs out for a joyride in a storm. They knew what they were doing, had the tools and expertise to track down their target in a storm. If Syd was right and Angie was their target, he and Kent would have no chance against their superior skills.

But they could have come in shooting and they hadn't. That gave him hope.

"I'm glad you won't get lost. 'Cause then I won't have to come looking for you."

"Come looking for us? What do you mean?" A hint of concern.

"I'm a cop. We're the ones who do search and rescue around here."

"Oh." The two men shared a look. "Don't worry. We'll head home right now."

"Where's home?" Kent asked, stepping out from behind the tree.

"Huh?"

"Where are you staying? I know pretty much everyone in this area. Who are you staying with?"

The men seemed stymied.

"Uh . . . we're renting a place," Max mumbled. "Just for the week-end. I don't remember the name." He looked at the other man. "We'd better go."

"Just a minute. You do have licenses for those, don't you?" Rick asked, glancing down at their rifles. "Not that you should have them anyway. There's no open hunting season at the moment."

"Uh . . . no, of course not. We weren't hunting." Max kicked the snow with his booted toe. A tic appeared in his left cheek.

"Protection. We heard about bears in this area," his friend told them. "Thought we'd be prepared in case we ran into one."

"Ran into a bear? In the winter?" Kent laughed. "Some hunters you'd make. Bears sleep in the winter, remember?"

Rick wasn't fooled. Kent might pretend affability, but his brain was running overtime.

"About the only thing you'll find out here are my horses and a few partridges. I sure don't like to think of somebody putting a bullet into one of those horses. Maybe you better take a look at their licenses, Rick; get some names. Just so I'll know who to come after for damages."

"No need for that. I told you, we're not shooting anything. Anyway, we left our wallets back in—our vehicles." The other man began backing away. "We're sorry we bothered you. We don't want to cause any fuss. We're just here for a break, a little holiday. You won't see us again." He turned and began retracing his steps.

Max stayed put, looking at the house. "I see you've got a security system. Wouldn't have thought you'd need it way out here."

"Guess you're living proof that I do," Rick said. He waited for it to sink in. "Are you sure I don't know you? Seems like we've met somewhere."

"We never met." One last look around. "Sorry for the intrusion. We'll stay off your land." Max stomped through the snow to join his partner.

"Sure you will," Kent muttered, scanning the area.

"So we've got two more players." Rick stared into the whiteness. "Angie works for CSIS, the Canadian Security Intelligence Service. She knows Max is a hired gun, but he's wearing the same outfit as the other guy, which leads me to assume that they have the same employer."

"CSIS?"

"I don't know . . . yet." Rick clapped a hand on his shoulder. "Too many questions. Not enough answers."

They paused, stared at each other as the muffled roar of two snowmobile motors faded into the hum of the wind.

"Guess they found some gas."

"You think that's the end of it?" Kent asked. He looked at Rick, shook his head. "Me, neither."

—————⊰◆⊱—————

Angie woke slowly, her head thick as if stuffed with cotton wool, the dream of her mother slowly fading as reality moved in. Moonlight streamed through the window, lighting the room with that strange blue white glow that only winter nights can cast.

"Cancer," Syd had said. Even told her to ask the doctor about it. That didn't mean he was telling the truth, but in all the years they'd lived together in that house, Angie had seen her father break down only once, the night after her mother's funeral. He'd ordered her to bed and she'd obeyed, but she hadn't slept. She'd lain there in the darkness and prayed to the God her mother always talked about. And then she'd heard them—muffled noises that frightened her.

She remembered creeping up the stairs to his room, peeking around the corner. He'd been kneeling beside the bed, his fingers knotted in the afghan her mother had made, tears streaming down his face. The muffled groans hurt to listen to, and she'd wanted to run to him, comfort him, and have him hold her. But something stopped her. What had it been?

*"I'm sorry, Eve. I'm so sorry I did it."*

Those words had preyed on her mind for years. Somehow, through all the abuse and anger and pain, she'd believed they were regret for killing her mother. And she'd hated him for it.

No! She thrust away the trickle of remorse. She hadn't been wrong then, and she wasn't wrong now. Syd was a user, practiced at manipulating people. She'd seen it a thousand times throughout her childhood. Bill collectors who left without any money but happy in spite of it. Repossessors who shared his bottle until they left agreeing to give him a little more time, just enough time for him to work another scheme.

Syd was guilty. There could be no pity for him. Not ever.

Angie sat up in bed and glanced at the clock—1:00 a.m. The house was quiet, no scream of wind tearing at the eaves, no creak of branches brushing the roof. The blizzard was over.

She slipped out from beneath the covers and grabbed the tattered old green robe that should have become a rag five years ago. After wrapping herself in it, she took a deep breath, clenching her jaw as the jackhammer in her brain took up a new rhythm. Tension. It had been with her for days, steadily intensifying as the minutes of dread counted down.

Tomorrow she would go to jail.

She would be forced to abandon Kelly despite her promises, despite her best intentions. There was no way out.

She trailed one finger over the dolls so carefully arranged on the top of the bureau. Kelly said they had hurts and as she stared at them, Angie saw with new eyes the rips, the tattered edges, the loose stitches. After Syd's rough treatment she'd tried to repair them. Now it seemed they needed it again.

It was a time-consuming, intricate task that she needed to do right now, something to keep her busy while she waited to be locked up. She'd fix each one as best she could, then hide them somewhere safe. *He* wouldn't find them. Not again. This one tender memory of her mother she'd keep for herself.

Angie gathered the dolls in her arms and carried them out of the bedroom. She eased down the hall to Kelly's room, saw the platinum ringlets spread across the pillowcase, and felt a smile lift her lips. Sweet Kelly. So trusting. God wouldn't let that tender spirit be harmed when she couldn't watch out for her anymore, would He?

Angie blinked away the tears and forced her feet to keep walking toward the living room. She could work there without disturbing anyone.

A sound behind her had her spinning on her heels.

"Relax, it's just me, Angie." Rick's warm firm fingers squeezed her shoulder. "You okay?"

"Yes. Just a little jumpy." She opened the hall cupboard, lifted out her mother's shabby sewing kit. "Couldn't sleep so I thought I'd do a little repair work."

"The storm's over." He followed her into the living room, watching her thread a needle with bright red silk thread, not saying what they were both thinking.

"Yes." Angie glimpsed the shadows in his eyes. "I know." She saw him look at his watch. "How much time have you missed?"

"A lot. Nothing I could do about it, though. This storm kept us boxed in."

"But you want to get back," she guessed. "You need to make sure that nobody has taken over your town while you were away."

"I'm not that bad," he protested.

"Yes, you are. You're very protective of the community. It's one of your most appealing attributes." She felt a shiver of uncertainty ripple down her back. "Anyway, you have to do your duty and take me in. We both know that. I just wish I knew what to do about Kelly. I think her father's dead, but I don't want to tell her that until I have proof. So far, there's been no announcement."

"Did you check your e-mail again? Maybe something's changed."

She knew it hadn't, but to please him she laid down her sewing, retrieved her phone, and checked both her voice mail and her e-mail. Nothing.

"I'm going to ask them to send another agent for Kelly."

Rick's jaw clenched, but he remained silent as she left her message.

The job complete, Angie snapped the phone closed and slid it into her robe pocket. "No point in trying to hide my location anymore," she mumbled, then blinked. "What if those men you saw this afternoon came for Kelly?"

He began shaking his head even before she finished speaking. "You said Max was a 'for hire.' CSIS wouldn't use him, would they?"

"No." Angie sighed. "I guess I'm grasping at straws."

Rick picked up his cell phone. "I'm going to check in with the office, see if there have been any new developments."

Angie shook her head. "Still clinging to hope? I tried praying but it didn't work."

"How do you know?"

"God isn't going to work some big miracle to save me from this mess. You're going to take me to jail; then someone will pick me up and I'll stand trial. Everything will follow its natural course, and if I'm very lucky I'll be able to prove that I didn't murder those two agents."

"Maybe." He dialed a number, waited for several minutes, then closed the phone. "Nobody's in the office," he told her. "It's switched to the service. Never mind. I'll know what's been going on tomorrow."

Angie finished stitching the band around the hat of one doll and set it aside. She picked up the next, rethreaded her needle, and began repairing the yellowed stitches around the neck. Her mother's work was fine, delicate. It wasn't easy to match but she did her best.

"My mother must have had a ton of patience," she muttered, sucking on her pricked finger. "And very good eyesight. I feel like I'm going blind." She glanced at him and smiled. "Do you know she kept on working, even on her very worst days? She'd have her kit nearby, and in between rests and reading her Bible she'd sew a few more stitches."

He leaned back in his chair and let her talk.

"I'd almost forgotten the fun we had choosing colors for the clothes. I got to pick out the ribbons off this rod she had hanging in the closet. She'd say, 'Cut off a piece as long as your arm, Angie.' And I'd measure and snip a piece and she'd look at it and then laugh. 'I'm so glad God gave you long arms.'" Angie gulped.

"It sounds like her faith was part of her everyday life."

Angie nodded. "Oh yes. She was a very strong believer." She knew what he was thinking. "You're wondering about me, aren't you? Don't worry, Rick. She passed her beliefs on to me."

"I know. You used to be so active in the youth group. Seemed like you had an announcement every week about a fund-raiser you were planning for Camp Hope or a youth trip. I especially remember that contraption you had built."

She giggled. "The dunk tank. I'd forgotten that. Did you get dunked?"

"About six million times. I'm pretty sure I single-handedly paid for that trip your group took to hear Billy Graham."

"You were the best-looking cop on the force, and you were single. We all had crushes on you." She watched his cheeks redden. "Rest assured that your sacrifice wasn't in vain. That was a wonderful weekend."

"But you stopped coming to church after that."

"Yes, I did. After Syd's arrest when he could no longer force me to go." She bit her lip, stared down at the worn fabric, and wondered whether it was worth trying to salvage.

"Mind telling me why?"

"He was a hypocrite. All those years of pretending and finally the truth came out. It was a relief."

Rick frowned. Angie hoped desperately that he'd let it go, give it up, but one look at his face told her it wasn't going to happen.

"*You* weren't playing at church, Angie. You were a leader, one of the best I've seen. You encouraged others, brought in teens who wouldn't normally have attended church. You were on fire. Are you trying to say it was an act? Because I don't believe that."

"It wasn't an act," she admitted finally. "I believed in God, still do."

"Then why—?"

"I didn't leave God. He left me." She saw his eyes flare, knew he was shocked. "There are some things God can't forgive, Rick. That's why it doesn't matter how hard I pray. I crossed that line." She swallowed. "So you see, the warrant, jail—all of it—are simply what I deserve. There are no big miracles waiting for me. No act of God is going to miraculously clear me."

Consternation filled his face, but Angie couldn't stop. Here, at least, she would finally tell the truth. "In God's opinion, I probably deserve exactly what I'm getting."

# CHAPTER NINE

$A$ngie, if God gave us what we deserve, we'd all be dead."

The longer she knew Rick, the more Angie appreciated his honesty. From the day she'd met him, through all the years, he'd always been straightforward with her. He was who he said he was, and she'd always been able to count on him to speak the truth. So now, when he knelt in front of her and took her hand, Angie felt she owed him the courtesy of listening to what he had to say.

"We don't die, though, because there's this thing called grace that God extends to us. His grace declares us not guilty. You see, Syd's not your only father." Rick smiled at her start of surprise. "There is another Father who loves you more than you will ever know or can even imagine. He sees everything. He knows exactly what you've done, and He loves you anyway."

"You don't understand."

"I don't have to understand. But God does. Listen." He released her hand before he reached for the Testament in his shirt pocket. He found his place and began to read: "'Does it mean he no longer loves us if we have trouble or calamity, or are persecuted, or are hungry or cold or in danger or threatened with death?'"

"You talked about this before."

"Yes." He grinned at her. "It about covers our situation; don't you think?"

She liked that he had made her problems his. She didn't feel so alone.

"But that's not all there is. There's hope here too. 'Overwhelming victory is ours through Christ who loved us enough to die for us.' That's quite a promise. And it isn't made lightly. God is here—now. He sees and knows what you've done, what Syd has done, what I've done. All of it. He knows. And He still loves us."

"I have trouble with that," Angie admitted.

"Of course you do. So do I. Grace isn't a concept humans get. How can God love someone as selfish and pigheaded as I am? I mess up over and over again. I do things that hurt other people, I want my own way, and I steal time I should spend praying and use it for my own selfish wants. How can He forgive me and still want me as His child?"

His sins didn't compare to hers.

"But God does forgive. He always does. The problem isn't with Him; it's with me. I don't understand His grace because I don't have the right vision, because I can't see as He does. Our law says that if we do something wrong, we should be punished. God's law says that if we are sincerely sorry, He will forgive us. It doesn't mean we won't suffer the consequences. It means that if we repent, we're still His child. No matter what."

"It's too easy."

"Easy?" Rick shook his head. "No, Angie. Grace cost God His Son."

"But—"

Rick tipped up her chin, forcing her to look at him. "You're forgiven, Ang. Whatever you've done, it's forgiven as soon as you ask. Let it go and know that God is doing what He has to in order to work things out for you."

"What things?" she asked.

"Things far beyond what you or I know. It really doesn't matter what or how because nothing will ever erase the love God has for us."

"I don't think my life is any example of heavenly love," she whispered. "My own father hates my guts."

"I don't think that's true, but even if it is, your heavenly Father loved you from the first moment He thought about creating you. Before your mother even knew you were coming, He knew and loved you. That kind of love is almost inconceivable. Read it for yourself if you don't believe me." He flipped through his Testament again, found the right place. "Start there."

Angie stared down at the words, felt the sting of knowing that what she'd done was something Rick would never have even considered. He was good; he did the right things. If he knew—

"Read it, Angie. Please?"

His soft whisper forced her compliance. Rick had stood by her through everything. What would it hurt to read a few words from his Bible?

"'I am convinced that nothing can ever separate us from his love.'" *Nothing?* She continued, "'Death can't, and life can't. The angels can't, and the demons can't. Our fears for today, our worries about tomorrow, and even the powers of hell can't keep God's love away. Whether we are high above the sky or in the deepest ocean, nothing in all creation will ever be able to separate us from the love of God that is revealed in Christ Jesus our Lord.'"

"You see? His love exceeds it all. In spite of what we've done or who we are, God loves us."

She heard him, but the past was too real, too horrible. "You don't understand. You can't possibly know."

"No, I can't. But, sweetheart, God does."

It was so tempting to pretend that Rick was right and that what she'd done didn't matter. It would be so easy to accept what he offered, to let him care for her, protect her, shield her. He would take on her battle if she let him.

But what about his hopes, his dreams? There was no way to tell what might happen. Association with her could ruin his chances of promotion, destroying the dream he'd held for so long. She couldn't do that to him.

"It's almost morning," she said when a long silence had passed. "I'll shower and get ready. Then we'll take Kelly to Georgia so she won't have to see me booked."

As Rick put away his Bible, she flinched at the dismay on his face but refused to allow the pang of regret to grab hold.

Instead, Angie forced a smile to her lips when she brushed his arm with her fingers. "Don't worry about me so much, Rick. I'll be fine. Whatever they think I've done will be explained and I'll get back to my life. It's Kelly we should be worrying about."

"Kelly?" He glanced around, his forehead furrowed. "Why?"

"She's the reason I ran, remember?"

"Yes, I remember."

When he didn't say any more, she looked more closely at him, realized something else was fluttering through his mind. "What?"

He chewed on his bottom lip while he studied her. "I was just thinking."

She crossed her arms over her chest and waited.

The action must have helped make up his mind because after a moment, Rick nodded. "Remember what you told me your father said that day in the garage? 'It's not about the kid.' I can't help but believe there's some truth in that." He stopped her from interrupting by holding up his hand. "This whole situation is weird, Angie. You ran from—wherever you ran from, to protect Kelly. Yet no one has come after her."

"Of course they have. Who do you think Max was after? Me, right? To lead them to Kelly. If they can get me out of the way, Carver Simpson can get rid of the witness against him." She squeezed her eyes closed at the thought of anyone hurting the tiny child. "Pray they don't get her, Rick."

"My point is, they seem to have found this place easily enough. Even Syd knew where to find you. Those two with guns were checking out their suspicions, but nothing was said about Kelly. Nobody even mentioned her."

"They're not going to broadcast their intentions to kill her." Angie frowned. "I don't understand what you're getting at."

"I'm not sure I do either. Let's think about it for a minute. This warrant business is way out in left field and totally unprecedented for an organization like CSIS. They like to keep their affairs hush-hush, in-house."

"True. In training that was stressed over and over."

"So what was the basis for issuing a countrywide warrant on you? Ballistic evidence? You said you didn't fire your weapon, so how could you have killed those men? Eyewitness? Who? The guy you said you recognized through the window? Known felon—hardly reliable. So what reason do they have for the charge?"

Angie's brain clicked into the familiar routine of assessing a case based on the evidence. "Actually," she said, staring at her hands as she mentally reconstructed that day, "there was nothing in that house that could have even remotely incriminated me. Unless they planted it."

"What do you mean?"

"I was never inside, Rick."

"But you were guarding Kelly."

"Technically. In reality I was backup. My orders were to stay in the house next door. The others were primaries; I was just a second line of defense. I notified headquarters that I was in place, but I never went into the house."

"Then Kelly—"

"She walked in my back door, asked me if I was her guardian angel. That was the first time I saw her since we moved from the last safe house. But even then, I never got close to her. I was the gofer. She was always upstairs."

"So that night, someone hit your front door, you saw men enter the safe house, heard what you thought was a shot, and took off. You made arrangements to meet someone from your outfit three times and were targeted each time. Correct?"

"Not exactly in that order, but yes, that's the gist of it." She knew he was assembling the scene in his mind. "What are you thinking?"

"I don't know what to think. I'm just postulating, laying out what I know and trying to fit the pieces together. But either something's missing or we don't know everything about Kelly's situation, because these pieces don't fit."

"Maybe we'll find out what it's all about when you take me in." She let her head drop to her chest, her body weary beyond belief.

"Wait a minute! I'd forgotten all about it." He lurched to his feet, stalked over to where his jacket hung, and dragged out the notice of the warrant and his phone. When he returned he said, "There's a contact number here. I was going to check it out before, but with the blizzard and things, I forgot. Whether they track you or not doesn't matter now because we're going to the office tomorrow. But I'd like to get a feel for what's happening before we show up. Especially since you said Syd mentioned a trap."

Rick held up the notice, then dialed the number at the bottom. When it began ringing, he sat down beside her, holding the phone so she could hear.

A nondescript voice answered.

"I understand you people are looking for someone. A former agent with your service." Rick kept his voice very low, a husky whisper that would be difficult to pattern.

"I don't believe so, sir. We're not—"

"I'm trying to find Angie Grant," he interrupted, breaking into the receptionist's practiced denial. "Do you want to know where she is or not?"

"I'll transfer you. One moment please."

Angie felt alarm prickle up her back as a series of clicks told her the call was being relayed and monitored, but she kept her gaze fixed on Rick. He would never betray her.

"Who is this?"

Rick winked at her before he began speaking slowly in a guttural whisper. "Is this Renner? I'm somebody who knows Angie Grant and can see a setup from miles away. Don't push it any further."

The transfer had deliberately taken too long, Angie knew. She tapped her watch, pointed to the phone.

Rick nodded.

"Agent Renner isn't in this area. Who are you?" the voice demanded.

"Pull the warrant. Or else I'll spill your dirty little secret to the whole world." Rick clicked the phone off. "Now we'll see what happens. You might as well get some rest."

Angie stared at him. "What *dirty little secret* do you know?"

"I don't have a clue." He shrugged. "But everybody has one. Who knows? Maybe I hit a nerve."

As long as he didn't know hers. Angie shuffled off the nagging worry. "You're very convincing as a bad guy. I never knew that about you."

"There's a lot you don't know about me. So don't plan on going anywhere soon."

The look he gave her made her nervous. She suddenly realized how close he was, mere inches away, as if he knew she kept her own secret. His probing brown eyes glowed black with an intensity she hadn't seen before. She leaned away automatically, worried he'd somehow scour out what she couldn't tell him.

One hand reached out to grasp her chin. "Promise me you won't run away again."

The comment stung. "I know you have to turn me in. I told you I'd go." A flush of shame burst up her neck at the scrutiny he subjected her to. "I wouldn't do that to you, Rick. Surely you know that."

"I'm not talking about the warrant. Once before you ran away. I don't want you to do it again. Not until we get things straightened out."

She was afraid to ask what things. That steady, unrelenting stare was getting to her. She nodded out of pure desperation. "Okay, fine. I'll be around till they cart me away."

His fingers smoothed against her jaw, cupped her cheek. "Nobody's going to cart you away. Not without going through me." His hand finally dropped away. "Angie, who is your contact at CSIS?"

"David Renner," she repeated. "I told you, he's my boss."

"He's the guy who assigned you to Kelly's case?"

"I don't know who decided what or how I was chosen. Renner's the one who called me and told me to drop what I was doing and get going."

"Was that unusual?"

She thought about it for a minute. "I don't know. I'd been working on a suspected terrorist case for several months so I wasn't expecting to be reassigned, especially since the man I was tracking had just made an unusual contact. But you know how it goes. Something else pops up and you drop what you're doing."

"Of course. But why you? Why not choose someone else as backup?"

"I'm not sure," she admitted. "Maybe to give me experience? Maybe they figured I could handle it. What are you thinking?"

"I'm still just putting all the pieces together."

"You're going by that little nudge inside, aren't you?" She made a face. "Don't give me that look! I know you, Rick. I can see how your mind works by watching your face. Something's eating at you."

"A whole lot of things, none of which I can connect." He glanced at his watch. "You need some rest. Maybe we'll learn something at the office, but for now you might as well get whatever sleep you can."

"I guess." Though Angie doubted she would sleep anymore, she put away the sewing supplies and picked up the dolls. "I'm so tired of this mess called my life. Who knows what will happen next?"

"God," Rick answered promptly. "And somehow He's going to make it all come together for good."

The question was, whose good? But Angie didn't say that. She simply bade him good night and walked into her old bedroom, where Kelly lay sound asleep. Trying not to make a noise, she slid under the bed, opened the cubbyhole, and placed the dolls at the very end of the passage. When she was gone, Syd might come back here. She couldn't help that, but he wasn't going to destroy this link with her mother.

She stole back into the hallway and tiptoed toward the kitchen for a glass of water, but when she got to the living-room arch, she froze.

Rick was still up, seated on the sofa. His Testament was open on his knees, but his eyes were closed. She realized he was praying.

Angie couldn't turn away or dismiss the look of peace that flooded his handsome face. He was a man to admire and a true friend. If only she could know that peace, find the comfort Rick did in a God who forgave him.

The difference was Rick hadn't done what she had.

He hadn't betrayed anyone.

———⟫◆⟪———

"Okay, I've got the yard cleaned out and the snowplow's been over the road, so I think we're almost ready. Are you all right?"

"I'll be fine," Angie told Rick as her stomach clenched tight in a new spasm. Would she ever be fine again? "Did you okay it with Georgia?"

"Yes."

Angie could hear the strain in Rick's voice, noticed the way he kept avoiding her glance. This is what their friendship had come to— she'd managed to make Rick feel guilty for doing his job. That would soon kill any affection he'd once claimed to have for her.

"We'll drop Kelly and Spot at Camp Hope first. She's going to love it there. Then you can take me in." She gulped down the wave of emotion that roiled up at the thought of abandoning the little girl.

During the night she'd tried to accept that it couldn't be helped and it was beyond her control. But that didn't make it any easier.

"You have to believe that God will work it out, Angie." Rick's arm slid around her shoulder as he tried to comfort her. "Kelly does.

She believes God is in control and that He loves her and cares for her. She believes God wants the best for her."

"She's a child. She's supposed to believe she's safe and secure." Angie knew better.

She slipped out from beneath his hug. Her emotions were too raw; she was too needy. Though she longed for nothing more than to lean her head on Rick's strong shoulder and let him ease her fears, in her heart she knew that wouldn't help. It would only make it harder for her to leave, and it was already hard enough. Because of Rick, of course.

Funny how coming back to this place hadn't been at all as she'd feared. It wasn't the house that tormented her peace of mind; it was her growing feelings for Rick and knowing she wasn't worthy of him. He was leather and she was vinyl, an imitation of the real thing.

"Are you all right, Angel?" Kelly's appearance was as noiseless as usual. She slid her hand into Angie's, her fingers threading into a tight grasp.

Angie's heart squeezed tight. She'd failed this lovely child. Somehow she'd done something she shouldn't have and now she was going to pay.

She crouched in front of Kelly. "I'm fine, sweetheart. It's you I'm worried about. I want you to be safe so you have to do whatever Kent and Georgia tell you to. Okay?"

"I wish you could come with me," Kelly murmured. She jerked forward, wrapping her arms tightly around Angie's neck.

"So do I, honey; so do I." Angie allowed herself to hold the frail little body for just a moment, then gently set her away. Now was the time to be strong, though body and spirit both sagged with apprehension. "Okay, let's go."

"Wait." Kelly stood where she was, tiny booted feet planted solidly on the tired linoleum. She cuddled Spot in her arms, letting him lap her cheek with his tiny pink tongue. "We have to pray first."

"You're right, Kelly. We do." The tight lines of Rick's mouth quirked in a smile at her. "How about if you lead us?"

"Okay." She leaned over to set the dog down at her feet. "We're going to pray now, Spot." The dog flopped on the floor with a whoosh as if he understood every word. Kelly's eyes closed. "Dear God, my daddy says You are always near us, always watching. Some bad people are trying to hurt my angel. Please don't let them. Please let her come back and look after me until my daddy can come. Thank You. Amen." She blinked up at them, eyes shining. "Now we can go. God is going to take care of Angel and me."

Angie stared at the heart-shaped face and felt her heart pinch at the obvious love Kelly had for her father—the one on earth and the one in heaven. If only she'd had that. If only she hadn't been forced—

"Let's go," Rick said.

Their breath formed cloud puffs as they walked toward the camp barn. Rick had left his truck behind it with the engine running to warm up. Angie glanced back. The temperature had dropped during the night, forming a hard crust on the snow that left their footprints clearly visible. Not that it mattered now.

She climbed inside and sat silent as Rick headed for the main house at Camp Hope. She was glad she didn't have to walk. The thought of what lay ahead dragged at her like a lead weight.

When they arrived, Georgia and Kent were waiting and beckoned them inside.

"It's going to really drop tonight. They're predicting minus twenty-five degrees."

No one responded to Kent's chitchat. The mood grew solemn.

Kelly gripped Angie's hand. "Don't worry about me. I'm going to be fine. God is going to help me." A sweet smile fluttered across Kelly's lips. She beckoned Angie to bend to her level. "He's going to help you too," she whispered.

"Thanks, sweetie. I loved looking after you. You take care." Angie drew her into her arms for one last hug, then quickly straightened. "Time to go," she said brightly. "Thanks for taking care of Kelly, you two."

Georgia, tears sparkling on the ends of her lashes, shook her head and gathered Angie into her arms.

"Bye," was all Angie could manage.

It felt like hours before Angie and Rick were back inside the truck, heading out of the camp. Angie twisted around to read the familiar words on the big entrance sign—maybe for the last time: Camp Hope—Where nothing is impossible with God.

Nothing? She wanted to do as Rick asked, to believe that God would help, but guilt from the past kept getting in the way of faith. That long-ago sermon clung to the back of her mind: *You could only run from sin so long; then you had to pay.*

When they turned a corner, the sign disappeared. The truck carried them away from the camp and toward her jail cell. Angie wrapped her arms around her middle and fought the rush of tears that threatened to swamp her.

"Don't be afraid, sweetheart. Somehow this is going to work out." Rick's quiet voice echoed his assurance. His attention remained on the slippery road.

"How?"

"I don't know that yet. Just let me do my job, and don't give up," he ordered, his mouth stretched tight. His fingers gripped the wheel so tightly the tips of his nails turned white. When he glanced at her, his eyes softened. "Promise you won't give up yet. Please, Angie?"

She wanted to argue, to tell him to stopping clinging to the dream of a miracle. But that soft note of pleading in his voice tugged on her heart. After several moments, she simply nodded her head. Let him have his dreams.

They didn't speak after that. As they approached town, Angie noted familiar landmarks she hadn't taken time to see on the way in. The number of cars lining the streets surprised her.

"I guess everybody's sick of being cooped up after the storm." Rick pulled up in front of the detachment office and switched off the engine. He turned to look at her. "Ready?"

"As I'll ever be." She reached for the door handle.

His hand on her arm made her pause. "Ang?"

"Yes?" She twisted to face him.

"Please don't say anything. To anyone. Understand?"

Because it could be used against her. She swallowed, nodded, and climbed out of his truck.

She had pulled on an old knitted hat—the product of one of her adolescent dreams of fashion—that covered her hair and half hid her face. Its rolled brim drooped in front, offering obscurity so even though several of the townspeople called out greetings to Rick, no one seemed to recognize her.

"So far, so good. Let's get it over with. Remember, God is on our side."

Angie could have disputed that. Instead she lifted her head, pushed her shoulders back, and walked beside him, matching step for step until they came to the door. Then summoning every last ounce of courage, she grabbed the handle and pulled. She had no intention of looking like a sheep heading to the slaughter.

———◆———

Rick worked his way through the gibes and teasing his coworkers heaped on his shoulders until they noticed him heading for the cell. Suddenly the room went very quiet. He waited till Angie stepped inside, then locked the door of her cell. Though the sound stabbed his heart, he walked out and closed the door behind him without a second glance. He couldn't bear to look at her face.

"You miss work for days, stuck out in the boonies, and yet still you manage to bring someone back in custody?" Arden Victor shook his head. "Unbelievable."

The rest of the group joined in the teasing.

Rick ignored them all. "Shauna!"

"Hey, boss. Long time no bellow."

They were all staring at him now, unaccustomed to the sharpness in his voice.

Rick honed in on the bustling secretary. "I had a message you relayed through Kent Anderson, something about a warrant?" He paused, waited, and found himself holding his breath.

A sad look washed over Shauna's countenance. "It's not the best thing I'm going to tell you today, boss man," she mumbled, popping her gum between her teeth.

The noise irritated him immensely. Rick fought down his fretfulness, told himself to practice what he preached. God was in control. "Then you'd better just say it."

"A warrant came through while you were out. A warrant for Angie Grant." Shauna folded her hands.

"She's now in custody."

The silence was so loud it was deafening.

"That's Angie Grant back there?" Arden asked, jerking one thumb toward the cell area.

"Yes. Listen up. I need your attention. All of you." He waited until every eye was on him. "A warrant was issued for Agent Grant. She heard about it and turned herself in to me. As you saw, I locked her in a cell. But under no circumstances are any of you to release her to anyone."

"The Feds have been here already," Shauna told him. "Once they find out she's in custody—"

Rick remained silent until the discussion had died down. "I am the senior officer in charge of this detachment," he reminded them. "We do not release Agent Grant into *anyone's* custody until I give the word. Any questions?"

"Preferential treatment?" Arden asked.

"Irregularities in the warrant," Rick told him, his voice cool at being questioned. Of all times, he needed their full cooperation now. "Until I get it straightened out, she goes nowhere. Are we clear?"

One by one they each nodded.

"Now let's get back to work." He glanced around, raised one eyebrow. "I'm assuming we do still have work? You didn't stop crime while I was away?"

The tension snapped as they laughed and returned to their desks, but the whispers soon began.

Rick disregarded everything but the job in front of him. "Shauna, get me a copy of the warrant, please."

"Right away. But can I speak to you first?"

"Sure." He noticed the way she looked around the room. "What is it?"

"Syd Grant is out."

"Out? Of jail?" he asked. "When?"

"The day the storm started."

"How?"

"I'm not sure. You had a call from head office and you need to call them back immediately." She leaned forward, then lowered her voice. "Word is he got off on a technicality. Apparently the warrant wasn't executed properly."

"That's nonsense!" A rush of anger spurted up inside. Rick clenched his hands. So that's how Syd had managed to come back and harass Angie. "I executed it myself. Everything was done by the book."

"I'm sorry. That's all I know, except that a judge released him on the spot after he'd heard the evidence the lawyer presented."

"What lawyer? Syd had a guy from legal aid who died three years ago."

"This fellow wasn't from legal aid, according to my sources. He was some hotshot from down East, and he raised a stink about Syd serving all this time when his case should never have gone to trial."

From the East. Rick stared at the desk, his mind racing a thousand miles an hour. "You better get me head office first, Shauna. Then the warrant. Pull up everything you can find about that warrant, will you? Who authorized it, what the grounds were, evidence, anything. I don't care what they say. I don't believe Angie murdered two other agents."

"I was hoping you'd say that. I've already done some preliminary stuff. As soon as you're done with your call, I'll hand it over." She patted his shoulder in the motherly way she had. "Don't be too upset at the guys. It was a real shocker when that warrant came through. Seeing one of your own targeted like that shook them. They'll stand behind her. Don't you worry."

"Thanks, Shauna."

"Don't thank me," she told him. "I'm just doing my job. I'll get the call for you."

Two minutes later he was on the line with his boss.

"Grant's search was by the book, Martin," Rick insisted after hearing the accusation. "The money was in plain sight, in a bag that was open on the backseat."

"His lawyer says he left it in the trunk and that you opened the trunk. Ergo, you violated the warrant. And Syd Grant had a witness."

"What?" Rick couldn't believe it. "There were no witnesses. That's a lie."

"The witness testified. The judge believed him. They threw out the conviction. I've ordered an internal investigation."

Rick forced himself to swallow the protest. Let them investigate. He had nothing to hide. But right now he needed answers to help Angie. "Who was this witness?"

"I don't remember the name," Martin admitted. "Some buddy of his from the service. He said he'd come to visit Grant, found him already regretting what he'd done, claimed he'd had too much to drink. According to this guy, your man was about to turn himself in when you showed up and tore up the place looking for the evidence."

"Another lie! There was no one else there. And Syd was packing a bag."

"Based on the witness's statement, the judge made his decision. Only way to get your perp back inside is to retry him. With this guy backing him, that's not too likely."

"I see. And you can't tell me who the witness is?"

"Well, I can, but I'll have to look it up. Just a minute."

Rick forced himself to sit perfectly still and only then realized the room was silent. Suddenly he knew exactly how Angie felt. He'd done nothing wrong and yet he felt ashamed and embarrassed.

"Guy's name is Parker. Michael Parker. He's moved up some since he and your boy were best buds."

"Really. What does he do now?"

"Was military, I think. Seems he's in line for a promotion. At CSIS. Head of operations. I guess that's why the judge took his testimony as truth. Why would a guy like that lie?"

"Why indeed?" Rick thought fast. *Military—the car. Parker was ex-military.* If he could find some connection to Angie . . . "How come Mr. Parker didn't step forward years ago?"

"Claims he was out of the country, lost touch with Mr. Grant, and didn't know anything about the case. He also claims Mr. Grant was represented by a legal-aid lawyer who gave up a little too soon." Martin's voice changed, hardened. "You understand what I'm saying here, don't you? It's one thing to say a witness isn't credible, but we can hardly defend your actions when the soon-to-be head of CSIS tells us you broke the law."

"I did not break the law. There was no witness. The money was lying open on the backseat."

"And he says it wasn't."

Shauna laid a file on his desk and pointed toward the bottom.

"I dispute that, but let it go for now. I've something else to ask you about."

"You're facing suspension, Rick. I'm not sure I can help you."

"This is a totally different case and yet the tie-ins are curious. I have a warrant on my desk for an Agent Angie Grant, formerly one of ours, now an operative for CSIS."

"Grant? Any relation—?"

"Daughter of Syd Grant, the bank thief I arrested."

"And you say she works for CSIS? Now that *is* strange."

"It gets stranger. According to the warrant, she is accused of killing two fellow agents at a safe house. The warrant was authorized by one Mr. Michael Parker."

"Hmm. Odd but not impossible. Perhaps it's a case of like father like daughter."

"Perhaps. The only thing is Ms. Grant was never inside the house where the agents were killed. She did not even fire her weapon at the scene." He paused to let that sink in. "You know CSIS, sir. You know they take care of their own, and they hate for us to get involved. So why issue a countrywide arrest warrant? Why not go after her themselves?"

"Maybe she eluded them. Maybe they lost her trail. I don't know."

"I'm sorry, sir, but it doesn't wash. She called her office regularly for updates on protecting the little girl. That was her assignment, to keep a child safe for testimony against Carver Simpson. Ms. Grant arranged to meet with her organization on three separate occasions. Each time someone tried to kill her."

"This sounds a little far-fetched."

"I assure you, it is not. The child can testify to the events," Rick added as an afterthought, then prayed that Kelly could remember it all. "Agent Grant has been on the run for over two months, but she's had a constant line of communication with CSIS. Yet they only recently notified her they were issuing a warrant. Why didn't they ask her to return first?"

"Maybe they did."

"No, sir. I was present when Agent Grant requested another agent to take over the child's protection so she could turn herself in. She was told to continue until further notice."

Silence.

"If she was wanted in these murders, why didn't they call her in long ago, sir? The event happened in October. Why leave her alone, on the run with a child, with no backup?"

"You want me to dig into this; is that it?" Marin asked.

"If you can, sir, I'd appreciate it. You have access to areas that I don't." How much was safe to tell? "I've learned that Mr. Parker was once part of a tactical squad sent to Iran to free citizens of another country, as was Mr. Grant. Some type of covert operation, I'm guessing. Apparently during their mission, Mr. Grant was injured and later released from the service. Mr. Parker must have moved on."

"And up," his boss added cynically.

One by one, Rick laid out the facts as he'd learned them. "Something's off."

"Yes, sir."

"You're one of the best officers we've ever had, Rick. I couldn't believe you'd violated the warrant, but I admit I fell for this guy's credentials. Still, your situation is tenuous at best. Everything could still fall on your head."

"Yes, sir."

"But given what you've told me, for now I'm prepared to back you while an internal investigation is conducted from this end. I'll see what I can find out about the evidence they have on the girl, and you keep digging." A pause. "I'm assuming you have Ms. Grant in custody?"

"Yes, sir. I brought her in this morning. She's unhurt and anxious to answer all charges. Apparently Mr. Parker or someone from his office has already been in here looking for her."

"Have they now? Well, let 'em wait. Agent Grant goes nowhere, Rick. Not yet. If CSIS gets ahold of her, they'll bury her so deep we'll never find out the truth and you'll be out of a job. Or worse. You keep her in that jail cell, and if anyone tells you different, you sic them on me."

"Can you fax me instructions to that effect, sir? I don't want to be charged with obstruction."

"Ten minutes," his boss told him, then slammed down the phone. "Shauna!"

"Right behind you. I'll watch for the fax and make copies for the others."

"You heard?"

She made a face. "He's kind of hard not to hear. I'm just glad it was you he was snarling at." She leaned down to whisper in his ear, "Maybe you should share the news with our captive. It might cheer her to know her friends are doing their best to help."

He turned in his chair, reached up, and hugged the woman who often seemed more like a mother than his secretary. "What would I do without you, Shauna?"

She hugged him back, patting his shoulder. "Probably drown in paper."

He burst out laughing but stifled it when he heard his name.

"Call for you on line two. Wouldn't give his name."

He grabbed the phone, punched the button. "Mercer."

"This is Syd Grant. You've got to see me right away."

"I don't have to do anything."

"You do if you want to keep my daughter alive."

The words hit home. "Since when do you care about her?" Rick whispered.

"Since always. Don't you get it? That's what this is all about. Are you going to meet me or not?"

Maybe it wasn't the smartest thing to do, given that he was under investigation for an offense against the man he was going to see, but nothing would have kept Rick away. "Where and when?"

"My place. Alone. Take your lunch break. If you don't see me, something's gone wrong."

The telephone clicked in his ear. Rick set down the receiver, glanced at his watch. He had almost an hour before he'd have to head out. Long enough to talk to Angie.

"The fax is in, Rick. Everybody has a copy," Shauna said. "If anybody comes for her while I'm here, I'll call you on your cell phone."

"Thanks."

"Just doing my job, Sergeant. That's why they pay me the big bucks." She chuckled at his groan. "Don't you have somewhere you should be? someone you need to see?"

"Yeah." Rick picked up his keys and headed for the cells. If everything worked out right, he intended to see a lot more of Angie Grant in the very near future.

But at the moment he needed to go over her statement and figure out what she was hiding from him.

# CHAPTER TEN

Rick scanned the yard while he waited for Syd. No vehicles. No tracks of anyone in or out that he could discern, though the area looked windswept. So far, so good.

He found the key but didn't need it because the door was unlocked. "Hello?"

Nobody answered.

With the reassuring press of his gun against his hip, Rick stepped inside. Syd had never been violent. It was unlikely he'd start now. Then Rick remembered Angie's confessions. It occurred to him that he apparently knew less than he thought about her father's true nature.

He unzipped his jacket as the warmth of the house hit him, only then remembering that he'd forgotten to lower the thermostat when they left this morning. How long ago that seemed.

"Hello, Rick."

At least the voice hadn't changed. Rick turned, studied the man behind him at the top of the basement stairs. The face was a little different. "Back to the scene of the crime, huh, Syd?"

"I know you're mad—"

"Mad? Oh, maybe just a teensy bit ticked off. I'm being investigated for something I didn't do." Rick closed his fingers around his sidearm, just in case. "You're trying to ruin my reputation, and I want to know why. You and I both know that search of your car was legal, that the money was sitting in the open, right on the backseat."

"Actually it wasn't, but forget about that for now. I have something—"

"Forget about it? Like Angie is supposed to forget what you did to her?" Rage surged inside. "You're trashing my career, Syd! Just like you tried to trash her life. I'm not going to forget about it. You're an abuser and a thief, so I guess it shouldn't surprise me that you'd also lie under oath."

"I did not lie. About anything." Syd stepped forward, opened the fridge, and removed the remainder of Georgia's roast. He set it on the counter and began to neatly slice it. "You want a sandwich?"

Rick felt his mouth drop as he stared at the other man so calmly making his lunch. When Syd sat down and began to eat, Rick flopped down opposite him, completely mystified by this strange behavior. "I don't get you. Don't you have any remorse for what you did?"

"You're talking about Angie?"

"Angie and everyone else who ever got in your path." Rick grabbed two slices of bread from the counter and made his own sandwich. Since this was his lunch hour, he might as well eat. "How can you come back here, pretending everything's fine?"

Syd had been about to take a bite. Instead he set his sandwich on his plate, his eyes hardening as he stared at Rick. "Everything is certainly not fine. But I'm protecting my daughter the best way I know how. So back off the blame game."

"Not gonna happen." Rick held his stare. "I care about Angie. I won't let you ruin the rest of her life, despite your belated attempts at fatherly love."

Syd froze. His green eyes so like Angie's clouded over before he dropped his lids and hid his expression. "I know I hurt her. I didn't mean to, but sometimes the pain got so bad—"

"So you buried it in a bottle and when that didn't help, you took out your frustrations on your daughter. How macho of you," Rick scoffed. "You want a medal or a chest to pin it on?"

"Neither. It wouldn't lessen the guilt one bit." Syd sighed; then his shoulders went back. "But now you have to listen to me. I'm here because of Angie."

"You're here because of you." He glared at Syd. "She was a little kid. One who'd lost her mother. And you treated her like a soldier in an army, ordering her around, pushing her too hard, then dumping her on the neighbors while you ran off. I wish I'd been around then; I'd have charged you with abandonment."

"I did not abandon my daughter! Never." Syd's fists turned white as he clenched them on the table. "Look, I haven't got time for this. You need to hear what I have to say. There is a book—"

"So I've heard."

"She told you?"

"Oh yes. But she doesn't have it. She doesn't know where it is. How many more years will pass before you get that through your thick skull? Angie is not hiding some stupid book from you."

All color drained from the damaged skin of his face until Syd Grant resembled nothing more than a haggard old man. "She *has* to know. It's the only thing that will save her."

"Angie?"

The bristly white head nodded.

"Save her from what?" Rick lurched to his feet and glowered down at the man who seemed to wither before him. "Talk to me. Now!"

"You're a cop. You've got the means to keep her safe. Do that by keeping her away from here. I'll have to go through the house, search every inch. It's got to be here somewhere."

"You're going to stay here to look for this book; is that what you mean?"

"Yes." Syd was already scouring the room.

"Syd, listen to me."

The old man glanced his way, then returned to his scrutiny of the room. "I'm listening."

"Haven't you already looked?" A light clicked on. "Isn't that why you tore apart Angie's dolls? In hopes that you would find this book?"

Surprise lit Syd's eyes before he nodded.

"But you never found it."

"No."

"So why are you back here? What good will going over the same things do? What's changed?"

"But it's here!" Syd insisted. "It has to be."

"Why?"

"Because—" He stopped, stared at Rick, his eyes dark with secrets. "Eve had it," he finally blurted out. "The night she died, she had it. It has to be here. She never left the house. She was too sick." His tortured voice broke on the last word, and he leaned his head into his hands and sobbed. "It has to be here. I can't give up Angie too."

"Give Angie up? What do you mean? What's going on?"

Syd opened his mouth to explain, but Rick's phone rang. "Mercer."

"You've got to come, Rick. Now. I can't stall them much longer."

Rick closed the phone and pocketed it, grabbed his jacket, and headed for the door.

"Wait! I haven't explained."

"It'll have to wait, Syd." He shook off the other man's grip. "Somebody's trying to get to Angie, and there is no way I'm going to let that happen." He threw the door open and stepped outside.

"But you don't understand," Syd called. "You've got to help me find that book. I've got to tell you—"

"Another time."

Without a second glance Rick raced to his truck, gunned the motor, and took off. Her old man might have failed Angie, but Rick wasn't going to. Not in this lifetime.

—————⊰◆⊱—————

"Will someone please tell me what in the world is going on?" Angie yelled, indignant at the lack of attention she was getting and frustrated by the rumble of commotion she could hear outside the cell area. If this was the way the detachment now treated their prisoners, things had certainly changed. "Hello?"

"Calm down, Angela. We've got everything under control, as usual." Arden walked toward her, a smile on his face. "Guess you're not the crook of the week after all."

"What do you mean?" Angie watched him unlock the cell door. "What's going on?"

"You're free to go. All charges against you have been dropped. Congratulations."

"What? Why?" When he didn't answer, she frowned. "This doesn't make sense, Arden. Where's Rick?"

"Out for lunch, at an accident, doing stuff. We had some 'friends' of yours causing a ruckus, but Shauna couldn't get rid of them till she threatened to call head office. That chased them away pretty quickly. Then her grandson had an emergency at school so she left. Lucky for you I was here to see the notice that the warrant's been pulled. You're a free woman." Arden motioned her out of the cell, walked behind her out of the room.

Angie couldn't shake the nebulous feeling that something wasn't right. "Can I see the notice?"

"Sure." He walked to his desk, picked it up, and handed it to her. "You don't want to be free?"

"Don't be silly." She read the notice. Everything seemed to be in order. "Okay, then. Well, I guess I'm off."

"To where?" He shrugged at her raised brows. "It's the first question Rick is going to fire at me and you know it."

"I'll probably head back to Camp Hope."

"You need a ride?"

Angie glanced out the window as she thought what to do. Just then, a big old car slid around the corner, almost taking out a stop sign. "Isn't that the Murdock sisters' car?" she asked.

Arden looked out the window, groaned. "Yeah. I told them not to drive today. It's icy and getting worse. But you know those two. They don't take suggestions well."

"I remember." She grinned. "Seems like nothing changes around here."

"Some things do and some things don't. Rick, for instance. He hasn't changed that much." Arden looked at her, then winked. "If you know what I mean."

"Thank heaven he hasn't." She ignored the innuendo, though her cheeks felt hot. "I don't know what I would have done without Rick."

"Yeah. Like I said, same old, same old. So, you want a ride or what?"

Angie shook her head. "I think I'll see if Fiona and Emily can give me a ride to the camp. If not, I might be back. Can you let Rick know when he comes in?"

"Sure thing. You take care," he ordered, wrapping her in a bear hug. "Watch what you get mixed up in next time."

"Very funny." She buried her face in his shoulder for a moment, then kissed his cheek. "You always were an old softie. Tell Serena I said hello." Angie and Arden's daughter had been good friends in grade school.

"I'll do that. Believe it or not, I kind of miss the two of you giggling upstairs till all hours of the night. Retirement doesn't look nearly as good as it did back then."

Arden's wife had died while Angie had been away.

Angie hugged him again. "Don't quit just yet. I might need you again."

"I'm here, kid. Whenever."

"Thanks." Angie zipped up her coat, pulled her cap down, and walked out the door, relishing the sense of freedom as she quashed her worry.

"Another sunny day in paradise. Why am I always so ready to look at the negative side of things?" she asked herself.

Fiona and Emily were delighted to give her a ride once they'd filled their grocery list. Angie trailed them through the store, wishing they'd hurry up and decide which brand of tuna fish was best for their porcelain skin. She felt a shivery nervousness from being stuck out in the open without even the protection of her gun.

She'd have to talk to Rick about getting it back.

When the sisters finally headed for the checkout, Angie put the magazine she'd been scanning back on the shelf and stepped forward, only to bump into a pair of tall men.

"Excuse me. Aren't you Angie Grant?"

"So?" She glanced from one face to the other, trying to remember if she'd seen them before. No. She took a second look. They weren't locals, not unless the people of the farming community had started wearing cashmere scarves under the lapels of their wool topcoats.

"We're friends of Syd. Stopped by for a visit."

"Really? Then you should go to the penitentiary. That's his current address." She tried to sidestep one, but one of them moved with her. "Was there something else?" she demanded, glaring at him.

"Guess you didn't hear. Syd was released a couple of days ago. So we were hoping that when you see him, you'd pass on a message."

The other man's fingers closed around her arm.

"Tell him we'll see him soon. To pick up the book."

Again with the book. Angie held his gaze while her mind raced ahead.

"Well, buddy, you aren't as well informed as you think," she sneered as she yanked away her arm. "I don't speak to Syd. Not since he went away. And I have no intention of starting again."

"You'd better think about it, then, sweetheart. For both your sakes."

"Angela, are these friends of yours?" Fiona's high-pitched voice surprised the two men.

"Do introduce us," chimed in Emily.

"I can't, Emily. I have no idea who these gentlemen are or why they're bothering me." Angie shifted to stand between the sisters, looped an arm through each of theirs. "Are you ladies ready to go?"

"Yes, dear. That nice young man is waiting to put our groceries in the car. I do so appreciate a little help, you know. My ankle isn't what it was after that fall in '89."

Angie let the chitchat roll past as she walked out to the car, conscious of the men watching them leave, wondering who they were.

As she sat in the backseat, clinging to her seat belt while the car drifted from the shoulder into the center of the lane and back again, she couldn't help the explosion of relief that flooded her heart just to know she was free. Why, wasn't exactly clear yet, but for the moment she'd accept her freedom and be glad.

At Camp Hope, Kelly hugged her so tight Angie had to pull away to catch her breath.

"I knew God would help you, Angel," she crowed.

Almost as excited, Georgia invited the Murdock sisters in for tea to celebrate. Angie reveled in the sensation of enjoying the ordinary give-and-take of normal conversation among friends, of feeling wanted. She sat at the kitchen table, holding her teacup, content to listen as the two sisters reminisced about the camp's origins.

Emily gazed at Kelly as the girl sipped her pretend tea. After a moment she turned to Angie. "You know, dear, she reminds me so much of you."

Angie frowned, studied Kelly's sweet face anew. "How?"

"Her faith," Fiona chimed in. "She has so much of it, just as you did. I remember we did some puppet stories here one summer. You were like a little sponge, soaking up all the knowledge of God you could get."

"Oh." Angie didn't want to talk about those days.

"Your grandparents would have been so proud of you."

Now this was a subject she could discuss or rather listen to, since she knew next to nothing about them. "You knew my mother's folks?"

The two ladies twittered.

"My word, yes. As well as we knew our own father. Why, your grandparents and our father were three of the original founders of Camp Hope. They had such vision in creating this place." Fiona tapped her nail against the tabletop. "Later on it was your grandfather who insisted the camp must have a pool to draw the kids. He and your grandmother worked like crazy to raise funds for the place."

Angie saw Rick come in the back door. He walked up beside her and stood there, staring down at her, worry blackening his eyes. A bubble of pure delight sputtered up inside, filling her heart with joy that he cared.

"Hi," she said, unable to hide her pleasure at seeing him away from the jail cell.

He shrugged out of his coat and sat down next to her. "Hi, yourself." His fingers curled around hers under cover of the table and he squeezed them. "Why didn't you wait for me? Shauna phoned all het up about someone trying to take you away."

"I don't know anything about that," Angie told him. The storm clouds on his face were melting. She didn't want to cause him pain, but it was so nice to have someone be concerned about her. "Arden said I was free to go and I went. I'm sorry if I worried you. I caught a ride with these ladies."

"No problem." He let go of her fingers to accept the tea Georgia handed him.

Sensing he needed a few moments to regroup, Angie recalled the discussion before he'd entered and turned to the Fiona and Emily. "How did my grandmother raise funds for this place?"

"Oh, many ways. Your grandmother, Esther, was quite a knitter, you know. Could look at something and re-create it with her needles. She knitted the cutest little sweaters. They sold like hotcakes. Then she crocheted tablecloths, which she sold all over the place. Your grandmother made quilts, drapes, all kinds of things."

That must have been where her mother honed her skill with a needle, Angie mused, thinking about the beautiful dolls.

"She also raised turkeys," Emily remarked. "I'll never forget the summer she hatched the idea of selling them to people for Christmas—two hundred turkeys! She thought the campgrounds needed benches, you see, so people could sit and relax, commune with God.

In those days there was no money for extras like that, but she was determined."

"Yes, she was like that," Fiona agreed, her usually stern eyes dancing with fun. "We plucked those birds till our fingers ached. It was such fun. Your grandmother could make a party out of anything. Barrons' Rest always rang with laughter in those days. A party every week in the summer. It was bursting at the seams, but everyone always felt welcome."

"Barrons' Rest?" Angie asked. "What's that?"

"The name of your home, of course. Your grandparents, the Barrons, were adamant when they bought the place—it was to be a home where others could find solace, rejuvenation." Fiona shrugged. "Hence Barrons' Rest. And that's exactly what it was. Even when the parties were going full swing, it was the kind of place you felt comfortable to relax in."

"Parties?" *Comfortable?* Angie couldn't imagine what they were talking about. The dismal house she'd shared with her father had never been a joyous place. Even imagining such a thing seemed ludicrous.

"Oh, dozens of parties," Emily said. "All through the summer your grandparents would host these . . . events, I guess you'd call them. Counselors, speakers, cooks—anybody who was helping out at camp—was invited to their place whenever there was no camp. Your grandparents hosted corn roasts, barbeques, baseball games, sing-alongs under the stars. If it was a wet year, we'd all gather inside. Board games, contests—there was always something going on."

"Yes, and don't forget the food, sister." Fiona licked her lips. "I can almost taste Esther's potato salad with dill. That woman loved dill in everything."

Angie tried to think of the present ramshackle house filled with people having fun. It simply didn't compute.

"Father would bring us over on Friday nights, and we'd help Esther begin her preparations while Father and your grandfather found chairs, benches, anything for folks to sit on. The men were in charge of the activities, and they dreamed up lots of them. Potato races, pea shelling, catching bloodsuckers in the creek, footraces—oh, I can't remember them all." Emily clapped her hands to her cheeks.

Fiona took over. "The camp staff would all show up at noon, after cleanup on Saturday, after the children had gone home. They were tired, hungry, and sometimes lonely for home, but your grandmother welcomed them in and pretty soon everyone was laughing. She always had a special cake tucked away, just in case someone had a birthday."

"I never knew any of this," Angie whispered.

"But surely your mother told you," Fiona mused. "Eve loved those weekends. She had a heart like her mother's, watching out for the hurting ones. It was her job to light the yard after dark, and she did a wonderful job with paper lanterns and candles. She opened her room to anyone who wasn't feeling well or just needed a rest. Of course, the boys who were counseling all fell for her and would try to keep her to themselves, but Eve didn't allow it."

"I remember her laugh," Emily said. "Reminded me of sleigh bells. Remember when she learned to drive the camp tractor, sister?"

The Murdocks looked at each other and burst into a fit of giggles.

"Many a gearshift that girl took out. I took a picture of her the day she ran into the barn. Oh, she was so embarrassed."

"A picture?" Angie asked hopefully. Maybe if she could see her mother in those bygone happy days, she'd believe that the house of ugly memories had once been a place of joy.

"Why, yes. I'm sure there must be lots of them." Fiona looked at Angie with one eyebrow raised. "Your grandfather kept photo albums—records of their 'family,' as he called the camp workers. Haven't you ever looked at them?"

Angie shook her head. "I've never seen them."

"Well, I can't imagine anyone would throw them out." Emily sounded scandalized by the thought. "I remember he made a huge chest to keep them in. Cedar, I think it was. Said Eve would want them after they'd gone." Her voice dropped. "I miss them still."

Angie recalled the garage. "I think I know where it is. I hope they haven't been damaged." She turned to Rick excitedly. "Remember the big cedar box in the garage? That must be it. I always thought it held my grandfather's books."

"Oh no, dear. Your father sold those books years ago."

Maybe he had, but Syd had never said anything about photos.

Rick leaned near, his voice soft, as if they shared a secret. "I promise we'll lug that chest out soon. But first I want the place checked out. Every inch and corner in daylight. You're not going back unless it's safe."

She stared at him, surprised by the tone of his voice. As if he suspected someone might actually hide inside the house and wait for her to show up. Carver Simpson's thugs didn't work like that.

"Of course there are also the Camp Hope albums," Emily said. "Your mother would be in some of those pictures because she was a camp counselor for several years. She loved teaching the youngest children best; she had an affinity with them."

"My mother taught here?" Angie tried to picture it.

"Yes, she did," Emily answered. "I remember her sitting on the grass beside the chapel with seven little girls surrounding her, all of them asking about Daniel in the lions' den. Eve was never stumped for an answer. She knew exactly what she believed and why, and she found great pleasure in sharing with the kids who came here."

"Georgia, dear, would it be too great an imposition to dig out some of the albums?" Fiona asked. "Perhaps it might help Angela to see things as they were back then."

"It isn't too much trouble. But you'll have to give me a few minutes to find the right years. Kent built new shelves for them, and when Abby was housecleaning she didn't have time to reference them by year. I've been meaning to get to it, but—"

"Maybe Angie could do it," Rick suggested. He smiled at her surprise, but his eyes weren't laughing. His voice dropped. "I don't want you at your house alone. I know you think everything's okay now, but I'd prefer it if you didn't go back there. For the next couple of days anyway. Just until I'm sure someone isn't still poking around."

He meant Syd.

"Please say you'll stay with us, Angie. You and Kelly. We'd love to have you." Georgia's quiet voice urged her to consider it. "I've been lonely since the exodus after Christmas. It would be nice to visit and share Kelly with you for a few days."

Angie glanced from her to Rick, recognized the concern he didn't utter, and decided to go with her gut. She trusted Rick; she could rely on him. "All right. For a couple of days. If you're sure we won't be in the way," she told Georgia.

"Of course you won't. It's going to be fun."

"There's a condition," Angie told her. "You have to let me organize those albums for you. It's the least I can do."

"You're welcome to it." Georgia grinned. "I hate being in the basement. Call me weird, but when I'm down there I feel like I've been entombed." She blushed at the curious stares her words elicited. "Well, that's what it reminds me of. I'd be very grateful if you'd take on that job, Angie."

It was apparent from the tremble in her voice and the bleached look of her skin that Georgia was telling the truth. Angie wondered if it had something to do with the fire that had killed her first husband and her son, but she wasn't about to ask. Time and Kent were healing Georgia. She would get over her fear in her own way.

"I can see the longing written all over your face, Angie. You want to take a look at those albums now, don't you?" Georgia asked. She smiled. "Why don't you and Rick go ahead. I'm going to check the oven. The chicken should be almost done."

"And we should head home." Fiona stood, stretched. "I don't like arriving after dark. Too many shadows lurking in the trees. I'm always afraid a deer will dash out in front. That will be one advantage of living in town. There's always someone about."

"You're looking forward to moving?" Angie asked, puzzled by their excitement about leaving the farm where they'd spent the last seventy-plus years.

"Oh, my dear, we can hardly wait!" Emily patted her hand. "Why, if it weren't for all that stuff we have to dispose of, we'd be in there now. New challenges are so exciting. We can hardly wait to see how God works it all out for us."

"But aren't you sad about leaving?"

"Sad?" Emily shook her head. "I don't think we're sad; are we, sister?"

"Why would we be sad?" Fiona looked confused. "We've had a wonderful life, but we're not dead yet! God has other things for us to do, and I want to do them. I'm sure there will be difficulties, but I prefer to think of them as challenges that I will overcome. Whatever time I have left on this earth, I intend to live it fully, without regret."

Silence followed these words. Angie couldn't help but compare their outlook with her own. She dreaded the next day, the next week. These women had learned to joyfully anticipate. That had to do with their faith in something beyond their own abilities, she knew. But it wasn't the same for her. She had—her past.

"Surely you two will stay for dinner with us?" Georgia insisted. "I'm sure Rick or Kent will be happy to follow you home, make sure everything's all right. Please stay."

Rick added his encouragement, and the sisters gracefully gave in. While Fiona went to help Georgia, Emily and Kelly conferred about a book, and the two huddled together on the sofa to read it.

"Should we go take a look at these albums?"

Angie nodded and followed Rick down the stairs. The basement was finished to look like a study, though a sofa bed was at the ready for unexpected guests. It, along with every other piece of furniture in the room, was covered with photo albums. Each one had a date printed on the spine.

"Let's start with this pile." Rick flicked on the gas fireplace to take off the chill of the room, then sat on the floor and opened the book. "Curious?"

"Yes." Angie sat down beside him, conscious of the way his leg brushed hers as he placed the album so they could both see. "Oh, look."

She stared at the face so like her own. Her mother as a small child, carrying cups of water to the workmen. Angie flipped through the pages. There she was as an adolescent dressed in jeans and a T-shirt, hammering fiercely on a log building.

Like an ever-changing kaleidoscope, out of the aspens and pines emerged Camp Hope, each building lovingly constructed by volunteers who shared a dream. Angie found another picture of her mother seated among several young girls, holding up puppets. *Eve Barron, 16, a counselor at junior camp,* the caption read.

Rick glanced from the page to Angie's face. "Beautiful, both of you." His forefinger traced the sculpted lines of Angie's cheekbones, down to her jaw and the rounded point of her chin. It paused at the center, then slid underneath to tilt up her head. "You look exactly like your mother."

"I guess I do." It had been a long time since Angie had seen a photo of Eve. She'd been forced to rely on her memory since the day they'd buried her mother and Syd had removed every picture from the house. A tear slipped from the corner of her eye and slid down her cheek.

Rick caught it, held it on his fingertip, his eyes riveted to hers. "Please don't cry. I don't think I can stand that."

"I'm not crying," she sniffed. "It's just so awful. She was so alive, so kind and gentle. She wasn't evil; she didn't do anything wrong. Why did my mother have to die so young? Why couldn't he have died instead?" She stared through the sheet of tears that wouldn't stop.

It was probably a sin to say those words. Another thing she wouldn't find forgiveness for.

"Oh, Angie." Rick wrapped his arms around her and gathered her close. "I don't know why. I can only tell you what Syd told me today when I met him at your house."

She blinked away the wetness, frowned up at him. "My father was at my—our house?"

"He asked me to meet him because he had something important to tell me."

"Wh-what was it?"

"I never got to find out. Shauna called me away too soon." He pressed his fingertip across her cheek, smoothed away the tears. "But he did say one thing that you need to hear."

"What?"

"Syd claims he never meant to hurt you, that his actions were the result of his pain. He says he's trying to protect you."

"And you believe him?" She was shocked. "He's a thief! A liar."

"I know. But you didn't see his face when he said it. I think we need to hear him out, Angie."

"No!" Fury drove away the tender moment she'd shared with him. Angie jerked out of his embrace, surged to her feet. "I don't want to listen to him ever again."

"Rick?" Kent stood at the top of the basement stairs. He was still wearing his coat, and his face was red from the cold. "I'm sorry to interrupt, but I think you two should come up here. It's important."

Dread dogged Angie's steps as she preceded Rick up the stairs.

*Now what?*

# CHAPTER ELEVEN

Rick pulled on his leather gloves and lifted the lid of the green metal box.

"It's my father's military locker," Angie muttered. "It wasn't in the garage when I was out there the other day."

"I found it in the woods. That was inside." Kent pointed to the sheet of paper that rested on top.

"'*One week. Find it.*' Cryptic."

The author wasn't giving anything away. Rick carefully lifted out the paper, set it aside, and began checking through the remainder of the contents. Holding up a small bronze disc on a wide ribbon, he glanced at Angie. "Syd left his medals in this locker in the garage?"

"Don't look at me," she responded. "I never peeked inside. Didn't even know he had a medal, if you want the truth. I told you, he didn't talk about his past."

"Somebody was searching for something." Kent gestured to the jumbled confusion. The velvet-lined box that had obviously held the medal lay open, tossed in with several other things. "Guess they expected Syd to find their note."

Rick didn't like the conclusions he was drawing. "Maybe. There was no snow inside, and the spot where you found this was cleared off, right?"

Kent nodded.

"Obviously they hoped Syd would find the locker. So if they didn't take anything and all they leave is this message, why bother?" Rick saw a flicker of something in Angie's eyes. "What?"

"Perhaps they left the locker there after searching inside for this book everyone wants. Oh, I just remembered. Two guys stopped me in the grocery store while I was waiting for the Murdock sisters. They said they were friends of Syd's and that they would see him soon to pick up the book."

"What is with this book?" Rick fumed.

"Don't know that, but they told me to pass on the message because they didn't know where to find Syd. Maybe that's why they left his box in plain view." Angie shrugged. "Just a guess. But when I said he didn't have their book, they said we had better find it 'for both our sakes.'"

"Meaning they'll go after you if you don't find it, or you're the threat against Syd?" Rick followed her line of thinking to the conclusions he didn't like.

"Either way."

Rick flipped through his thoughts, searching for the niggling question that he'd been ignoring. "Syd said something about a book too. I didn't pay a lot of attention at the time, which in retrospect might have been a mistake. But he did say your mother was the last one to have it, the night she died." He paused, frowned. "He said, 'I can't lose Angie too.'"

"Dad's concern is overwhelming," she sneered. Her chin jutted out in the stubborn angle that telegraphed her mood. She wasn't prepared to cut Syd any slack.

Not that Rick blamed her, but in his own mind he was more certain than ever that Syd was the key to it all. "Angie, we've got to talk to him. I'll do it on my own if I have to, but we need to hear what he has to say about all this."

"Why? So he can blame his problems on me or my mother? Anybody but himself."

"No." Rick caught her arm, forcing her to look at him. "Because I'm pretty sure he knows what's behind your problems."

She jerked away from his touch. "You hope! Then ask him. If you can find him. I have no idea where he's hiding out." She turned away, walked over to the sofa, and sat down beside Kelly, her tough-girl front firmly in place.

A lump rose in Rick's throat as he watched the little girl climb on Angie's knee. Though Kelly's attention was still on the storybook, she was perceptive enough to sense Angie's inner turmoil. After a few moments she looped her arm around her protector's neck and pressed a gentle kiss on her fair cheek.

Rick envied Kelly that touch. He wanted to comfort Angie, to help her get past the pain that ate at her soul. But he didn't know how, other than to face Syd, finally get at the truth, and to keep praying for her.

"Come on, everyone. Dinner's ready." If Fiona Murdock sensed that something was wrong, she didn't let on. Nor did anyone else. But Angie's anger wasn't easy to ignore.

After the meal, Rick excused himself. "I'm sorry to leave so fast, but I ducked out of work a little early and I've got some things that need doing at the office. Thanks for a great meal, Georgia."

"Anytime. You know that."

"Thanks." He watched Kent sling an arm around his wife's narrow waist and stuffed down a stab of envy for his best friend's happiness. Not that he wasn't delighted that Kent was so happy, but he wanted the same kind of relationship for Angie and himself. He wanted the past to stop coming between them. He wanted Angie to look ahead instead of over one shoulder.

Kent hurried out to start the Murdocks' car to warm it up.

While the sisters talked with Georgia, Rick drew Angie aside. "I know you don't want to talk about this anymore, but I can't leave it alone. A threat was made against you, for one thing. I'm not going to stand by and wait for something to happen."

She glared at him but said nothing.

"I'm trying to help, Ang. This thing between you and your father has festered for years. Isn't it time to drain the wound and let out some of the pain? He was genuinely concerned for you; it was not an act."

"Sure." The utter despair bound up in that one word stung.

"I'm not betraying you. I would never do that."

"Really? Then why are you taking his side? Why do you take the word of a liar and thief against mine?"

"People can change." Rick touched her shoulder, felt her slipping away. "That's what Christianity is all about. Getting a new life and starting over. If Syd says he's different, that he's trying to help, then who am I to question him?" He leaned down to meet her angry glare. "He's a free man, Angie. He could have gone anywhere. But he chose to come back here."

"You're assuming that's a good thing."

"It could be. Maybe he'll help us unravel the mystery of what's been happening these past few days."

"What's been happening is that Carver Simpson ordered someone to get rid of Kelly. It's my job to make sure that doesn't happen. For now my orders are to stay put and wait, so that's what I'll do. But that doesn't mean I'm going to kindle some fairy-tale relationship with my father even if he begged me on both knees." Her hands clenched into fists, pressed against her thighs. "I cannot wipe out the past just because he doesn't want to remember. Not even for you."

"You have to forgive him. It's the only way to get past it and face the future."

She shook her head firmly. "I'm not going to do that. Not today, not tomorrow. Not even next year. I will never forgive him for ruining my life."

She would have turned away, but Rick grasped her hand, unfolded her fingers, and threaded his own into them. "Your life isn't ruined. Not yet. But it will be if you don't let yourself move on and grow beyond the past. Is this what you want—to always be on the run, like a fugitive, looking over one shoulder at the past and reliving how he hurt you again and again? Was the life you were leading a few days ago, skulking from place to place, so great that you want to spend whatever days you have left like that?"

"You don't understand."

"I can't understand, Angie. It was your life, your experience. It's your pain. I can't imagine how horrible it must have been." He felt her pulse steady and strong and knew he had to say it. "But I can see what it's doing to you. I can see that you're dragging the past into your future, and it's ruining whatever joy you might find. You have to forgive yourself."

"Forgive myself?" She frowned. "What are you talking about?"

"You can't—or won't—forgive your father, because you can't forgive yourself. Underneath it all, isn't that what really hurts?"

Her face blanched. She withdrew her hand from his and backed away. "I-I don't know what you mean."

Rick saw the fear in her eyes. Yellow gold glints darkened and grew until the green had almost disappeared. He'd hit on something. If only he could understand what was going on in that beautiful head. "You know. But for real clarity, I suggest you talk to our heavenly Father. He has the answers you need."

"God doesn't answer me," she whispered. "I've tried but . . . He isn't there."

"He's *always* there. Always waiting to hear from you. I'll be praying for you."

"Don't bother," she told him, keeping her head down so he couldn't see the secrets she kept hidden. "It won't help."

"It will help me," he stated. "Besides, that's what you thought about the warrant and look what God did. I've been praying for you a long time, Angie Grant. I can't possibly stop now." His voice dropped. "Not ever. Sleep well and know that despite everything God is watching out for you, that He loves you so much."

The Murdocks' conversation with Georgia had died down, so he knew the sisters were waiting for him. He said his good-byes to the others, received Kelly's tight hug, then escorted the ladies to their car.

But as he puttered along behind them, Rick let his mind paint a picture of the courageous woman who'd held his heart for so long.

He couldn't imagine life without Angie, couldn't imagine going back to the life he'd led while she'd been away. Just seeing her made his day. He let his fingers recall the texture of her skin—so delicate, so fine, as if a puff of wind could ruin it.

"Good night, ladies," he said from his truck, waiting as they unlocked their front door.

They fluttered their hands, then scurried inside.

On the way back to the Grant house, Rick tried to remember a time when Angie had seemed as defenseless as he'd seen her tonight. Never, that's when. Even on the day he'd arrested Syd, Angie had stood alone, proudly and defiantly proclaiming that she didn't need anyone. But she was wrong.

She needed Rick to figure out what was going on and to help build a bridge between her father and her. Keeping her safe and figuring out what was behind Syd and his curious comments would be a challenge.

But Rick wouldn't walk away from it—not with Angie counting on him.

If only he could hang on to his job and his integrity.

If only she didn't end up hating him.

---

For the first time since she'd taken on the task of protecting Kelly, Angie was glad someone else was there to care for her. She'd slept fitfully through the night. Vivid dreams of the past—of her mother, of her father angry because she'd hosted a birthday party for a friend in their home—had made her toss and turn.

Barrons' Rest. She'd never found any real rest there. It had never seemed the peaceful sanctuary the Murdock sisters spoke of. Truthfully, her best memories came from the hours she'd spent here at Camp Hope.

Late at night when Syd thought she was in bed, she'd stolen away from the house. From her perch high in the trees and secreted by their shadows, she'd watched as other children with normal lives ran, played, laughed, and gathered around huge bonfires to roast wieners and sing. Sometimes she'd found tears on her cheeks after their songs had long since faded into the night.

The need to know more had driven her to the basement of Kent and Georgia's home, where she'd grabbed three of the albums and taken them to her room. Now as she stared at the pictures, the soft gentle smile on her mother's lips made her realize how happy their lives had been. Was that why Eve had come back here, to recapture the happiness from the past? Had she been as miserable with Syd as Angie had been?

Angie picked up another album, opened it, and froze at the caption: *The newlyweds stop by for a visit.*

She recognized her mother, but Syd? It couldn't be. He was so good-looking! Dark hair, dark eyes that seemed to pierce the distance between the picture and herself. He was laughing, his mouth open wide in a grin that begged the photographer to share in the joke. One muscular arm encircled Eve's waist, and her head of tumbling curls rested on his shoulder.

Angie turned the page. There were several more photos—Syd putting shingles on a cabin roof, Eve and Syd serving hamburgers to kids, Syd at the front of the chapel.

What? Angie flipped back and stared at the photo, desperate to see something that proved she was wrong—that it wasn't him, that it wasn't inside the chapel.

To no avail. It was him. He had a Bible in his hands, and he was talking to a full house.

"Angie?" Georgia's concerned face swam into view. "I thought I heard something. Are you all right?"

"Oh, just peachy." She held out the album. "Look at this for a minute, will you?"

She watched Georgia's face closely for a reaction.

"It's your father. He's speaking . . . in the chapel?"

Angie nodded. "What I want to know is what right he had to do that."

"Then why don't you ask him?"

Angie blinked, uncertain that she'd heard correctly.

"I mean it. If you get the chance, why not ask him. Lay out all your questions and give him a chance to explain."

"But—"

"Of course, it would mean letting go of all your preconceptions and really listening to what he has to say." Georgia crouched down in front of her. Her voice was soft, gentle. "I know you don't want to hear this, but maybe you've been mistaken about some things. Maybe the past wasn't quite the way you remembered."

Angie opened her mouth to protest, but it struck her that she'd harped on all the same old complaints ever since she'd come back here. Obviously Rick was tired of hearing them, but Georgia too?

She licked her lips, trying to come up with some explanation. There wasn't one. She knew what she knew, had lived it, felt it. But to someone who hadn't, it would be impossible to explain the feelings that would not go away.

"I'm not saying it didn't happen, Angie. I know you're not faking it, that your suffering is real. I'm just saying there might be some explanation that could help you understand why it happened."

"Do you think I haven't asked myself that?"

"But you don't have the answer, do you? And your father might." Georgia pointed to the album. "The captions and these photos suggest that your father once practiced his faith. What happened to change that? I'd like to know, wouldn't you?"

"He could lie."

"Yes. But he might tell you the truth. Isn't it worth asking?"

Angie chewed her lip as she mulled over Georgia's suggestion. Her father didn't tell the truth; she knew that. But maybe, if he was confronted by these pictures in front of Rick, he'd have to explain.

"You know what it says."

"Hmm?" Angie pushed away her thoughts, studied Georgia's smiling face. "Who says what?"

"The Bible says the truth shall set you free. Wouldn't it be wonderful to finally be free of all your questions? We spend so much time hiding our true feelings, trying to fake our way through life, pretending. The truth gets rid of the pretense, opens things up so we can face the shadows and dread and move on."

"You think Syd knows the truth?" Angie watched Georgia's golden head nod. "Maybe he does. But will he speak it? I'm afraid to trust him again."

"I know—because of the anger inside and the fear that he'll hurt you again." Georgia patted her shoulder. "But if you put your trust in God to be your comforter, then you'd be free to ask Syd for an explanation. Who knows what might come of that?"

"Angel?" Kelly's soft voice carried an urgency through the door. "There's someone knocking at the door."

Angie raced out into the hall, maligning herself as she did. She was Kelly's protector. She had no business getting so wrapped up in her own problems that she forgot that the child was alone in a room, even if she was only a few feet away. "Go into the bedroom with Georgia, Kelly. I'll look after this."

She waited until they'd disappeared, then opened the door, feeling only marginally protected by the locked screen door. "Yes?" She fingered the gun she'd slid into her pocket.

"Agent Grant, I've been ordered to speak to you personally."

She surveyed the lean man in grey wool just beyond the door. "And you would be?"

"Tony Nickel. CSIS." He held up his badge so she could take a good look at it.

"To speak about what?" She wasn't letting him in, no matter who he was. "Why are you here?"

"I've been ordered to inform you that we now have confirmation of irregularities in the organization. We're tracking down several leads, but until this person can be identified and neutralized, you are to keep the child in your custody, preferably here, but wherever you feel safest."

"So why the warrant? I'm following my orders. Why issue a warrant on me?"

He nodded. "I was told you'd ask that. I can only say that as far as we know it was not authorized by CSIS."

"Are you kidding me? Somebody signed the thing."

"Mr. Parker's name was on the bottom. We believe it was a forgery, though we're not sure why."

"Parker? The guy who is going to be our boss?" Angie asked.

Tony nodded.

"How could anyone—never mind. And Carver Simpson?"

"He's been advised that if anything should happen to the child, he will be our primary suspect. We have agents on him constantly. This morning a cohort of his named Max Vogler was apprehended. As far as we know, Simpson has not recruited anyone else. In fact, as I understand it, Vogler's now trying to work a plea bargain. The child's testimony may not be required."

Meaning the past few weeks need never have happened. Angie bit her lip. Well, it wasn't all a waste. At least Max was out of the way. "So let me get this straight—you don't want me back in Ottawa?"

"Not yet." He sighed. "As you may be aware, there was some concern when that warrant went out, supposedly with our blessing. That is not standard procedure, and we're unable to account for it. Until we do—" He left the rest of it hanging.

"Are you assigning someone else to Kelly, a backup?"

"I've been ordered to remain in the area and to check out all threats. Here's my pager number." He held out a small white card, then tucked it into the doorframe. "Just call if you need me."

"Fine. Thanks." Angie kept the screen door closed. She wouldn't make any moves until she'd checked him out. "Let me know when you learn more."

"Of course."

She needed to think about everything she'd just learned.

But Tony Nickel wasn't finished. "Wait a minute. Agent Grant, I need to ask how close you've become to the local police office."

"I've always been close," she told him with a frown. "I used to work with them. Why?"

"There is a . . . situation with the acting staff sergeant. I believe his name is Mercer."

"Rick Mercer. Yes." She nodded, barely able to stem her curiosity. "And? Why does CSIS care about Rick?"

"May I advise you to stay clear of Sergeant Mercer?"

"Not without some reason you may not. Rick is a friend of mine and as straight as an arrow. If he's under suspicion, I want to know why."

"I can't tell you that," Nickel stated. "I can only advise extreme caution in your dealings with him." He turned and began to walk down the steps.

Angie unlocked the door and rushed outside. "Hold on! You can't leave me here to protect a child after you've made some nebulous accusations about my friend. What's going on?"

Tony Nickel looked around as if he suspected someone was listening in on their conversation.

Angie looked too but saw nothing more than snow and ice and pine trees. The grounds looked deserted.

"They could have my badge," he admitted.

"Nobody's going to tell, least of all me."

"Okay. Your friend chose the wrong case to cut corners on and the wrong adversary. Word is he's up against Parker and that's one man you don't want to cross. I've heard this Mercer fellow is going to be used as an example against bending the rules. It won't be pretty. He'll lose his job, his reputation, and probably his freedom. If I were you, I'd distance myself from this guy as fast as you can or they'll take you down with him."

"Rick doesn't cut corners," she insisted, stunned by his suggestions.

While she stood there, Tony turned, strode to his car, climbed inside, and drove away.

The wind cut through the thin fabric of her shirt like a knife, but Angie ignored the cold as icicles of fear formed around her heart.

Rick was going to pay. Gentle, kind Rick whose integrity had never been called into question until he got involved with the Grants. Angie knew the way it worked—Rick had fulfilled the terms of the fake CSIS warrant and embarrassed someone in the process. She could imagine him making a fuss on her behalf, pointing out that someone's error had caused her a lot of embarrassment and their office extra work for no reason.

Members of CSIS prided themselves on their in-house management of affairs, and they didn't suffer remonstrances from outsiders easily. They'd look for a way to make Rick pay and if they succeeded, he could lose more than the promotion he'd longed for. If Tony Nickel was right, Rick was going to lose everything.

All because of her.

The guilt was unbearable.

It didn't matter if someone was out there waiting for her. Angie didn't care if she froze every finger and toe getting back to her old house.

She had to warn Rick.

# CHAPTER TWELVE

$A$ngie, calm down. You're not making sense."

Rick glanced around the yard, then tugged on her arm to draw her inside. He closed and locked the door behind her, took her jacket. "What are you doing over here? Is Kelly okay?"

"She's fine. Kent and Georgia are with her. I'm concerned about you."

"Me?" He frowned, dusted his hands on his pants, and tried to ignore his annoyance that he hadn't thought of an excuse to prevent her sudden appearance before his project was complete. "I'm fine."

"I'm not."

"Sit down. I just made a pot of coffee. Want some?" He saw her eyes widen at the mess he'd made in her house. "You did say I could rent the place, remember? I'm just making some . . . alterations."

"Alterations? That's what you call this?"

"Is it okay?" The changes weren't for him. They were for her, to help her see beyond the bad memories to the potential this house held.

"I'm not sure it's an improvement," she told him, raising one eyebrow at the pile of broken boards stacked in the middle of the living-room floor. "But I don't really care what you do. I won't be living here again."

Rick sucked in his breath at the finality of those words, then turned his back to pour the coffee so she wouldn't see how her certainty affected him. *Wait!* his mind silently screamed, but he remained silent.

When they both had cups of steaming brew, he sat down opposite her. "Now what's wrong?"

"Didn't you get my message that I needed to see you?"

"Yes, but I was going to call you later this evening. You didn't say it was urgent."

She was more agitated than he'd ever seen her. Spots of red dotted her cheekbones. Her hazel eyes flashed with anger and something else . . . fear?

"Clearly I should have called right away," he apologized. "Tell me."

Rick watched the flare of emotions blaze across her face as she related her discussion with Agent Nickel.

"You're in danger, Rick. Parker needs something to show he's in charge, some big action that will echo through the agency. Making an example of you will reinforce his theory that we need someone outside the RCMP to monitor it."

A flicker of worry tugged at him, but he pushed it away. He'd done nothing wrong. Trusting meant hanging on in spite of the way things looked. He wasn't going to stop trusting God now.

"I'll be fine, Angie. I have a few contacts too, you know. They're checking into the story this fellow gave. They'll figure things out."

"This fellow is none other than Michael Parker. Do you know anything about him?" She groaned when he simply looked at her. "You should. He's up for the top job at CSIS, and the word is that he'll get it."

"You sound like you know him." Rick studied his nails, hating the pretense but needing to garner whatever information he could before he told her what he knew.

"I never met the guy. Wouldn't know him if he personally handed me a raise. But I've heard about him, and not all of it is good." She pulled her phone out of her jacket pocket. "I had a friend e-mail me whatever information she could find in the files on our Mr. Parker."

She punched a couple of buttons, then began reading: "'Former military, four medals, six overseas postings, Order of Canada—'" she scanned the screen—"looks like he retired from special forces with several commendations, then worked for a while in an undisclosed location training men for an elite tactical force. He moved from there to a desk position—analyst or something—at CSIS. That was last year and since then he's moved up the ladder faster than a speeding bullet."

"Impressive." He'd read all this on the sheets his boss had faxed late this afternoon. Rick held her gaze with his. "What connection does Mr. Parker have with your father?"

Her wide-eyed astonishment couldn't possibly be faked. After a moment, Angie hooted with laughter. "With Syd? Absolutely nothing. Why would you even think that?"

Rick reconsidered. If Angie knew what was going on, if he explained how much trouble he was in and why, she'd try to dash to his rescue. It was bad enough she thought the CSIS warrant was the basis of his problem. If she knew it was because of Syd—no. Though he'd love to have Angie there backing him, he didn't want her fighting his battles at the expense of her relationship with her father. If there was to be a future for father and daughter, it wasn't going to be tarnished by his problems.

"Rick?"

"I remembered you said your father was in the military. Guess I was just trying to get a handle on things," he told her.

"That's not all, is it?" she asked, perceptive as ever.

"There are a couple of things going on at work that I'd like to clear up—your suddenly vanishing warrant being one of them."

Obvioulsy Angie wasn't fooled by his sidestepping. "This isn't about me. Tell the truth. You haven't been cleared of whatever they're upset about, have you?"

"Not yet." He saw the surprise in her eyes and rushed to explain. "Don't worry about me, Angie. I'll sort it out. My boss is backing me so there's nothing for us to do but sit tight and let him ferret out the truth."

"You're sure? You don't want to talk about it?"

That was the last thing he wanted. "I'm fine. But what about you?"

She didn't avoid his question as he'd expected. Instead she leaned her elbows on the table and cupped her chin in her palms. "Me? I guess you could say I'm more confused than I've ever been." She held up her hand at his offer of more coffee. "After Tony Nickel stopped by, when I couldn't get ahold of you, Georgia and Kelly and I went over to the dining hall. I said I'd help make decorations for that Valentine's thing they have coming up. You know, the couples retreat?"

He nodded. Kent was branching out by putting some of his ideas for year-round use of the camp into action.

"While we were there I noticed some books on the camp in that big glass case beside the fireplace. I pulled a couple out. They were written by former camp directors, sort of little histories of the ways they'd seen God move in lives during their time at Camp Hope."

"And?" He wished he could soothe the turbulence from her face.

"I don't know how to explain it, but the more I read, the more I felt connected to Camp Hope, as if I was somehow part of it all."

Rick stayed silent, content to watch her as she mused aloud.

"I have had absolutely nothing to do with the success of Camp Hope. And yet I have this little glow of pride inside that my grandparents, my mother—even Syd, for pete's sake—had something to do with creating it. Hundreds and hundreds of kids have come through that camp, listened to Bible stories, learned about God. All because a few people had a dream."

She wasn't talking to him, not directly anyway. Rick had seen it before—Camp Hope had a way of impacting people. Angie was only now figuring out that she wasn't the island she'd thought, that her past and her history mattered.

"A couple of those books mention my grandparents and my

mother. They speak of the open houses on the weekends, of the fun they had in this house." She looked around as if she couldn't believe it. "I never thought of my home as anything but a prison. I could hardly wait to get away, but according to those writers, they could hardly wait to come here."

Emotions—yearning, joy, a flicker of hope—flitted across her beautiful face. Like the shooting stars he often saw at night, love burst white-hot inside his chest. In this moment he would gladly give up everything—his life, his career, his own family—if he could only change Angie Grant's past.

"There was so much potential here," she whispered. "Now it's all gone."

Rick couldn't sit silent anymore. He leaned across the table, grasped her hand in his. "It isn't the place. God could have used anywhere. The potential came from the people. They used what they had to spread joy. Do you think your grandparents were any different than you? that they didn't have disappointments and defeats? that your mother didn't experience times when she questioned everything?"

Angie's riot of curls tumbled from side to side when she shook her head. "I don't think she did. I think she had an inner peace and security that her parents provided."

"She found that in God," Rick argued. "Your mother wasn't a saint. Neither were your grandparents. They were human, the same as you and I. I'm sure they struggled with the same issues we do."

She stared at him. "You think—"

"I'm glad you've learned something about your family, but you only know part of the story. You've got this dream going because you know only about the good times."

"I barely know anything," she admitted softly. "Syd never talked about the past, and I never knew who or what to ask."

"Then ask now. The Murdocks know quite a lot. I'm sure they'd love to tell you anything they can remember."

"And there are the albums."

"Pardon?" In his opinion, she'd looked at those Camp Hope albums too long.

"My grandfather also made albums," she reminded him. "The Murdocks think they're inside that big cedar trunk in the garage. I need to get it inside so I can go through it."

Rick had promised to take the box over for her to look through. But he didn't want her here during the day—not while the carpenters were working. Especially not after what she'd just told him about Tony Nickel's information. He wanted her safe among friends, not isolated.

"If it's so important, I'll drop the box off tomorrow morning on my way to work," he told her.

"Thank you." She kept her eyes down, focused on the table, her nails tracing the marks and dents that had accumulated over the years. "I don't know what I would have done without you, Rick."

"You would have managed."

"I'm not sure that's true." She lifted her head, met his gaze. "You're the best friend I've ever had. I don't think you'll ever know what you mean to me."

"You could always tell me," he joked. But the laughter disappeared as he watched her face. "Please tell me," he whispered.

Angie reached across the table, placed her palm against his cheek, and held it there. "You're like my rock," she murmured, her voice so soft he had to lean nearer. "When I'm with you I feel whole, a real person who has a place in the world. Accepted, that's what I'm trying to say."

She laughed at her own words, a harsh sad sound. "I guess what I mean is that for a little while I can forget that I'm Syd Grant's daughter, a no-name brat from a dysfunctional home who doesn't deserve to have a friend like you."

He was appalled by her words, then worried when she suddenly jumped up and grabbed her coat. "Angie—"

"I've got to go. I told Georgia I wouldn't be long." She avoided his scrutiny.

"Wait a minute." Rick stepped around the table, slid his arms into his own jacket. "I'm not sure of your meaning. And I don't understand what you said about not belonging. But I know one thing."

Rick placed himself in front of her so she couldn't escape, couldn't avoid him by running away. Again. "I care about you, Angie Grant. You have become much more than a friend to me. When you're not around, I look for you, wonder if you'd laugh at my joke or poke fun at me. I wake up in the morning thinking about you—if you'll have a good day, if you'll think of me—and I go to sleep wondering the same thing."

Surprise washed across her face, but he kept going, letting the words flow past the dam he'd failed to keep intact. "It doesn't matter where I am or what I'm doing. You're there in my thoughts, in my heart. It's not something new. I've felt this way for a long time. And it's not going to go away. So when you talk about feeling whole, that's how I feel when I'm with you."

"Rick, I can't—"

He couldn't stop now. "Sometimes I see Georgia and Kent together, watch them share a private look or see her squeeze his arm and I think, 'Will Angie ever feel that way about me? Will we ever communicate with a look? Will she ever know how much I want to be more than her friend?'"

Rick stepped an inch closer, so close he could see the tiny pulse throbbing in her neck. "Will you?" He cupped her face in his hands and stared into her eyes for timeless moments before he bent and pressed his lips to hers.

For an instant, for one infinitesimal moment in time, she responded, and her kiss was far beyond any response he could have wished for.

Then she stepped away. "I can't."

The bleakness in those words sent his hands falling to his sides.

Tears welled at the corners of her eyes. "I don't want to hurt you. But I can't love you. I won't."

"Why?" he whispered as his heart shattered.

"Because there are too many things we don't share." Her shoulders went back as she drew in a deep breath. "You don't see the real me. You think I have a distorted view of the past, but it's you who isn't accepting reality. You have this picture of some fantasy girl who could be all those things you want. I can't be her."

"You *are* her."

She shook her head, brushed his arm with her hand. "I wish." Angie smiled but there was no joy in that solemn uptilt of her mouth. "I'm nothing like her. I'm nothing like the kind of person you are. I'm not generous or tender or gentle. I'm mean and dirty. I've done things I'm ashamed of. I've used you a thousand times. That's not the kind of person who deserves to be loved."

"I never said you deserved it," he said. "It's not something I chose. Loving you just . . . is."

"It can't be." She turned, walked to the door.

Frustration ate at him. Why couldn't she explain? What stopped her from reciprocating his feelings? Her kiss had not been that of an unfeeling woman. So why did she keep putting up barriers?

"Wait a minute!"

She paused and turned, one eyebrow quirked.

"Tell me one thing. Why can't it be?"

"Because when it comes right down to it, I am my father's daughter."

Before he could say another word, Angie was out the door.

Rick responded without hesitating. No way would he allow her to go back to the camp alone. He watched until Angie was across the yard, then followed as silently as he could, keeping his distance, but with his gaze riveted on her.

Not until she was safely inside the house did he draw a calming breath. And let it out almost immediately when a hand clamped onto his arm.

"I need to talk to you and Angie," Syd Grant said.

"Not tonight, Syd." It was rude, it was inconsiderate, and it was probably the worst thing he could do given Angie's questions. But right now Rick just wanted to be alone.

"Then when? It's not easy to get away. I haven't got much time left, and you need to know—"

"Know what? Why you're trying to ruin me? Why you're lying?" Rick glared at him. "Yeah, I'd like to know that. But why wait? Why not tell me now?"

Syd didn't answer.

Rick trudged back through the snow toward the house in which he'd invested so much hope. Defeat dragged at his heels.

Syd followed him. "I can't tell you now because I need Angela to be there too."

Rick whirled around to face the man who'd caused Angie so much pain. "She won't listen to you."

"Did she check out the doctor I told her about—the one who treated Eve?"

Rick shook his head. "She doesn't believe anything you say. Frankly I'm wondering about you myself."

"Get her to see Dr. Magnusson. You both might be surprised."

"I'll do that. Tomorrow." Rick almost continued walking, then remembered his promise to take the trunk to Angie. "But you can help me out for a change, Syd."

"How?"

Rick pulled open the garage door. "Help me get this trunk loaded. Angie wants to look at it while she's staying at Camp Hope." He led the way to the trunk, grabbed one end.

"Why's she looking at old pictures?" Syd grunted as he helped Rick lug the trunk to the truck.

"Because she's never seen them before. Didn't you think your daughter would be interested in her past?" Rick deliberately jarred the other man's grip, trying to force him to admit his faults. "Are you so self-centered you couldn't even give her that much?"

"But she always disappeared for hours at a time. After I found the trunk open, I thought . . . I figured—" Groaning, Syd dragged a hand through his bristled hair. "They were out here. Poking through our things without even telling me."

"I have no idea what you're talking about, Syd. And frankly, I'm not really interested."

"Maybe not. But do you care about my daughter?"

"Yes. Do you?" Rick shot back, knowing his own voice was sharp with condemnation.

"I love my daughter more than anything in life. That's why you've got to get her to listen to me. Please."

There was something in the old man's voice, some note of desperation that Rick couldn't ignore. "All right," he agreed when the silence had stretched too long. "I'll try. Tomorrow night Kent and Georgia will be away. Angie will be alone at Camp Hope with Kelly. You meet me here and we'll go over together. But don't be surprised if she won't talk to you. You've got a lot to answer for."

"I know." Surprisingly, Syd was smiling. "I'll see you tomorrow night at seven. And, Rick?"

"Yeah?"

"Don't leave this trunk in here overnight. Take it to her now."

"Why?"

"Why not? Things, important things, have a way of disappearing around here. I still haven't found that book."

"You probably never will."

Syd's face lost all color. When he reached out to slam the truck gate closed, Rick noticed his hand was shaking.

"Don't say that," Syd pleaded. "For all our sakes that book has to turn up soon or Angie will—"

"Will what?" Rick gripped his shoulder and hung on. "Tell me."

"She'll pay the price."

The threat was implied. Rick could only stare as Syd turned and moved silently across the yard and toward the trees. He remained in place, watching the bent figure fade into the shadows as questions chased through his mind.

When he'd finally accepted that there were no answers, that Syd was probably paranoid about his book, Rick thought, *Maybe our Syd is telling the truth. About this at least. Tomorrow I'll find out.*

Rick made sure no one else was around. It took two minutes to activate the house's security system, two more to climb into his vehicle and drive down the lane to Camp Hope.

Kent opened the door to him, then called to Angie.

She stood in a halo of light, staring. "What's this?"

"A trunk, courtesy of your father. Apparently he was unaware that you'd never looked inside." He nodded at Kent, and the two of them hauled the cedar chest into the house.

Rick leaned toward Angie and said in a low voice, "I'll be back tomorrow after work. You and I have an appointment."

"To do what?"

"Clear up past mistakes. See you."

As he drove away from the house, Rick became aware of an ominous feeling invading the truck's cab.

He should have pushed Syd to tell him first, so he could ease the path for Angie. Yet his own problems weighed heavily on his mind. A routine warrant served years ago—no reason to think then that he'd need a witness. No reason to believe Syd would challenge it after spending so much time incarcerated either. But here he was, his integrity as an officer and a person in question, and no way to disprove the allegations.

Perhaps that's why Rick felt compelled to help Angie as much as he could now, because there was no guarantee that he'd be able to do anything if he was suspended—unless Syd and his buddy withdrew their claims. Which, given their last conversation, didn't seem likely.

⟢◈⟠

It was four on a silent snowy morning, and Angie couldn't sleep.

That big handmade chest her grandfather had crafted sat in the corner of her room, calling out to her. She had to answer.

Angie slid from beneath the covers, put on a thick fleece robe and slippers, then stared down at the trunk.

What secrets did it hold?

The house was quiet with only the occasional hum of the furnace and the swish of warm air to disrupt the hush. She knelt in front of the chest, laid her hand against the solid, timeless surface.

*Please, God, let the answers be in here.*

It was not locked, merely latched. She unclasped the brass works and gently lifted the lid, mindful of the creaky hinges. The aromatic cedar scent wafted up. A black velvet lining surrounded the many binders. The faint musty odor of pages long hidden rose to her nose.

Angie lifted out the first book, carefully examined the pages. This wasn't simply a photo album; it was more like a history-filled scrapbook. She recognized no one in it and, after checking the date, realized it had been created years before her birth, even before her mother's.

One by one she removed the books, arranging them in yearly sequence. The most recent one lay on the bottom of the chest, which puzzled her until she thought of her father. No doubt he'd wanted to get them out of sight.

Heart pounding, Angie lifted the cover and stared into the face of her mother. *Eve graduates from high school.* A face almost identical to her own peered back with wide-eyed naïveté. Her mother wore a long green gown, filmy with some sort of tiny pattern chasing across the billowing skirt. She was beautiful.

Angie turned the page. *Eve's last summer home. Eve home from college. Eve's wedding day.*

Tears rolled down Angie's cheeks as she followed the path of her mother's life, of her father's part in it. How dare God let her father share these halcyon moments when Angie had almost nothing to remember.

She flipped the page, anxious to avoid contemplation of that tender smile on her father's face while he gazed at his new wife.

*Eve's great news!*

Angie's heart bounced, then stopped. She traced a finger over the pale pink birth announcement and drew in a deep breath. *Angela Valentine Grant—our Valentine's angel.* It was her father's writing.

How dare he use Kelly's special name for her! Angie couldn't bear to look at the picture of herself lying in her father's arms.

She turned the page. Snapshots of her crawling, walking, eating, sleeping in her father's arms—they were all there. She shifted and one picture slipped free of the page, landed on the carpet. Her grand-mother—it had to be her—was kneeling on the floor, arms out-stretched, beckoning a toddler near.

*Our angel learns to walk.*

Never, not once in all the years she'd lived with him, had her father called her anything other than Angie. She couldn't fathom why he'd written it down on this picture as if she were some treasured bit of his heart instead of the nuisance kid he couldn't tolerate.

Anger, pain sharper than she'd ever felt before, throbbed through her. It was accompanied by a sense of loss that she'd never known Syd when he was like this, had never experienced the look of love she saw on his face. If the pictures were true, she must have done something wrong to lose his love.

It didn't matter now, not really. Angie knew she would never get it back. It was too late for that. Besides, if Syd found out what she'd done—no, better to forget about the past.

"Let it go," she muttered to herself, as she replaced the photo and tried to close the book.

But it wouldn't close. The last page refused to stay in place so she had to adjust it. Her fingers paused, then fell to her lap.

Angie's gaze rested on the suntanned smiling countenance of a gentle-looking man sitting on a tractor, his arms tenderly surrounding a chubby child dressed in the grubbiest clothes imaginable. The red gold hair looked like ruby-spun silk in a wash of setting sun, but there was nothing unreal about the child's face. Her eyes danced with joy, her tiny hands confidently resting on the wheel, supported by gnarled fingers.

*Grandpa and his angel.*

She wept for everything she'd lost, for the family that had loved her, for the grandparents who'd given so much love to others, but left behind a grandchild who couldn't remember any of the soft touches she glimpsed in these pictures.

But weeping did little to assuage her heart. Maybe if she'd been more understanding, maybe if she'd been the kind of daughter he needed, maybe if she'd seen these pictures sooner—no!

There were no excuses. She'd done what she'd done—a shameful, horrible thing no daughter would be proud of. But he'd deserved it. He'd treated her like a slave—worse, like an interloper. But her deeds hadn't made her feel any better. And Rick would never understand her actions. Never condone them.

After a long time, Angie rose, placed all the albums back in the chest, and then softly closed the lid.

The past was over. It was time to think about the future. About leaving here. She squeezed her eyes closed. *Please let there be a message telling me to go back. Please let me get away from all these memories.*

As usual, God had no response to her pleas.

She picked up her cell phone and began dialing the numbers by heart. One message held her attention: "Have found some evidence that child's father may still be alive. Cannot confirm at this time. Remain in current location. We confirm visitor to your previous location—identity unknown. Simpson under surveillance. Use extreme caution."

So the threat was still out there.

A heavy burden lodged on her shoulders, weighing down her spirit. Angie accepted that she wasn't going anywhere. Which proved that God wasn't there for her; otherwise He would have helped her escape. She knew why, understood that her sin had created the gap and that there was no way she could span it.

Rick was wrong. Some things couldn't be forgiven.

She was living proof.

# CHAPTER THIRTEEN

She looked like a bag lady.

Rick's lips twitched at the sight of his passenger, but he kept his mouth shut.

Kelly, however, saw his glance and grinned. "I love dress-up games," she told him, adjusting the big floppy hat that Georgia had provided.

"So do I, honey." He clapped a hand over his smiling mouth at Angie's rumble of disgust. *Grumpy* didn't begin to describe her mood today. "Dress-up is fun for grown-ups too, isn't it, Ang?"

"Oh, hilarious. I love looking like I just went Dumpster diving. But I guess it was worth it. At least I know Syd wasn't lying about my mother. Cancer." She shook her head. "I never even dreamed it was that. How on earth did my mother manage with me to look after?"

"I think the Murdock sisters were there a lot before your dad came back."

"I suppose so. That's probably why they know so much about me. One of these days I'm going to ask them some more questions. I want to know the truth. All of it." She tilted her head sideways. "You haven't said much."

"Not a lot to say."

She was too intuitive. Rick reiterated his orders to himself to watch that she didn't dig the truth out of him and run away from her own problems by burying herself in his.

"Are you apprehensive about seeing your father tonight?" He'd told her earlier, hoping to prepare her.

"No—" her jaw hardened—"because I'm not going to."

"But I promised Syd—"

"*You* promised, Rick. I agreed to nothing." Angie crossed her arms over her chest. "It's better if I don't have anything to do with him."

Dismay filled him. Rick was more certain than ever that his relationship with Angie would never progress until she had the answers she needed. And Syd held the key to her past, to the guilt that robbed her of any hope and joy.

"But, Ang, you said yourself that you have questions. He can answer them better than anyone. He was there; he lived it."

"Answers, maybe. But there's no guarantee he'll tell me the truth."

"He did about the cancer. Dr. Magnusson confirmed everything Syd told us. Besides, why would he lie?"

"Why indeed?" she scoffed. "I don't pretend to understand how my father's mind works. I only know it's better if I don't get anywhere near him."

"Why?"

She glanced at Kelly, sitting between them, then pressed her lips together.

"Angie, I know you're angry at him, but that's exactly why I think you need to talk to him. Let him know your questions and frustrations. He might say something that can help."

"I don't think there's anything that can help. There are no words he can utter that would erase his actions." She stared straight ahead through the windshield. "It's better if I concentrate on my job and forget about Syd."

Rick pursed his lips. Maybe she was right. Maybe it was silly to keep hoping for the best. Heaven knew he had his own doubts about Syd's veracity.

This afternoon a package had arrived from his boss. The contents were not encouraging. Syd's statement indicted him. His friend's testimony, this Michael Parker, only added weight to that. It didn't matter that the money had been found in Syd's car, nor that he had been preparing to escape. It didn't matter that he'd confessed to the crime. It was all obviated by the illegality of the warrant. The one Rick had served.

Soft music from the radio filled the cab. He saw Kelly's head move from side to side as she studied Angie first, then him. "What are you thinking about?" he asked.

Her heart-shaped face tipped up, her smile blazing out. "Valentine's Day."

"Oh, what's so big about Valentine's?" Aside from the fact that it was Angie's birthday and the day he would have to stand before the investigating committee.

"Georgia's having a big party. I'm helping her get ready," Kelly crowed, chest puffed out.

"Good for you." He ruffled her golden curls. "How?"

"Well . . ." She dragged the word out as she decided how to explain. "Kent's sister—did you know he has a sister?"

"Yes, I did. Her name is Christa."

"She sent us a great big package. We have to make huge hearts to hang around the dining hall and funny little bags with candy hearts inside and toothpick umbrellas and a whole bunch of stuff. I'm very good at gluing."

"Yourself or the paper?" Rick smiled as her giggle echoed around the cab. "I know Georgia couldn't do it without your help," he said as he pulled into the yard and parked beside the camp's main house.

"That's what she said." Kelly didn't wait for Angie to get out. Instead she wiggled underneath the steering wheel and held out her arms, waiting for Rick to lift her down. "I have to go help her now."

"Wait a minute." Rick hunkered down so he was at her eye level.

"Can I ask you a favor?" he whispered, knowing Angie would take a moment to remove a few of her less-than-beautiful garments before she entered the house.

"Sure." Kelly danced from one foot to the other. "Is it a secret?"

"Yes, a big one. Georgia and Kent are going out tonight."

"I know. It's a big meeting at church."

"Yes. I'm going to come over with a surprise for Angie after they're gone. Do you think you could go to bed a little bit early so she can talk to her dad by herself?"

"Angie's mad at her daddy. She might get mad at me too." Kelly's face drooped.

"Uh-uh. Angie couldn't get mad at you. She loves you."

The truck door slammed on the other side.

"Please, Kelly. I want Angie and her father to talk out their hurts, and they need time to do that."

"So she can love him again." Kelly nodded. "Okay, Mr. Rick. I'll watch on the clock and when it says seven zero zero, I'll get ready for bed. Okay?"

He nodded, then straightened as Angie came around the back of the vehicle, carrying her discarded disguise.

"What are you two whispering about?" she demanded.

"I wasn't whispering." Kelly tugged on Rick's arm. When he leaned down, he slid something into her hand. She grinned, then pressed her lips to his cheek. "Thanks for the chocolate bar."

"You're welcome, Kelly." He grinned as she dashed across the yard to grab her puppy, who could hardly walk, his backside was wagging so hard. She lugged the dog up the stairs and burst into the house, calling Georgia's name.

When he glanced at Angie, Rick saw the way her face had changed, softened. "It's going to be awfully hard to let that little girl go."

Angie nodded. "Thanks a lot for taking me to see Dr. Magnusson. It feels good to finally know the truth."

"Does it?" He stared down at her, his heart welling with love he knew she wouldn't accept. "Then why not find out the whole truth?"

"I can't. It hurts too much to keep going back, and I-I don't want to do it anymore." She looked at her feet for a moment. "Sorry."

"Yeah. So am I." Rick sighed.

As he reached for the truck door, a shot rang out and the windshield shattered. He grabbed Angie's arm and tossed her to the ground, shielding her body with his.

Another shot clipped what he thought was his headlight.

"Let me go! I have to get Kelly."

"She's all right. She's inside," he whispered, scanning the ground beyond them from his prone position. "Can you see anything?"

"No." She edged away from him, drawing the gun he'd returned to her this morning. "We're sitting ducks."

"Get in the truck," he ordered. "Lie on the floor."

She studied him, her face inches away, then nodded. "Gotcha." She scooted inside, crawled across the seat, and dropped to the floor.

Rick inched up the side, trying to get a better look at the area. From the hole in his windshield he guessed the trajectory and scanned that spot. Nothing.

He could hear Angie's soft voice in the background, talking on his radio, but he kept his focus on the shield of trees. A great place to experience nature, but Camp Hope also offered terrific cover for anyone who wanted to blend into the shadows. The winter afternoon had turned to dusk during the drive home. Now he could only pick out gloomy obscurities that wavered in the shade. There was no way of knowing whether or not they were human.

He slid behind the wheel, reached for the ignition, paused.

"Help's on the way," Angie told him. "What now?"

"I'm going to drive closer to the house and park in front of the steps. I want you to use the truck as cover and get inside. Make sure everyone is okay, then have dispatch let me know if Kent's home or walking around out here."

"Okay." Her fingers closed around the door handle.

"Angie?" Rick made the short journey with his heart racing. He couldn't help himself. He touched her hair and then her cheek. "Please be careful."

She drew away after a moment, her green eyes swirling darker in the dashboard's glow. "You too." She held his gaze for a moment, touched his cheek with her fingertips. Then she pointed upward. "Light's gonna come on when I open this door. Better duck."

He obeyed. Angie slid out of the vehicle and climbed up the steps into the house. In her dark bulky coat she was almost invisible against the dark siding.

*Okay, Lord, now it's my turn. Please give us some protection. Keep Angie and Kelly safe.*

He moved out of the truck, toward the house. The door opened and he ducked inside. "Everything okay? Kelly?"

Angie pointed and Rick saw the little girl huddled under a table in the corner, the dog still clutched in her arms. "Kent? Georgia?"

Angie shook her head. He saw the fear in her eyes, and his whole body went cold.

"What's wrong? Are they hurt?"

"I don't know where they are. But this was lying on the table."

He took the big red heart from her and read the chalk-written words aloud. "'*One week left. That's all.*'"

"One week till what?" Angie asked. "Is this message for me, for Kelly, or for you?"

"Maybe it's none of us," he mused, remembering a conversation he'd had last night. "Maybe it's for Syd."

———◆———

"So what you're telling me is that no one has any idea who was shooting at us."

Arden nodded at Angie. "There's no way to tell which one of you they were shooting at either. I know you think it was you, but it could as easily have been Rick. Judging from what you've told me, the bullet that came through the windshield was nearest him."

Angie sighed. "It just gets better, doesn't it?"

"I suppose it's too much to expect that someone found the bullet," Rick said.

Arden snorted. "Are you kidding me? It's dark, it's snowy, and there are tracks all over the place. It's a mess."

"At least no one was hurt." Angie glanced from the kitchen into the living room, where Kent and Georgia sat on the sofa with Kelly between them. Now they were suffering—because of her. "They've got a meeting they should be at tonight. Do you think it's safe?"

"Sure. Why not?" Arden answered. "That phone call they had was obviously meant to draw them away from here, so they wouldn't be hurt."

"Thank God," she whispered.

"Exactly," Rick agreed, offering her a brilliant smile.

"Now, this is—" A knock at the door interrupted Arden.

At the door, Arden held a whispered conversation with another officer, then closed it. "They just found a man bound and gagged behind the pool house. Claims he knows Angie. A Tony Nickel?"

Angie felt her knees begin to wobble so she sat on the nearest chair. "CSIS sent him here to be my backup. Is he all right?"

"The back of his head is going to hurt for a while. Somebody clipped him pretty good."

"With what?" Rick demanded.

"There was no weapon at the scene. Maybe their hand?"

Angie felt Rick's stare and knew his thoughts echoed hers. Military training taught people how to use their hands in combat. Syd's former friend?

"There's not much more we can do tonight. If it's okay with you, Rick, I'll leave a man here till Angie's pal gets back on the job. He thinks overnight should do it, though I'm guessing he'll have second thoughts tomorrow morning." Arden waited for Rick's agreement, then slapped a hand on his shoulder. "I'm glad he missed. We need you at work."

"Thanks, Arden."

"By the way, you had a phone call after you left. Somebody at head office is real anxious to talk to you."

Kelly padded out to the kitchen. Busy with the little girl, Angie missed the rest of the conversation. By the time she'd sent Kelly back to Georgia, the men had stopped talking.

"See you, Angie. Take care." Arden walked out the door.

"Thanks," Angie called after him, then glanced at Rick. He was staring at something beyond her, his eyes dark and brooding, his face tight with tension. "Is everything okay?"

"No." He sighed heavily. "I was supposed to meet Syd tonight and bring him over here."

"What? I can't believe you'd do this," Angie complained, even though she knew she was repeating herself. "I told you I didn't want to talk to him."

"Yes, you did. But I didn't know that when I agreed to it. Besides, I've got some questions for Syd myself, and I think it's time he answered them."

"Did you stop to consider it could have been him shooting at us?"

"For what reason?" His surprise was obvious. "I've seen him several times. He could have hurt me any time he wanted. Why now?"

"I don't know!" She raked her hands through her hair, frustration chewing a hole in her composure. "Nothing makes sense anymore. Ever since I got here, things have been skewed. Sometimes I think I'm going crazy."

Rick stepped forward, smoothed one hand over her disordered curls. "Then isn't it time we started getting some answers? Whatever Syd knows, whatever he doesn't, we have to hear him out. If there's even a trickle of information he can provide, we need it."

"You think Syd knows something about that shot?" She chewed on her bottom lip.

"Truthfully? I don't know—for sure. But think about what he's said, Angie. He's after a book. Your mother had it before she died. Somebody wants it, and he thinks they'll come after you to get it." He

LOIS RICHER

nodded at her skeptical look. "I know, it's a stretch. But we haven't got anything else. We've got to hear what he has to say."

"I don't trust him."

"I'm not sure I do either. But what else have we got?"

"Nothing." Syd was her father. She owed him respect. The old Sunday school lessons lingered in the back of her mind, raging against the reality of what she'd endured at his hands.

One after the other old hurts, accusations, reminders tumbled through her brain, and the anger festered anew. But in the end only one thing mattered—there was no one else to turn to.

"Fine. Let's talk to him and ask him some hard questions. Not because I expect the truth, but because you're right. What's the alternative?"

Rick looked relieved by her decision. "He was supposed to meet me at your house. But there's no way I'm leaving here now."

"Call Arden back; get him to go with you." She pulled up her pant leg, indicating her gun. "I can protect us. Besides, Kent and Georgia won't be leaving for a while, long enough for you to get there and back."

Rick didn't respond immediately, which prompted Angie to scrutinize him more thoroughly. "What's the problem?"

"I don't like leaving you here alone," he admitted, his eyes holding hers, saying things she didn't want to hear.

"Arden said someone would be outside." Angie turned away. "I told you—we'll be fine. Stop fussing."

"This could go wrong," he whispered, his breath brushing the tip of her ear. "What if it's a setup?"

Angie whirled around, furious at his implication. "You think I'd hesitate to do whatever's necessary, just because he's my father?" she demanded, glaring at him. She shook her head. "I wouldn't. Kelly is the most important thing. I'm not letting anyone or anything get to her."

"So fierce. So protective." He smiled softly. "I never doubted you for a minute, Angie Grant. You're going to make a wonderful mother one day."

His words sent her into a tailspin of shock. She stood frozen in place, watching mindlessly as he called out the door to Arden, then donned his coat and gloves. Rick offered some last-minute suggestions to Kent and Georgia, accepted Kelly's hug.

*A mother. Me?*

"Angie?" Rick stood staring at her, his brows drawn together. "Are you all right?"

"Yes."

"I'll be right back. If he isn't at your place, I'm not waiting. Okay?"

"Yeah." Nonchalance didn't work when he looked at her like a man who desperately needed comfort and thought she could help.

Maybe that's why she didn't move away when Rick leaned down and brushed his lips across her forehead. Maybe she wanted to offer him some scrap of comfort, just as he'd soothed her fears so many times before.

"Be safe," she whispered, the lump in her throat preventing further speech.

"Always."

Angie moved to the window, trying to keep him in sight as he strode across the compound, spoke to Arden for a moment, then disappeared into the night.

A mother? Her? She traced her fingertips over the spot where he'd kissed her. A child—her child. She could hardly imagine being in charge of such a fragile gift. So much responsibility.

Perhaps that's how Syd had felt that first day he'd held her in his arms. When Eve had died and he'd been left to raise her himself, he could have been apprehensive, overanxious about his capabilities as a father. Maybe—

*No!* Angie reined in the wayward sympathy. She would not allow these soft feelings to creep in. Other men lost their wives, but they didn't take it out on their kids.

For something to do and not because she wanted something to drink, Angie put the kettle on for tea. The waiting, that's what got to

her. That and the uncertainty. She'd sent in a report of this afternoon's incident, but her orders were unchanged. Remain until further
notice.

"We don't have to go tonight, honey. We could stay here with
you." Georgia assessed her, then called over her shoulder, "Kent?"

"Georgia, go. Please?" Angie rested her hand on the other
woman's shoulder. "I'll feel terrible if you don't. Besides, Rick will be
here and there's another officer outside. We'll be fine."

"You're sure?" Kent stood in the kitchen doorway, frowning.

"Positive." She looked around. "Where's Kelly?"

"Brushing her teeth. She said she was tired and she was going to
go to bed as soon as we left. Seems a little odd, don't you think?"

Angie's heart ached for the little girl who so willingly did what
she was asked.

"She's such a strong child," Kent continued, unaware of her inner
distress. "So self-sufficient. She asked me to explain what doubts are."

"What did you say?" Georgia sank onto a chair to listen.

"I told her we all have them. Young and old, we wonder if we're
doing the right thing, if we made a bad decision." He shrugged. "It's
true."

"What doubts do you have?" Angie couldn't believe he'd ever had
any serious doubts about his life. Kent always seemed so strong and
independent, helping everyone else.

"I have the same ones you have. But after I check with God and
find out what He wants, I shove the doubts away and get on with my
job. Jesus didn't condemn Thomas for doubting. He held out His
hand and said 'feel it.' Once that was settled, I'm sure He expected
Thomas to get on with the job set before him."

"The Bible says that if anyone lacks wisdom they should ask God
and He will give it." Georgia gave Angie a funny look. "Christians
don't become perfect simply because they're Christians, you know.
We're still human. Thank heaven God loves us in spite of our
messes."

A ribbon of silence stretched across the room.

"Herein endeth tonight's lesson." Kent motioned to Georgia. "We should leave shortly."

"I'm ready whenever you are."

Rick's solid tread on the stairs outside was echoed by a lighter step.

"My father wanted to talk to us," Angie explained. "Don't ask me why. I think he's said more than enough."

The screen door creaked open.

"I know it's hard for you," Georgia said. "I'll be praying for you both tonight."

"Thanks."

Once Syd was inside and introductions had been performed, Kent and Georgia left.

Moments later Kelly appeared. "You're my Angel's daddy."

"Yes I am."

Angie couldn't believe the change in him. Despite the scars and markings from past surgeries, he looked more like the man in the pictures than she would have imagined. Softer, gentler, more caring.

Not at all like the father she'd endured.

"My daddy told me it doesn't matter if you're big or little, when you do something wrong you should 'pologize." Kelly's round face looked stern.

"I will apologize," Syd told her, "if she'll let me."

Kelly studied him for a moment, then nodded. "Okay," she agreed, her irrepressible smile slipping out. "I'm going to bed now so you can have some alone time." She held up her arms.

Syd looked at her, a puzzled look crossing his face. Finally he leaned down. His webbed hands wrapped around Kelly's tiny waist as he drew her close.

Kelly hugged him back. After she stepped away, she traced the marks on his hands. "I don't have a grandpa. Could you be mine?"

Syd's eyes watered. One damaged hand reached out to touch the wispy waves of hair against her forehead, then quickly pulled away, but he left his other hand cradled between Kelly's. "I was a terrible father. I don't think I could be your grandpa. I might hurt you, and I'd never ever want to do that."

"I would forgive you." When he didn't respond, Kelly frowned, and her eyes became glossy with unshed tears. "Please? I'm so lonesome for my daddy. I really would like to have a grandpa—just until my daddy can come and get me."

Angie's heart hurt so badly she struggled to control her feelings. *No!* she wanted to scream. *Stay away from her. Don't get near her. You'll only hurt her like you hurt me.*

As if she'd said the words aloud, Rick's arms encircled her waist and drew her back against him. His touch was like a delicate blanket, a shimmer of soothing comfort bathing her heart in a tender balm.

"It's okay, sweetheart," Rick whispered for Angie's ears alone. "He won't hurt her." And she believed him.

Silently they both watched the exchange.

"I'll be your grandpa if you really want me to, Kelly. For as long as I can." Syd's scarred cheeks glistened with wetness, and his voice emerged as a strangled whisper. "But you must tell me if I do something wrong."

"You won't." Kelly's eyes danced with happiness. "You made a mistake before, but you know better now."

"I hope so." He looked up at Angie. "I really hope so."

Angie slid away from Rick, cursing herself for depending on him. Rick had enough problems. He didn't deserve to take on hers too.

"Come on, sweetie. Let's get you tucked in." She tried to take Kelly's hand, but for the first time since they'd met Kelly refused to comply.

She remained where she was, tugged on Syd's hand. "Good night, Grandpa," she murmured.

"Good night, Kelly. Sweet dreams." He opened his lips to say something else, then glanced at Angie. Like a chameleon, his face changed into an emotionless mask.

Angie deliberately walked in front of him on her way to Kelly's room. She paused a fraction of a second to look him in the eye. "You have a lot of questions to answer."

"I'm not going anywhere."

As she tucked Kelly in and listened to her prayers, Angie felt a shiver of apprehension skitter up her spine.

She already regretted her decision to hear Syd out.

# CHAPTER FOURTEEN

Rick swallowed, then cleared his throat, shattering the hard silence that had fallen on the room. "So, Syd, maybe you'd better tell us why you had to talk to Angie." He mentally braced himself for the pain he knew would follow.

But Syd couldn't say a word because Angie burst into speech. "Before I listen to you, I want you to listen to me."

"Fine. You can say what you want. Ask me anything." Syd sat silent, his hands folded together.

Rick had the impression he was steeling himself for a verbal battle and silently prayed for help for them all.

"These past few days I've been learning things about my past, things you never bothered to tell me."

"Your grandfather's picture diaries," he said.

"Those and the Camp Hope albums. I want you to tell me about my mother. I know she was happy with her parents. I know she had a wonderful childhood."

"And you didn't." He nodded. "It's my fault, I know." A sigh emanated from a place deep within him. "I could never bring myself to talk about Eve—but for your sake I'll try. I met your mother when I came to Camp Hope to work one summer."

Rick saw Angie's look of surprise and knew she hadn't expected that.

"I was seventeen. I had no family, but I had dreams of going to college. Camp Hope needed a kid to mow lawns, paint, whatever. It was a great opportunity for me. I could live here with free room and board and save every dime. And on weekends I got to go to Eve's."

He pictured something that neither of them could see, and it brought a smile to his face. "Your mother was like a burst of sunshine, always laughing, always singing. There were ten other guys who had more money, better looks, and a lot more to offer, but Eve and I hit it off. I came back the next two summers, and in between we wrote to each other."

He paused, then continued. "That last summer I knew there couldn't be anything between us. I was going back to school, and in those days a trip to Calgary was a big deal. The military was paying for my college degree. Then Eve surprised me, told me she'd enrolled in a Bible college there."

He smiled at Angie's tiny gasp. "That's the way I felt. I was surprised and ecstatic. We studied hard and saw each other only on the weekends, but every moment was wonderful. The next summer I knew I had to return to Camp Hope. I asked her to marry me and she said yes. We knew it wouldn't be easy. I'd finished my degree, and the military expected me to be in active service. They were organizing an elite outfit for special assignments. I passed their tests, so we settled in a house on the base. We were married for four years, and it seemed like it would go on forever. Then Eve found out she was sick."

He stared at his hands. "For the first time in my life I couldn't fix things. She had treatments, we prayed constantly, and one day the doctors said that magic word: *remission*. They'd told her she would never be able to have children. I didn't care as long as I had her. Neither of us could believe it when she found out she was pregnant the following year. Your grandparents were overjoyed when we came home to tell them that summer."

"I saw a picture of you holding me," Angie whispered.

"Yes." He held her gaze as tears trickled down his cheeks. "I was scared and proud and a hundred other things. You were perfect and Eve was deliriously happy. I was being sent on missions by then, but each time I'd rush home to see what had happened with you two while I was away. It's what kept me going."

Angie was having a hard time with this. Rick could see the longing in her eyes battling with anger and disbelief.

"If I was wanted so much, if you loved me so much, then why—?" She couldn't go on.

"Why did I act as if I hated you?" he finished softly. "I think for a while I did. Isn't that terrible? You were my whole world, both of you. Then I was sent away and while I was gone God played a trick on me. At least, that's how I thought of it."

"Eve got sick again," Rick said, intrigued in spite of his determination to remain neutral.

Syd nodded. "I heard about it the day I was airlifted from Iran to Germany after my unit rescued the American hostages. I was in agony from the burns caused by the explosion, and nothing seemed to touch the pain. Except every once in a while there would be this spot of clarity when I could escape, think about something else. It was during one of these times that a buddy read Eve's letter to me." He stopped, closed his eyes.

Angie remained silent, but her eyes spoke volumes.

Rick moved nearer to her, threaded his fingers through hers.

"Go on," she finally told him.

"In a way, that letter became my motivation. I had to get home to see her. I had this idea that if I could somehow be with her, I could fix things, make them better. All through the scrapings, the attempts at grafts, hours of lying there while that terrible machine peeled off the damaged skin—the only way I made it through was by thinking of you two."

"It must have been terrible," she said. "But it doesn't excuse—"

"You wanted to hear," he reminded Angie. "Please let me finish. I need to say this. I should have told you years ago, but I have to tell you now."

Angie nodded. Rick squeezed her hand.

"I got an infection and was back in this country for two weeks before I learned that Eve had moved home, to spend whatever time she had left in her parents' home. As soon as I could, I checked myself out of the hospital and got back here. We had only two weeks together before she died."

Rick shifted uneasily. Syd hadn't told the whole story, not if the information from head office had been correct. Would he admit it? The silence stretched for long interminable minutes.

"How did the accident happen?" Angie asked, riveted on the father she'd never really known.

"It was no accident."

Rick jerked out of his introspection at those words. But father and daughter ignored him.

"What do you mean—not an accident?" She shook her head. "I don't get it."

"That's why I'm here. You have to help me, Angie. If you'll just let me explain, you'll understand why."

"I'm listening."

Syd wasn't going to tell her. Somehow Rick knew that the older man intended to sidestep parts of the truth, just as he'd done when he'd told the court about that bank money being in the trunk. Only this time Rick couldn't let it go. Angie would be able to decide on her future relationship with Syd only if she had all the facts.

"As long as you're baring your soul, you'd better tell her all of it, Syd."

"All of what?" Angie glanced back and forth between the two.

Syd clamped his lips together.

Rick shook his head. "It should have come from you." He faced

Angie. "Your father was a top-level agent in his day. He was notorious for being able to get into and out of places without anyone knowing."

"Is that true?" Angie asked.

Syd nodded.

"But not all the truth, is it?"

Still Syd did not respond.

Rick sighed, hating what he felt compelled to do. "I ran a check on his military record. His team was sent to Iran to free some hostages. Two days after the hostages were freed there was a quiet little furor about some statues that had been stolen from the ayatollah's palace. Four of them. The Iranians considered the statues very holy and were not amused by their absence. Your father was questioned about the matter."

Rick hated seeing Angie's face crumple like that, hated knowing he'd pricked the bubble of trust she'd barely begun to form. But he'd always lived by truth. He couldn't change that now, not even to spare the woman he loved. "I'm sorry, Angie."

"Why should you be sorry? You didn't do anything." She jumped to her feet, her hands clamped on her hips, her scathing gaze raking over her father's whitened face. "You just can't do it, can you, Syd? You can't relate to me honestly, without losing some of the truth or trying to cover yourself. It must be all your time spent in covert operations that made you like this. Or was it the burns? Maybe it was—"

"Stop it!" Syd was standing too, his eyes blazing with anger. "Just be quiet and I'll explain."

"You know what? I don't want to hear it, Syd. I've heard about all the stories I can take from you today. I'd like you to leave. Now."

He shook his head. "I can't. We're not finished here, and until we are, you can't leave either."

"Try and stop me."

Rick clenched his hands at his sides. He'd wanted to help her, but he'd made things worse. "Maybe you should go, Syd. Obviously this isn't the time. And—" His breath whooshed out of him in a gasp of surprise.

Meek, quiet Syd stood in front of them both, pointing a gun at Angie. "You are going to hear me out," he told them, his voice like honed steel. "No more waiting for the right time. None of us can afford that anymore. I heard your men here earlier," he said to Rick, his mouth tight with tension. "They said someone had left you a note. One week isn't much time, but it's all we have."

He knew! He understood what the note was about. So why hadn't he explained? Rick's temper soared.

"Will it ever stop, Syd? The skulking around and the listening in on other people?" Rick used every skill he had to inject reason into his voice while he surveyed the room, looking for a way to protect Angie from the muzzle of that gun.

"It has to," Syd answered. "Within the week. So both of you can just sit down and listen to what I have to say. Then you'll decide whether to help or not."

He looked hard at Rick, his gaze reinforcing his threat. "Just remember, you could be deciding on Angie's life."

# CHAPTER FIFTEEN

The Luger was in its usual place against Angie's ankle. If Syd made one wrong move—stumbled, slipped, lowered the gun—she could have hers out in an instant.

"Forget it, Angie." Syd shook his head. "This isn't debatable. I will make one promise. You listen to me now and you'll never have to listen again."

"It's a deal," she snapped, barely aware she'd even said it. "Talk."

"Rick was right. I was very good at what I did. I had to be. It kept me alive. It also paid top dollar, and I got lots of time with you and Eve between missions. That's what I wanted. What *we* wanted. We had a plan, your mother and I. We intended to come back here to Camp Hope. Both of us loved this place. We wanted to take over her father's dream and help build the camp into the outreach center he'd planned."

Syd sighed. She frowned at him. Her mother had never said any of this. "I'd already resigned from the tactical unit; in fact I was at home when the call came for the Iranian job. I declined, but my old boss insisted, telling me I'd be paid a huge sum if I went."

"So of course you jumped at the chance." She hated the sneer in her own voice.

"No, I talked it over with Eve. The money would help us come back to camp sooner, and we felt this was God's way of getting us here. The mission in charge of the camp had agreed to our offer of help. Everything was a go. I left her that day with a promise that I wouldn't be long." Syd drew in a deep breath.

Angie swallowed a response. *Just listen and then he'll go,* she reminded her skittery nerves.

"All of the team was there. It was like old times, flying in, deciding how we'd work it. Old times until I overheard my boss talking about a little trick he was going to play on the Iranians. Understand that relations between the ayatollah and the U.S. were already strained. Taking some of their holy objects would only add to the tensions. Besides, it was stealing and I wanted no part of it."

"Too bad you didn't hold those high principles years later."

He ignored the dig. "I told them I refused to be a part of it, thinking the stuff they were spouting was just hot air. Mikey laughed it off, said okay, it was just an idea he had. But that night I figured out they were going ahead with it." His eyes narrowed. "You have to understand—we were there as liberators, to free hostages. We were not mercenaries. If we were found out, it would kill any hope of building a relationship with Iran. I went to Mikey. I told him that if he persisted in his plan, I'd tell the ambassador."

"That must have gone over well," Rick remarked.

"Mikey argued with me for a long time, even hit me, but I refused to back down. Finally he gave up, and we reviewed our plans for the following day. I was given my orders. As detonations expert I was supposed to set an incendiary device to draw attention away from where the hostages were being held."

He shuddered, and his voice dropped to a dull monotone. "Everything went on schedule until we were loading the hostages into the helicopter. I was supposed to rig another device to go off after we left, to give us cover. I was just finishing when I heard a noise so I turned. There was a flash; then I was in flames."

Syd gulped, his face twisting at the agony of those remembered hours. "I faded in and out, I guess. But once on the helicopter I came to. Mikey was sitting beside me, holding something. As soon as I saw the gold I knew what he'd done. I didn't wake up again until much later in a military hospital in Germany."

"Did you tell someone?" Rick demanded.

"Let me tell it my way. Please?" He waited for Rick's nod, then went on. "I was in and out of consciousness for days. Sometimes there would be tiny lucid moments between the morphine and the pain. Mikey was always there. It got so the nurses talked about how devoted he was to his friend. Several times I asked to talk to someone, but no one ever came. At least not when I was awake."

Angie couldn't dismiss the torment on his face or the anguish threading through his words. But she was afraid to believe him, afraid that something else would come out, something that would shake her world even more.

"One day Mikey paid me a visit and said he'd heard about my request. He told me that if I did or said anything, he'd make sure I never saw Eve alive again. He threatened her! And you, Angie." Syd's eyes raged with anger and despair. "I knew he would do it. He had pictures he'd taken of me the day I arrived at the hospital. The statues were just visible next to me. He said he'd tell everyone I'd taken them and he'd covered for me because we were such good friends."

"So you lied for him." Angie felt her heart torn between the agony Syd had suffered and the knowledge that he was not a man of courage.

"I couldn't talk for a long time." Syd's mouth tightened, and he bit his lip. "My throat was damaged—I don't want to talk about those days," he said hoarsely. "Living through them was nightmare enough. Many times I only wanted to die, but the thoughts of you and Eve, of Mikey visiting her and spinning some story about my demise kept me going."

He closed his eyes, tilted his head back, as if he'd forgotten he held a gun on them. "Eventually I was transferred to a burn hospital, and the grafting procedure was started. I begged the doctors for a phone, and I called home over and over. I couldn't reach Eve, didn't know what to think. I was frantic for news of her health."

"Let me guess. Mikey told you?" Rick's voice was hard.

Syd nodded. "I could hardly believe that he'd actually visited my home, my wife, held my daughter. There was nothing I could do but get well as fast as I could and get home. I was given a medal for my bravery, arranged by my 'friend.' Twice while I was still in the hospital I tried to speak to my superiors about the statues; twice Mikey intervened. After the second time, I learned that Eve had a fire at the house, so I got someone to help me call her. I knew it was no accident when she said, 'Thank goodness your friend was here to help.'"

"How does this connect to me?" Angie demanded, hating the rush of sympathy she felt for him. It would be so much easier to go on hating him for what he'd done to her.

"About three months after Iran, Mikey made another visit to the hospital. By then the nurses all thought we were the best of friends, and they snapped some pictures of him by my bed. One nurse packed a couple of the shots with my clothes the day I was finally discharged." He scratched the rumpled skin at the edge of his eye. "Eve saw the picture when I unpacked. She said something about his unusual ring, and I recognized it as part of the icon collection. Mikey knew he'd gotten away with stealing it, and now he was wearing it! Eve sensed something was wrong, and she pressed until I finally told her the whole story."

Syd sat down, the gun loose in his lap. "She was so sick by then, but she begged me to go to the police to keep Angie safe. I knew it was dangerous, but I didn't like keeping Mikey's dirty secret, so I agreed to go the next morning. That night he phoned. He was in a tough spot and wondered if I could lend him some money. It was blackmail, pure and simple. Eve and I both knew it. I told her to put the picture of him wearing the ring somewhere safe in case we needed it."

Her mother had the picture! Angie's brain began processing.

"That night Mikey came to the house. I gave him some money and he went away, but not before he made sure I understood that if

I talked, my family would suffer." He grimaced. "He gave me a fairly graphic description of what he would do to you. I was scared stiff. I followed him all the way into town to be sure he was nowhere around my family. I got home late. Too late."

He fought to regain control. "Eve died in the wee hours. Her last thoughts were worrying about me. My last day with her and *he* had to ruin it!"

Angie sensed he was telling the truth. Nobody could have faked that kind of soul sadness.

Syd looked at Angie. "I never saw that picture again."

"So what then?" Rick asked. "You kept paying him blackmail money?"

"More and more. He had extravagant tastes. I refused a few times. That was pointless and I paid for my stupidity." Syd stared at Angie. "Do you remember the time you got locked in the old chicken house?"

She shook her head.

"I spent hours searching for you. I was frantic, had everybody at the camp and half the town hunting. Mikey 'happened' along and pretended to search. He claimed he'd heard a sound and—voilà!—there you were, Angie. Even though other people had checked that building moments earlier and found nothing. I knew then that we were never going to be safe. I made up my mind to go to the police. That afternoon a letter arrived. Inside were three pictures of me with the statues and a warning."

"I'm beginning to get the message. If you said he stole the statues, he'd claim that you'd taken them yourself and got burned stealing them or something."

"And that he had no idea the ring I'd given *him* was stolen property." Syd nodded. "You've got the gist of it."

"That's why we never had any money—because you gave it all away to this Mikey creep?" Angie was furious. "How could you?"

"How could I not, Angela?" Syd's eyes begged her to understand. "I would have given my life if it would have kept you safe. That would have been easier than living with the pain, without your mother, constantly afraid that if I didn't pay attention, he'd kidnap you— or worse."

He sounded as if he was afraid for her. As if he loved her.

Angie couldn't make that compute, so she searched for other answers. "But his buddies—they must have been your friends too. Wouldn't they have helped?"

Syd shook his head. "They're dead."

Rick sat up straight, focused on Syd. "All of them?"

"Yes." A corner of his lips lifted. "Sounds impossible, doesn't it? But it isn't. They didn't all die at once. He wouldn't have wanted any suspicions raised. Two were killed in another mission a few months after the Iran incident. They'd been to see me at the house. They knew how badly I was burned, that Eve had died, that Mikey was bleeding me dry. Maybe they protested, or maybe he'd done the same to them. Who knows?"

"The rest of them?"

"One died in an unexplained car accident. One ruled suicide. One death by drowning—this by a man who had every diving certification there was."

"So nobody could back up your story?"

"No."

"But those men who came here to see you—they were your friends," Angie protested.

"They were Mikey's friends. His thugs." Syd watched Angie for a few minutes, then handed Rick his gun. "It isn't loaded," he admitted. "I didn't have any bullets."

Rick took the weapon. "So you paid him off and for years everything went along peachy keen. What happened?"

"The buddies Angie just mentioned. He used to drop by with them from time to time," Syd answered. "They were some new cohorts he'd picked up. No notice, suddenly they were just there. Mikey liked the idea of keeping me on edge, guessing when he'd appear next. While I was in the hospital, I got a little too dependent on morphine for the pain. The milder painkillers didn't touch my migraines so to ease that I'd begun to drink. More after each surgery. I was never falling-down drunk, but usually I had some in my system. Dulled the pain. And the loss," he added, his eyes on his daughter.

"I remember you bought it for your friends," Angie accused.

"Yes, I bought it. And watched them guzzle it down, but I never let myself have a drop while they were here. As long as Mikey didn't know about the picture, I figured I still had some leverage, if I needed it." He smiled, but it was nothing more than a grim uplift of his lips. "I always made sure you were well out of the way when they came around. I was glad you were afraid; it kept you safe. Until that last time."

Suddenly Angie knew exactly when he meant. "The day of my graduation."

"You were the most beautiful girl in the world in that dress," he said. "You reminded me so much of Eve. I was determined that for one night I'd be the kind of father you would be proud of."

"But you were drunk!"

"I never touched it that day. Nor since."

"Why?" She had to understand what had changed on that day and why.

"I knew you'd soon be leaving. I wanted this one last time to show you that I could be the kind of father you should have had. I wanted to be there, to watch you and to feel the pride other fathers felt. I wanted to make up for everything."

Angie saw genuine remorse in his eyes, but she couldn't respond. All she remembered was the pain of knowing he couldn't be bothered to see her achieve that milestone, just as he'd never been there for her. Had she been wrong about him all these years?

"I was in town on my way to the school when they drove up. Mikey was loaded. All he could talk about was my beautiful daughter and how she was so much like my wife. He said that if Eve hadn't been so sick he'd have taken her away from me, that he knew how to treat a woman. He began to talk about you, Angie. Vile, filthy comments that no father should have to hear about his daughter." His face changed, hardened, the lines of the scars standing out white against his leathery skin.

"He was sick," Rick muttered, his own anger evident.

"Worse than that; he's evil. There was no way I could let it happen, no way I'd let him near Angie. So, yes, I loaded up on the booze and got them out to the house. I watched while they drank themselves into a stupor, but I didn't touch it, and I made sure you didn't come home that night."

"You called Arden," she said. "They invited me to a sleepover, and the next day we went to the lake. I never understood why you agreed."

"I loved you, Angie. God knows I'd messed up, ruined your life with my wild moods and poverty lifestyle, but I did everything I could to keep Mikey away from you. I couldn't let him ruin the only good thing in my life. I sat there all night listening to their disgusting laughs and I made my plans."

The haunting shadows in Syd's eyes chewed past her defenses and touched her soul. "It was stupid and wrong and didn't have a hope of working, but I was at my wit's end. I knew Mikey would soon be leaving on a mission. I figured if I robbed a bank, took the money, and got you away from here—somewhere he couldn't find us—that you could finally have a decent life. I have no excuse, except that I was desperate."

Angie couldn't stop the tears or the flood of emotions that her own father, a man she'd hated for most of her life, had gone to such extreme lengths to protect her. Because he cared about her. Because he loved her.

"That's why you weren't at my graduation. I didn't know," she whispered.

"I never wanted you to know. You were sweet and innocent."

"You could have asked for help, Syd. The community would have backed you."

Syd smiled at Rick, shook his head. "You don't know Mikey. You have no idea of the things he can do. I was her father, so it was my

duty, my responsibility to protect her. Besides, I-I promised Eve."
He bent his head.

Angie saw tears drip onto his fingers.

"But when I arrested you, you left Angie alone."

"Did I?" Syd glanced up, his stare intense. "Do you remember
that day?"

"More clearly than you, I think," Rick answered.

"What did I ask you?"

"To get her to the Murdocks', to make sure she was safe."

A look Angie couldn't interpret passed between the two of them.
Rick sighed. "You knew."

"Of course I knew," Syd agreed. "I knew you cared deeply for my
daughter, that you would protect her with your life if you had to.
Mikey wouldn't touch her if you were there. I couldn't help her
anymore. I had to leave my daughter in your hands, and you more
than fulfilled my expectations."

"Too bad you never said that to me," Angie blurted out.

Syd smiled, and it transformed the ugliness. She caught her
breath at the glow that lit his face from inside.

"Oh, Angie, don't you know? From the moment you were born
you far exceeded anything I ever expected. Every night when you lay
asleep in that bed, I'd stand in the doorway staring at you, unable to
believe that such an angelic child was even related to me. You were
always Eve's child, with her sense of decency, her faith, her caring,
and her compassion. I was so afraid I'd mess that up."

"You abandoned me," she accused, still unable to let go of the
hurt.

"Never." He held her gaze, his eyes shiny with . . . love? "I had
to leave every so often to have grafts done or to have scar tissue
removed. They were horrible, agonizing procedures, and I didn't want
you to know about them."

"So you handed me over to the Murdock sisters. I thought you
hated me," she whispered. "That you didn't want me around."

"I was scared of the day you would leave because I knew that then

I'd have nothing to live for. And at the same time I wanted you to leave, to get away from me and Mikey's awful threats. If I'd had relatives, someone I could trust, I'd have sent you there, even though it would have killed me."

Angie couldn't believe he'd felt like this and she hadn't known, had never guessed the reason behind his surly attitude. And yet, her mother had told her this on that very last day.

"I'm sorry." The bitterness was still there, but she had to say the words. She'd sentenced and condemned him without knowing all the facts. "I accused you of so many things—"

"I'm guilty of all of them, Angie. Every one. I apologize for ruining your life, though I don't expect your forgiveness. I was not the kind of father you deserved, not the parent God expected me to be, not the kind of man your mother wanted me to be. I failed both of you, and for that I am so sorry."

She sat frozen, unable to tear her gaze away, unable to tell him the one thing he didn't know.

That dirty secret kept her from accepting her father's love. But she couldn't tell him now that they'd finally built a connection.

What if he never forgave her?

———⟾⟩◆⟨⟸———

Rick rose, moved behind Angie. He could almost feel her pain, her shock, her defenselessness. He laid his arm around her shoulders and hugged her against his side.

"There's one thing I don't understand. Why is he back here, threatening Angie?" He pulled out the note in its plastic bag. "It's from him, isn't it? This Mikey of yours?"

"Yes." Syd took the bag, stared at the lettering. "Several months ago I was sent to a specialist to have some keloids around my eyes removed. My skin doesn't heal evenly, and the scar tissue was affecting my eyesight. Mikey showed up before the operation, said he was up for a big promotion and wanted me to help him celebrate after surgery. That must have been on my mind. I had a reaction to the anesthetic. The recovery nurse told me I was blabbing about a book that had a certain picture, that I talked about Eve noticing Mikey's ring. She asked him what I was referring to, but he didn't know."

Syd glanced at them both. "I can see what you're thinking. Yes, it was the first Mikey had heard of any picture. He became so furious the nurses made him leave. I knew he wouldn't rest, and I was right." He squeezed his eyes closed for a moment, then sighed. "By the time I returned to the penitentiary, everything was in an uproar. I had to meet with a lawyer I never hired. Later I found out Mikey was going to testify on my behalf."

Rick saw Angie glance sideways at him and knew he had to hurry Syd on or she'd start asking questions. She'd just learned that her father loved her. Rick didn't want her to start doubting Syd again, not yet and not because of him. Let her enjoy her happiness for a while longer.

"Mikey is Michael Parker, isn't he?" Rick asked.

"Michael Parker?" Angie's attention shifted to Rick. "How do you know about—?"

"It doesn't matter how he knows, only that he's right," Syd muttered, his forehead furrowed in thought. "It's what we do next that counts."

"Wait a minute!" Angie peered at Rick. Her eyes narrowed and he knew her brain had begun to piece together what she knew. "I wasn't randomly chosen to look after Kelly. I was set up by Michael Parker. Is that what you think?"

"I considered it," he admitted. "I think Mikey expected you to come home. That's why Max 'stopped by.' Obviously he didn't buy into my story about you going east, because he came back."

"But why ambush me? Why put out a warrant?" She frowned. "Parker signed the warrant, didn't he?" She heaved a sigh at Rick's nod. "Oh."

"He must have been frantic. You'd dropped out of sight. His little plan to reunite you and your father so Syd could find that book had to work if he was going to remove the threat. A crooked operative is one thing, but there's no way he could be in the public eye in his new CSIS job with the threat of exposure hanging over his head. Even the gossip about a crime like that would ruin him."

"It's always back to this infamous book, isn't it? But I don't know where it is. Why would he think I did?" Frustration nipped through Angie's voice as she struggled to tie up the loose ends. "I've never met the man, and I don't even know what this book looks like."

"Neither do I, but it has to be small. One of those little coil-bound things that holds five or six photos." Syd pinned her with his stare. "I've had lots of time to think about this while I was in jail. When I came home that night, Eve was making up several of those little booklets with pictures of you in them. She wanted to send them to some friends. After she died I noticed the ones she'd finished were sitting on the night table, but the photo of the ring was gone."

Silence stretched around the room as they each sifted through the information, searching for a clue.

"You've got to go public with what you know, Dad. It's the only way to finally be free of him."

Rick saw the flare of surprise in Syd's eyes when she called him that name. It seemed like it had slipped out so easily. If only she could wipe away the pain as swiftly.

"But you could be hurt." Syd shook his head. "He's a powerful man, Angela. He won't go down easily. Besides, I'm a convicted felon. Who's going to believe me? It's my word against his."

"More than that—he has those photos of you with the statues." Rick scratched his chin. "I suppose you could claim those were a setup, that a man with burns as severe as yours would hardly be aware of those statues, let alone carry them back with him, but it's not a strong indictment against him."

"No."

"Either way, it's no cakewalk." He studied Syd, then Angie. "We need to spend a lot of time praying about this, because right now only God knows the way out."

"God?" Angie muttered. "He's the one who let it happen in the first place." She glanced at her father, her eyes blazing with anger again. "Look at him, look at the marks on him. Does it seem right that God would allow an innocent man to endure that?"

Syd knelt before her, his scarred hands clasping hers. "Honey, you know better than most that I'm no innocent. Anyway, God didn't do this. Mikey did. A million times I've asked myself why God punished me so harshly, but I always knew I deserved these scars and more because of the way I treated you." He reached a tentative hand to touch the smoothness of her cheek. "But you know what? God isn't about punishment."

Rick watched the older man's face light up and knew Syd had come to terms with his Lord.

"Angie, God is about forgiveness. He's about accepting my life as He's given it to me today and making the most of it. It took me a long time to understand that there is more going on here than my petty problems. God has a purpose and a reason for what He allows."

"That's easy to say, but—"

"It's hard to say. Very hard." Syd paused, swallowed. "My view of God doesn't want to include a God who allows pain. I want roses and sunshine and happiness. But it's in the pain, in the darkest times when I can't seem to see an inch in front of my face, that I depend on Him the most. It's then I learn what Psalm 23 is all about."

Rick saw her confusion.

"I don't understand."

"For so many years neither did I. Did you know that was your mother's favorite passage? She used to recite it over and over. Listen. 'Even when I walk though the dark valley of death, I will not be afraid, for you are close beside me.'" His eyes blazed with assurance. "Not carrying me past the valley, not moving the valley or me, but walking *through* it with me. Close beside me, feeling everything I feel. It's incredible.

"He can do that because He's been there. He's experienced it with me, He understands, and He forgives. He looks at me and says,

'Not guilty. You're forgiven.'" Syd squeezed Angie's fingers. "Don't stay rooted in the past. Even if you can't forgive me, you can still turn to Him. He knows what you went through. He understands. And He forgives."

Angie slid her hands away. "You don't understand. How could you? All this talk of forgiveness. You have no idea—" She stopped. "I don't want to talk about this anymore."

"Okay." Syd gave in gracefully, rising awkwardly to his feet. "But now that you know the facts, we've got to come up with a plan to find that book."

"Well, it's not in your military kit. We know that much. And I didn't find anything like that in my grandfather's books, though I haven't completely gone through each one."

Syd shook his head. "It wouldn't be in there. Eve was too sick. It has to be somewhere inside that house. A hiding place, a secret place that only she knew about."

Angie froze, remembered the night her mother had died and the noise she'd heard. "I might know where to look."

Syd grinned. "You've thought of something. Smart girl. We'll go look."

Angie turned to get her coat.

Rick's arm stopped her. "We'll have to go tomorrow, Syd, when I can get some help. After those shots today, I'm not prepared to take any chances with Angie or Kelly."

"Okay. I'll be out here tomorrow. We'll go over then."

They set a time when Rick would be off work; then Syd pulled on his jacket, mitts, and hat. "Good night, honey," he murmured, standing in front of Angie. He touched the tendril of hair that had strayed into her eyes. "I always loved you, even when it seemed like I didn't, even when I was drunk and abusive and never supported you the way a parent should. I know that doesn't mean much now, but I hope that someday you can learn to forgive me."

Rick knew Angie well enough to know that she was fighting an internal argument. The yearning he'd glimpsed flicker across her face made him suspect that Angie wished she could tell Syd what he wanted to hear. But to Rick it was obvious that some hard kernel of pain from the past reminded her that her father had hurt her before and he might do it again.

"Be careful," she said. "This friend of yours is getting desperate. Remember the hearing for his promotion is only days away."

"I know." Syd let his hand fall away, then turned toward the door. "Good night. Tell Kelly I'll see her soon."

Rick was silent until Syd's crunch through the snow had faded into nothingness. Then he faced Angie. "He really does love you. Can't you accept that?"

"I don't know," she answered. "I know you're not like me, Rick. You're the kind of Christian who would never let your hate take control. You probably don't have a lot of regrets about your past." She swallowed, stared at her feet.

He waited, knowing she wasn't finished.

"I'm doing the best I can not to hurt Syd again. It's just—" she shook her head—"some secrets are better kept."

# CHAPTER SIXTEEN

Where is he?"

Rick scanned the kitchen at Camp Hope. There were masses of red hearts covering every surface he could see, but Syd was nowhere in sight.

"He didn't show up," Angie said.

"Not at all? But he's two hours late!" Rick nodded at Angie's uplifted brow. "I know; I am too, but my boss called me, and I couldn't tell him to call back later. I assumed Syd would be here waiting."

"Well, he isn't. And I have no clue where he was staying so I can't go check on him or drag him here."

There it was again, Angie's note of stolid fatalism that told him she hadn't really expected the man who'd disappointed her so often to keep his word now.

Frustrated, Rick tried to figure out what to do next. "So do you think we should go ourselves without him?"

"I guess." Angie turned away, her face a blank mask.

Rick hated that look, that robotic response that killed the sparkle in her eyes.

"What did you remember so suddenly last night?" he asked.

The mask dropped away and vitality took its place. She smiled and it was a beautiful thing to see, her green irises lambent now with precious memories.

"Oh, that. It's probably nothing," she murmured.

"Tell me anyway." What he wouldn't do to make her happy, to keep from seeing the hurt return.

"My mother had these places she used to hide when she was a little girl. There are several of them in the house actually. When we first moved there, before she got so sick, the two of us used to play hide-and-seek in those secret cubbies. I used one myself when Kelly and I first arrived."

"So you think the book might be in one of them. Maybe Syd missed it."

"I'm not sure he knew much about them," she responded. "Unless my mother told him. I certainly didn't."

"Well, let's take a look ourselves. Arden told me three guys from the detachment who worked with you volunteered to spend the night patrolling the area. They didn't see anyone."

"The whole night?" Angie's eyes opened wide. "I had no idea. I could have given them coffee or something."

He laughed at her. "The whole purpose was for them *not* to be noticed, remember? Come on; get your coat. Kelly?"

The little girl appeared in the doorway. "Hi, Mr. Rick."

"Hello, yourself. Want to come with us?"

"Where?" she asked, jacket already in hand.

"We're going on a secret mission to find a book. Without Spot."

"I love secrets!" Kelly clapped her hands around Angie's face as she bent close to clasp the child's jacket. "Don't you like secrets, Angel?"

"Not really."

Rick didn't miss the quick glance she darted his way and immediately wondered what she was hiding.

"Maybe we should leave her here?" she suggested softly, so Kelly wouldn't hear.

"She's safer with us, I think. Besides, I brought reinforcements. One man will stay here and one will come with us."

"Okay." Angie pulled on her gloves. "I'm ready."

"We're going to drive. Just in case." He held her arm when she would have passed him. "Angie, I'm not going to let anything happen to you. Or Kelly. You can trust me on that."

She scrutinized his face, finally nodded. "I know."

He squeezed her shoulder, then let go. "Put Kelly between us. Okay. Here goes." He'd parked as close to the steps as possible, limiting the amount of time they'd be in the open. The two other officers provided cover, and they made it inside the vehicle with no problems.

Though Kelly hummed a little tune on the drive out of the camp, she stopped when they turned at the big sign. "The secret," she said, her forehead rippled in thought, "is it important?"

"Very important." A truck was coming, and Rick was forced to wait for it to pass. "Why?"

"Because nothing is impossible with God. That's what it says on that sign. Georgia told me that's how Camp Hope got made. Angie's grandpa and grandma and some other people knew God could do it." She grinned. "I think God can fix the secret too."

Rick glanced over the platinum head at Angie, saw the last dredges of hope in her eyes, and whispered a plea for help. "I think God can do it too, Kelly," he agreed.

"I'll pray and ask Him. Okay?"

"That would be very okay." He shoved the gearshift into neutral and waited until she'd offered her prayer. "Thank you, honey."

"Welcome." Obviously content to wait for God to answer, Kelly slipped back into her humming.

Rick drove slowly up the side road, his heart in his throat as he wondered how Angie would take his offering. Would she see the changes he'd made upstairs and down as interference, or would she understand that he'd wanted to erase her painful memories by replacing them with new ones?

He clicked his radio on. "All clear at Grant's?"

"All clear."

"Okay, let's go inside."

Fat fluffy snowflakes drifted down like a feather bed emptying itself over the earth. Reassured that he saw nothing out of place, he got out, walked around the back of the truck, and opened Angie's door. "Inside as fast as you can," he ordered, scanning the area as he followed her.

Once inside, Angie stopped so short that Rick bumped into her. "Oh." Turning in a circle, she took in the gleaming hardwood floor, the sparkling white cabinets, the sunny yellow walls. "What have you done?"

"I've been doing a little restoration. The Murdock sisters were kind enough to describe the interior of your grandparents' house. This is as close as I could get, though it's not quite finished." He waited impatiently, heart racing when she bent to slip out of her boots.

"This is a different house." Kelly flopped down on the new tile in the entry and tugged off her own boots. "I like it."

"Oh, Rick!" Angie exclaimed from the living room. "It's beautiful."

The soft cry drew him. Rick took Kelly's hand and walked through the kitchen to the living room.

Kelly pulled away. "I'm going to look for the secret."

Rick nodded, turned, saw Angie staring at the fireplace.

"You restored it," she said. "I thought I'd dreamed that it was here." She ran a hand over the brick. "Syd must have covered it over."

"I guess. Do you like it?" He'd pay mightily for the late nights the drywaller had spent fixing the damaged plaster, but looking at it now was worth it. The smooth cream walls complemented the floor and the oak trim.

"Like it?" She turned to face him, tears rolling down her cheeks. "It's beautiful, but French doors?"

"Kent gave me the idea. He said he could imagine picnics out here. When the Murdock sisters talked about the parties your grandparents used to give, I figured someday you might want to do the same." He studied her rapt face. The next words slipped out. "When you come home."

"This isn't home." She glanced around.

"But it could be. Don't you see? You've only ever seen one side of this house, but it could be so much more. Your grandparents had a dream for it. You could make it come true."

She shook her head slowly, as if waking up. "There are too many memories."

He tipped her chin up, kept his voice soft. "There are good memories here too. Before the sadness, there were joy and peace and laughter. That's why your mother came back, because she knew what this place really was. Barrons' Rest can be a place of respite again— if you want it to be."

*Please, God, please let her see the possibilities. Please let her dream.*

"You and I could make it that way," he whispered. "Together we could build something that would outlast us both and live on into eternity. Your grandparents dedicated this place to God. You and I could finish what they started."

Tears welled as Angie peered up at him. She touched his forehead, his cheek, his chin. "Oh, Rick. You are so precious, so generous, and I don't deserve it."

He tried to speak, but she pressed a finger against his lips. "Shh. You've done this wonderful thing for me, and I will never be able to repay you." Her soft shaky voice told him how moved she was. "If I could stay with anyone, I would stay with you. You're the one I turn to when life gets mean, the one I think of when I need to talk, the one I look up to when everyone else lets me down."

"I love you, Angie."

She nodded, her face shining with tears. "I know. And I feel so proud, so honored that you do. I don't understand why you chose me, why you think I'd be worthy of your love, but knowing that you do— it's like a precious jewel that I hold inside my heart."

"But you don't love me." Pain washed through him in waves.

"I do love you, Rick. More than I've ever loved anyone in my life." She held back when he would have embraced her. "But I can't. Don't you understand? I can't love you."

"Why? What's wrong?"

"I hurt the people I love." She stepped back. "You don't know the real me. You see the Angie you want to see, but you don't see me. I'm not the kind of person you should spend your life with. After I'm gone you'll understand that."

"What are you talking about?" Rick asked. "This isn't some fling I've decided to indulge in. I've been in love with you for years. The day I saw you here, the day I arrested Syd—I knew I was in love with you that day." He nodded at the shock filling her face. "Way back then. I knew I was too old for you, that you needed time to rebuild your life. So I did everything I could to help you and prayed that God would send you back. And He did."

"That wasn't God. That was just coincidence."

"There are no coincidences with God." He tweaked her ear. "Every day I hoped and prayed you'd see how much I cared about you. But you were carrying this pain that wouldn't go away. When you left the last time I realized that God was working things differently. But I knew in my heart that you would come back."

"But not to stay." She dashed her knuckles against her cheek, then waved a hand. "The work you've done here—it's incredible. And that you did it to replace my ugliness with beauty, to fulfill a dream, is very precious to me. But I'm not the one to help you make *your* dream come true, Rick."

He wanted to protest, but she didn't allow it. "Coming back here has taught me something. I am not my mother. I cannot be Eve, welcoming strangers, offering comfort to people. I'd like to be, but sooner or later my true nature would take over and I'd do something to spoil it all. And you'd begin to hate me."

Rick shook his head. "I don't want you to be Eve. I don't want you to do anything. I just want you to love me the way I love you. Stay, move, I don't care. As long as we're together."

"You say that now. But in a year, two years, when I've hurt you over and over, what about then?" Her eyes brimmed with tears. "I am not the kind of girl you should marry, Rick. I'm on the other side of you, a sinner."

"So am I. Saved by grace."

"But I'm not saved. I'm damned." She turned away from him. "Let's just look for the book. Please?"

There was nothing he could do but agree. And pray.

By the time Rick returned Angie and Kelly to Camp Hope, empty-handed, he needed to get away and spend some time alone with God.

"I'll see you soon," he told Kelly. He tried to read Angie's heart, but her face was back in its mask mode. "I'll see you tomorrow. If Syd comes, tell him to call me."

She nodded.

Rick left, returned to the house he'd worked so hard to restore. He collapsed onto the tattered and worn armchair in the center of the living room, then closed his eyes.

*All these years I was certain You'd chosen her for me. Was I so wrong? Have I made a mistake?*

The Father was silent.

———◆———

The office was unusually quiet when Rick entered the next morning. He glanced around, saw concern on Arden's face, read Shauna's anxious look, and knew it was bad.

"You have visitors in your office, Rick. You'd better go straight in." The secretary took his jacket and touched him on the shoulder. "I'll be praying."

What now?

He walked into the office, his steps faltering as he saw three of his superiors seated. "Good morning, gentlemen. To what do I owe this honor?"

His smile was not returned.

"Sergeant Mercer, where were you last night?"

The tone of that question alerted him. Rick paused over his answer. "Why do you ask? Is something wrong?"

"A Mr. Sydney Grant was last seen in your company. Today he missed an appointment with his lawyer to discuss a possible suit against you in regard to an improperly executed warrant. Do you know Mr. Grant's whereabouts?"

"No. Syd was supposed to meet Angie, his daughter, and me yesterday, but he never showed."

"Why would Mr. Grant want to meet with the man accused of wrongfully putting him in jail?"

Rick opened his mouth to explain about the book, then hesitated. How much was he supposed to tell? Would mentioning Michael Parker make things better or worse?

"I didn't see Syd yesterday. Whoever said I did is mistaken."

"I don't think that's possible."

"Why?"

"Because someone with this person's credentials doesn't make that kind of mistake."

Rick knew exactly who'd made the accusation. "You're talking about Michael Parker, aren't you?" He had his confirmation written all over their faces. "Well, in this case, Mr. Parker is dead wrong. I did not see or speak with Syd yesterday."

The men looked at each other.

Then his boss rose. "I'm sorry, Rick, but this has gone too far. Until Mr. Grant is found and this matter resolved, you are suspended. We will conduct our investigation, but in the meantime I want you to stay away from this office. Let things take their course, and the truth will come out."

Rick could see the sympathy on the older man's face, but it did nothing to alleviate the nightmare he was living.

"Mr. Parker also claims he saw me remove the money from Syd's trunk the day I served the warrant," Rick reminded them. "He's wrong about that too."

No response.

He wouldn't change their minds. Better to get out of the way while he figured out what to do.

"Very well." He turned, walked to the door.

"Rick—" his boss followed him out of the office—"I think you'd better get yourself a lawyer." The words were so soft, Rick was almost certain he'd imagined them, until he saw the expression on Martin's face. "Don't answer any more questions until you do." Then the man Rick had trusted like a father went back into the office.

Dazed, confused, Rick walked out to his truck, started the motor, and found himself driving toward Camp Hope. He'd believed Syd, trusted every word he'd said. But maybe Angie was right. Maybe a leopard couldn't change his spots.

Maybe Syd was working with Parker—against him!

# CHAPTER SEVENTEEN

Angie sat frozen on her chair as Rick explained his predicament to Doug Henderson, Georgia's childhood friend and a prominent lawyer in Calgary.

"Can you recommend anyone?" Rick asked.

A rattle of papers transmitted over the speakerphone. "I could take a look at things myself, if you want." Doug's voice came back slightly muffled. "I've just rearranged my schedule to take a week off for a skiing vacation, but Camp Hope sounds much more inviting. Georgia, can you put me up in one of those cute little cabins?"

"Don't be silly, Douglas. You'll stay with us." Georgia made a face. "Unless you're still dating that secretary. Then you'll have to find a hotel."

"You're heartless; do you know that? I feel sorry for Kent."

Their light banter helped ease the tension in the room, and Angie was grateful. She'd never forget the sight of Rick's face when he'd walked in an hour ago. Georgia's suggestion to call Doug for advice was brilliant.

"Don't feel sorry for me, buddy. I'm happier than a pig in mud."

Kent brushed his lips over Georgia's nose. "But I agree with my wife. We have a much more interesting lady here that you could renew acquaintances with."

"Abby's the one who gave me the brush off, remember? But you're right, visiting Camp Hope offers the perfect opportunity to see her again. In the meantime, Rick, talk to nobody. If your bosses want a meeting, I'll arrange it. I should be there sometime tomorrow afternoon. Until then, you don't know anything. Got it?"

"Yes. And thank you. I appreciate your giving up your ski holiday for me."

"Not a problem. I might as well tell you, since Georgia will anyway. The last time I went skiing, I broke my leg. She claimed God was trying to tell me something about my athletic prowess. Bye."

The click of the phone line left them staring at one another.

Georgia broke the silence. "Kelly, you and Kent can help me make up the basement room for Doug."

Moments later Angie was left alone with Rick. "Where do you think Syd is?" she asked, embarrassed to look at him after yesterday and his pledge of love. He must hate her now. Syd too.

"I don't think he's run away. Particularly not since it was Parker who claimed to see us together. I've been set up, but I don't understand why."

"I'm afraid I can't help you there," she murmured. "I've been ordered to return to Ottawa at the first of the week."

"But that's only four days away!"

She nodded. Her every sense was aware of him. Her eyes noted the lines of sleeplessness around his eyes; her ears heard the sigh that slipped out when he thought no one listened; her nose picked up the tangy lime scent of his aftershave; and her fingers still clutched the smoothness of his jacket. But most of all, her cheek still tingled from the brief touch of his lips when he arrived.

She knew she would never get over this love, but she had to face the possibility of its never being realized. Her father's face swam into her mind and the sour memory of what she'd done along with it.

"Angie?" Rick stood in front of her, his gaze probing hers. "I asked if you wanted to help me at the house. I haven't completed the upstairs. I guess the rest will have to wait since I don't know if I even have a job or not. But there's some scraping we can do, windowsills and such. At least it will pass the time."

And give her a few more precious moments with him. She both feared and wanted that. It hurt to be so close and know that she couldn't allow herself to give in, to let him see that she longed to be beside him, carrying out that dream he'd spoken of. But it would be easier to bear if she had a few precious moments to remember during those long lonely days coming up in Ottawa. Her spirit came alive whenever Rick was nearby.

"Sure, I'll help. If nothing else, you'll have a decent place to live in."

*Without you,* his eyes said.

She turned away. "Why don't we go over now?"

He agreed and she called Kelly, who was ecstatic about their return.

"What's so exciting about coming back here?" Angie asked Kelly as she helped the little girl out of her coat when they were all inside the old house.

"I want to see the dollies 'cuz they're so pretty. Come and look." Kelly grabbed Angie's hand, motioned to Rick, and led the way to the bedroom. "See?"

Kelly lifted each doll from the secret cupboard and set them on tiny chairs around a table where Angie had once played. "This is Polly," Kelly explained to Rick. "She doesn't like boys or snakes or anything yucky. This is Margaret. She's a very good reader. She reads all the books out loud. This is Amanda and she's very happy. See her smile. Amanda loves tea."

Months ago Angie had entertained Kelly with long stories about her childhood dolls and the many tea parties she'd held for them in this very room. She was surprised at the child's accurate memory.

"The only one who's missing is Betsey," Kelly mourned. "I've looked and looked, but I can't find her. Where did you put her, Angel? She's not in the hiding place."

Angie tried to recall when last she'd seen the doll years ago. "I don't know, sweetheart. Maybe she got all ruined and someone threw her out."

"But you said you kept her special, that she didn't get her head chopped off like the other dollies."

"Did I? Then I guess she's here somewhere. Did you find a book in the hiding place, Kelly?"

"No." Kelly clapped her fingers over her lips. "Maybe Betsey's in a secret place?"

"Maybe." Angie smiled as the child scampered off to begin her search. "So much for that idea. I thought maybe my mother had hidden the book in that cupboard where I used to keep my dolls. She once said it was her favorite hiding place. Should I go with Kelly, make sure she's okay?"

Rick shrugged. "I think Kelly's fine as long as she stays inside. She can't get out without help. The chain on the door is too high for her to reach. Besides, Tony Nickel is back on duty. He called last night. Said we wouldn't see him but he'd be tracking your every move."

"Okay. So where should we begin?"

He showed her and they worked companionably for half an hour, interrupted only by Kelly's brief updates on her search for Betsey.

"I don't understand where Syd would go. He was adamant that we hunt for that book right away. Why didn't he show up?" Angie grated the sandpaper across the wall with extra strength. "Why pull this now?"

Something passed over Rick's face. "Maybe he didn't have a chance. My boss said Parker told him he'd seen us together. Which means Parker is around."

"You think Dad's Mikey snatched him?" She closed her eyes. "But Mikey is the one who deliberately burned him. Oh no."

"I don't know that for sure. It's just a guess."

"But it makes sense." She rubbed the heel of her hand against her eyes. "If only I could figure out where this book is. I could get Dad back, and you could get this Parker out of the way."

"The picture would help, but I'm not sure it would make everything go away." He smiled at her. "Don't worry about me. I'll be fine."

He was just saying that and Angie knew it. Rick had always wanted to be a cop. Now he was losing that dream. Her heart ached for him. If only it could have been different. If only she was a regular person with a past that had taught her how to love. If only she could believe that God was on her side, that He wouldn't make her pay for her sins.

Angie's cell phone rang.

She met Rick's scrutiny, shrugged. Very few people had this number. "Hello?"

"Did you find the book?"

"Who is this?" She held the phone away from her ear so Rick could listen in.

"That doesn't matter. But it would be better for your father if you could find what he asked you to."

"I wouldn't know where to look," she responded, stalling as she tried to think of what to say. "You seem to know all about it. Any suggestions?"

"Since you ask, I'd suggest looking around right where you are. Your mother was a sick woman. She couldn't have gone far."

"You're Mikey, aren't you? Dad's friend? Or should I call you boss, Mr. Parker?"

"Don't get cute, Agent Grant. Your father isn't feeling too spry at the moment. He could get much worse."

"Haven't you done enough to him?" she demanded, the hard core of resentment toward her father melting at the edges. "Wasn't setting him on fire enough payback?"

"I see Syd's been telling stories."

Angie bit her lip. Maybe she'd made it worse.

"You listen to me, kid. You and your boyfriend have thwarted my plans ever since this thing began. But you're not going to do it again or Daddy dearest will pay, so tell the cop to butt out or he'll lose more than his job. So will you. That shot the other day was just practice. Next time my aim will be better." He paused to let that sink in. "I want that picture. I'll give you twenty-four hours to find it, and that's my final offer. Don't call me; I'll call you." A harsh laugh.

"But—" He'd already hung up. Angie closed the phone.

"At least now we know who shot at us. But he won't hurt Syd. Not as long as he hasn't got the proof. Especially not since you know who he is." He hugged her against his side. "I think he's really running scared."

"He must be crazy. Why else would he be skulking around Camp Hope shooting at us?" Angie pulled away to peer into his eyes. "He said you'd lose more than your job. What did that mean?"

Rick eased away from her. "He seems to know everything that's going on. I think we need to do one more search of the house and finish scraping this wall later."

They retrieved Kelly, started upstairs, and worked their way to the basement, searching every place Angie could think of.

They found nothing.

"I couldn't find Betsey either," Kelly said. "I looked in all the secret places you told me about, Angel, but I couldn't find her."

"I'm sorry, sweetie. I don't know where she is anymore."

Outside, darkness had fallen. Angie glanced at her watch, shocked to see that it was after six. "We'd better go back. Georgia will be worried."

They closed up the house, and Rick set the security system.

On the road back to the camp, Angie absorbed each detail and stocked them away in her mind. This was Thursday. The plane left early Monday morning, which meant she'd have to leave here on Sunday afternoon to drive to the city.

Two days, that's all she had left. Less than one day to find that picture.

*Why don't You help, God?* she demanded silently. *It's not for me. It's for Syd, Rick, and Kelly. Why can't You help?*

Her phone rang as they pulled into the yard. Angie clicked it open, her heart rate accelerating as she listened.

"Hello, Angela?" The whispery voice was familiar.

"Fiona? Is that you?"

"Why yes, dear. It is. I hope you don't mind that I persuaded Georgia to give me your number. I thought it was important that I speak to you."

"Is something wrong?"

"Not wrong exactly." A twittering voice in the background, then Fiona Murdock sighed. "I'm trying to tell her, sister. I don't imagine Angie's heard that we're moving."

"You got a place in town already?" Angie asked, trying to picture the Murdock sisters anywhere other than on the property where they'd lived for so long.

"Yes, dear. A lovely place. And we have someone interested in our home. We're packing madly, as you can imagine. Actually, that's why I called."

Because they were packing? "Do you need help?"

"Oh no, thank you, dear. We've had tons of help from the church. Most things are in boxes already. Emily and I have been cleaning out the attic, and we found some things your mother made. We'd promised to sell them, you see, and then . . . well, she died before the Christmas fair and we didn't know what to do, so we tucked them away, thinking we'd give them to you. We forgot all about them, of course. Until today."

A garbled transmission followed; then Emily's voice came on. "We thought we'd stop by and give them to you tonight, if you wouldn't mind. Before we lose them again."

The sisters' soft voices in the background made Angie smile. "Of course I don't mind. I'd love to see you again before I leave. Is seven all right?"

"Leave? Oh, dear. I didn't know you're leaving."

After some whispered consultation between the sisters they decided seven suited very well. Angie hoped Georgia would think so too. Which she did.

"I've got a huge pot of stew on. I'll invite them to come for supper. Doug phoned to say he'd be here in half an hour. It'll be fun to have the house full again."

And it was. For those few happy moments while everyone ate and laughed and talked, Angie let herself pretend that she belonged here, that God was as big a part of her life as He was in everyone else's. She sat quietly, noting everyone's mention of some way God had touched their lives, helping them through some difficulty.

Was it only she who felt bereft, abandoned, alone?

Georgia must have sensed her discomfort for she turned from teasing Doug, leaned over, and whispered, "I'm sorry your father didn't come, Angie. And that you weren't able to find what you're searching for. But don't lose hope. There is an answer."

"Thanks," she whispered back, but inside that stone of doubt sank to the pit of her stomach.

"What were you searching for?" Fiona asked.

All conversation stopped as everyone turned to stare at her.

Angie felt her cheeks heat. "Just . . . something of my mother's. I've looked everywhere, but it doesn't seem to be there."

"As I recall, Eve was fond of those side cubbies, as she used to call them. I remember her as a little girl, stashing all manner of things in those cubbies. Her mother got some shocks, I can tell you."

"Really?" Angie leaned forward, thrilled to learn more about her mother's childhood. "Like what?"

"Well, there was a horrid smell once. I remember that. We were asked to go over and help Eve clean out everything. Finally we found it, pale blue robin's eggs still in the nest, rotted and unbearably smelly. Which room was that in, Emily?"

"It was upstairs," the other woman replied. "In the bathroom. Remember how carefully we carried them outside on those newspapers? Oh, I can smell it still." She made a face and tilted her nose to the ceiling.

"In the upstairs bathroom?" Angie shook her head. "It couldn't be." She paused at the looks on their faces. "I'm sorry. I don't mean to contradict you, but there's no cubby in that bathroom."

"Really?" Fiona looked concerned. "But I'm sure Emily's right. She always remembers the details."

Realizing she shouldn't have said anything, Angie rushed to ease their minds. "Of course, it might have been there all those years ago, but it isn't there now. That's what I meant to say."

"Someone renovated? Who?" Emily looked more confused than usual. "Not your grandparents, I know. I'm sure Syd never had the interest or time to change things, and I didn't think you had the money."

The sister was right. The memories of her miserable childhood were too firmly etched. Angie had never wanted to do anything to the place until she'd seen Rick's work. Which meant that the bathroom should be the same as it had been during her mother's childhood.

Then where was this cubby? And how, during all these years, had she missed it?

"Ladies, would you be willing to come with me to the house and show me where you found that bird's nest?" Angie glanced apologetically at Georgia. "I'm sorry to spoil your meal."

"It's not spoiled. It's finished. I think we should all go and take a look."

Everyone was in agreement. It took only a few moments to gather coats, hats, and gloves. Spot sulked in a corner.

"We'll drive," Rick decided. "Come on, Ang. The party's moving to your place." He used the cover of darkness outside to brush his mouth against her cheek. "Don't give up yet."

They arrived en masse and trooped into the house Angie had hated for so long. She couldn't help but feel a shiver of pride at the exclamations Rick's work aroused, even though she'd had nothing to do with it.

"Now, my dear, let's see if we can figure this out." Fiona stepped into the bathroom and glanced around. "It looks the same to me. What do you think, sister?" The two of them touched and probed their way around the room.

A memory of that pain-filled night so long ago shimmered on the edge of her brain. Angie sought and found Rick's hand, held on tight. It had been summer then, the scent of wildflowers in the air.

In her mind's eye, she could see herself creeping up the stairs, trying to understand what was wrong. A man, there was a man talking to Syd. They exchanged loud, angry words. When they moved into the hall, she'd crept into her mother's room, but Mama was sleeping. More voices, someone moving up the stairs.

It was so clear to her now. She'd scooted into the bathroom, opened the secret door, and slipped inside.

Angie opened her eyes and found Rick frowning down at her.

"It's all right," she whispered, opening the cupboard door beneath the sink. "I remember now. I hid in here the night my mother died. A noise woke me up. The doctor was here." She peered up at Rick through her tears. "I think he was trying to make my father understand that they had to take her away, but Syd didn't want to let her go."

"Good, sweetheart. Now what else did you do?" He squeezed her shoulder. "How did you get it open?"

"It's easy." She bent down and lifted out an almost empty bottle of shampoo. "Mama showed me. She couldn't get inside so we didn't play our game in here, but see, if you push this over, you can go side-ways into the cubby. That's what I did."

"I want to see." Kelly pushed forward, and before anyone could stop her she'd slipped through the opening.

"Kelly, come out. You'll get all dirty."

A scrabbling against the boards, then Kelly's face appeared, wide-eyed, filled with excitement. "I found her, Angel! I found Betsey." She wiggled out and held up a dusty doll.

Angie stared at the green glass eyes that were loose now with stitches that sagged. "Yes, that's her. I remember I put her in there to keep her safe. I thought if I could find Mama, I would give her Betsey. Mama liked to hold her."

"Can I have her, Angel? Can I? I promise I'll love her very much." Kelly's eyes pleaded with her, and Angie couldn't say no.

"Kelly, this doll is Angie's very special dolly. I don't think—" Rick reached out to take the doll.

Angie stopped him. "No. Let her have it. It's okay."

"Are you sure?"

She nodded.

"If that's what you want." Rick hunkered down in front of Kelly. "Was there anything else in the cubby? Like maybe a book?"

"I'll look." She gently laid Betsey on the floor where no one could step on her, then crawled back into the gap. "It's dark. I can't see."

"Just a minute. This connects with the other room." Angie walked around the gaping group into Syd's room and flicked on a light before opening a cupboard door. "Better?"

"Oh yes. I can see. But there's no book."

Angie turned, walked back to the bathroom, disappointment dragging at her heels.

"You're sure, Kelly?" Rick's voice had an edge to it. "Very sure?"

"Yes. Can I come out now?"

"Of course you can." Angie leaned down to help Kelly emerge from the cubby, brushed at the cobwebs stuck to her hair and clothes.

"I think it's time for you to take a bath, sweetie." Georgia took Kelly's hand, then looked to the others. "Don't you think?"

"Yes. And we need to get home and finish our packing." Fiona patted Emily's shoulder.

"I knew it was there." Emily's warbly voice echoed up the stairwell as the two ladies followed Georgia down the stairs. "My mind is sharp. I remember that day as clearly as today."

"Yes, sister."

Angie stood beside Rick in the tired old bathroom, listening as the voices died away. She took one last look and knew she would never return. Some things changed, but some things remained the same. This old house would always hold too many painful memories.

"I'm sorry, Angie." Rick's face expressed her own feelings. "I'm so sorry we couldn't find the book."

She summoned a smile. "At least we found the doll. Kelly's been bugging me about her ever since I first told her."

A noise downstairs broke the silence between them. Kelly raced up the stairs, followed by Georgia.

"Angie, Kelly wants to stay with you. Kent and Doug will drop me off, then follow the sisters home. I'll see you back at the house." Georgia left as silently as she'd appeared.

"What is it?" Angie knelt down to Kelly's level.

"Please can I take the other dollies too? They're lonely. They don't like it here all by themselves. They want someone to play with. I promise I'll be careful with them. You can come and visit all of us. Daddy will like that."

"Kelly, the dollies are Angie's memories of her mother."

"I know." Kelly looked at Rick as if he couldn't possibly understand. "Angel's mommy made them for her. But they don't like being in a cupboard all by themselves. They want to be loved."

Didn't everyone? As she stared at the little girl, Angie realized that she'd locked away her heart just as she'd locked away the dolls. She loved Rick. He'd always been there, watching out for her, protecting her, caring for her. Maybe if she tried very hard—

"I see you've arrived a bit early. I saw the lights and figured something must be happening. But don't expect help. Everyone's left. Everyone but you three."

The voice was unfamiliar, but the man standing with a gun pointed at her father could be none other than Michael Parker.

Angie pushed Kelly behind her. "Let him go."

Parker's lips tilted at one corner in a sardonic grin. "I'm afraid I can't do that, Agent Grant. Not until I get what I need. Do you have it?" He scanned the room in an all-seeing glance that left out no detail.

"Angel?" Kelly's fingers locked on her pant leg and tugged.

"I have to talk to this man. Just wait a minute, sweetie."

"Betsey's sick."

Angie took her eyes off Parker to glance at the insistent little girl. "What do you mean?"

She knew Rick was doing the same as her, watching for any sign that Parker would try to hurt the child. Her gun was at her ankle. Perhaps if she pretended to stumble or—

"Betsey has a hurt. Look." Kelly pressed the doll's head. A lump appeared. "Can you fix her?"

"I don't know." For the first time in so many years, Angie held her beloved doll. The feel of it recalled that last night, her mother's soft voice. *Would it be all right if Betsey kept me company while you finish building that house?* Mama had kept the doll for several hours.

Angie glanced up, saw Syd's eyes on her hands as she traced the lump. Her hands seemed to move of their own volition, finding the corner, outlining the shape of a small book stuffed between thick layers of batting.

*"Never forget that I love you, Angie. With all my heart. I've prayed that God will show you how much He loves you too. He'll always love you. No matter what."*

Her mother had hidden the book with its incriminating picture inside her precious doll.

She closed her eyes. Parker would kill Syd if he didn't get that book. Syd, Kelly, maybe even Rick.

"Please help me," she prayed quietly. "Please help me do the right thing, no matter what."

Maybe—just maybe—if she handled this right, she could finally do something to atone for her past sin against her father.

Angie opened her eyes.

Parker was watching her. "Are you sick or something?"

"No, I feel perfectly fine."

"So answer the question. And be certain you have the right answer. It could cost your father his life."

Angie ignored him. "Kelly," she said, studying the heart-shaped face she'd grown so fond of. "Betsey needs an operation. Do you understand what that means?"

Kelly nodded. "You have to fix her to make her better."

"That's exactly right. And when we do operations we have to

send everybody else out of the room. So here's what I want you to do. I want you to go downstairs to the room where the dollies are, and I want you to find our special place. Do you understand?"

Kelly's eyes widened, then shifted to the man who held the gun. "Is he going to hurt my new grandpa?"

"He's not going to hurt anyone. Just do as I ask. Okay?"

"Okay." Kelly stepped toward the door.

Parker raised his gun. "She's not going anywhere."

"She goes and so does Rick. If they don't, you don't get the picture. Isn't that what all of this is about?" She lifted one eyebrow, pretended a calm she didn't feel.

"They both go," Parker finally agreed.

Behind her, Rick protested. "Angie, I am not leaving you alone."

She kept her focus on the real culprit of her years of misery, but she directed her words to the only man she'd ever really loved. "I'm not alone. My mother's last words were that God is always with me. If you believe that, you have to leave. Now. This is something I have to do. On my own." She saw the pain in his eyes. "Please? For me."

"You're sure everything is okay?"

She nodded. "Almost certain sure." *Almost* was the key word that meant for him to wait nearby. She prayed he'd remember.

Without another word, Rick took Kelly's hand and led her out of the room. The scamper of feet down the stairs told Angie that Kelly was obeying her request to hide. Rick would make sure the child was safe. He was that kind of man.

"Okay, they're gone. You got what you wanted, now give me the picture." Parker clicked the hammer back. "Now. Before my finger slips and your father is gone." He kicked the door closed.

Angie held up the doll, tried to tug on the tired stitches, hoping to preserve the worn and weary fabric for Kelly's sake. In spite of her efforts, the cotton tore, the sound loud and angry in the silent room. Her mother's delicate work ruined. It was like hearing a piece of her heart tear away but Angie ignored that, slipped her fingers inside, and eased out the booklet.

"Is this what you wanted?" she asked. She opened the cover, stared at the photo of Parker with his arm wrapped around her father, a distinctive ring glittering on his left hand. "What a lovely ring. But I notice you don't wear it anymore."

"Cute." He kept his gun against Syd's head. "Give it to me."

"First you let my father go. This is one time you're going to keep your promise, *Mikey* Parker." If she hadn't been trained in observation, Angie wouldn't have seen the flicker of anger that touched his face.

A knife appeared in Parker's hand. He slit the ropes that bound Syd's hands but left the strip of duct tape across his mouth. "Happy now?"

"Ecstatic." She held out the picture, pretended to drop it, and while picking it up, slid her gun free. She raised it, pointed it directly at Parker. "Change of plan. Come toward me, Dad. Slowly. Good. Now take a piece of that rope. We're going to tie Mr. Parker's hands, and then we're going to call the police."

Everything happened at once.

Parker growled, shoved her father forward, and grabbed the booklet from her hand in one motion. Angie fell backward, impelled by her father's weight, and hit her head on the edge of the sink. Her gun fell from her hand. She saw stars for a minute.

Parker's gloating face loomed over her. "Not such a hotshot now, are you, Agent Grant? Daddy thought he was untouchable too, so I had to teach him a lesson. Like father, like daughter. Guess I'll have to teach you both this time."

She saw the intent in Parker's eyes a second before the shot rang out and her father's body crumpled on top of her as he was trying to get up.

"No!" she screamed, yet not a sound echoed around the room. "Dad! Dad!" she moaned, trying to shift his body so she could see where he was shot.

"I should have done this years ago." Parker tore the picture with his teeth until only tiny bits were left. These he flushed down the toilet. Then he aimed the barrel of his gun at her.

Angie felt the warm sticky blood from her father's wound seep onto her fingers, drip into a growing pool of red on the floor. "Put the gun down," Angie said.

"Or what?" He grinned, a sick evil grin. His gun lifted an inch.

"Put it down. Now."

His finger tightened around the trigger.

Angie drew her Luger from under her father's body and fired once. The mirror on the opposite wall shattered.

The door burst open. Rick stood in the doorway, his aim on the man in front of him. "You heard her. Put it down or I'll shoot, and I'm not aiming for your shoulder."

"Aren't you in enough trouble?" Parker turned his gun on Rick. "I'm the head of CSIS. You don't interfere with CSIS."

"When the head is infected with evil I do. Put it down!"

Angie had her gun trained on Parker, but she couldn't shoot. If Parker's gun went off, he'd hit Rick at point-blank range. She watched Parker's thumb slide the hammer back.

"Rick, look out!"

He turned to her. That was a mistake. As if in slow motion, Parker's hand came out in a left uppercut. The blow knocked Rick off his feet. Parker stepped through the door and rushed down the stairs.

Angie spared only a glance after him before checking to be sure Rick wasn't hurt; then her attention returned to her father.

A moment later Rick was by her side. "Angie?" he whispered, his eyes on the blood all over her clothes.

"Get an ambulance," she cried, trying to stanch the flow. "My father's been shot."

# CHAPTER EIGHTEEN

Technically, suspension meant that Rick had no right to use the flashing lights and siren on his truck, but he kept both going as he followed the ambulance to the hospital. Angie sat huddled in the seat beside him, staring blankly into the distance. Her fingers were clenched around a wad of clothing she'd held against Syd's wound.

"Kelly?" she whispered.

"Your Tony Nickel took her to Kent's. He'll watch over her till you get back."

"Thank you."

"Syd will be all right, Ang," he whispered. "God will take care of him."

"God?" She laughed. "Like He took care of him back there? Like He took care of him when that maniac burned him? Yeah, I'll put my faith in that, shall I?"

"I heard you praying earlier," he said, heart aching at her anger. "God heard you too. Don't let go now; don't give up."

"I'm so s-scared."

"So am I. But someone bigger than both of us is in charge now.

He knows what to do." Rick pulled in front of the emergency doors, hit the brakes. "Let's go."

They rushed inside, then were forced to wait. Nobody had any answers to their questions until the doctors made an assessment of Syd's condition. Sometime later Syd was rolled out of the emergency room on a gurney, his body unmoving, his face white and still.

"We're taking him to surgery. He's lost a lot of blood, and the bullet pierced a lung and nicked his spine. His prognosis is not good."

Angie crumpled under the news, unable to do anything but watch her father being wheeled away from her.

Rick gathered her into his arms, letting her weep on his shoulder. He didn't know how long he held her like that, drawing comfort from the weight of her head on his shoulder, the way her fingers curled into his.

He thought it was about five thirty in the morning when a noise in the distance alerted him. Moments later his boss walked through the door, a man on either side of him. Rick recognized the look. Internal investigations.

"Angie, I have to talk to someone for a minute. Will you be okay here?"

She glanced around, saw that it was not a doctor, and nodded with total disinterest.

"Good. I'll be right back." Rick felt a surge of relief that she didn't bother to question him further. He preferred she didn't overhear whatever this was about. She needed to concentrate on Syd now. He patted her shoulder, then strode toward the waiting men.

"Rick." His boss wore an angry look. His face was tight with strain. "What on earth is happening?"

"Syd Grant is in surgery. Punctured lung and some damage to the spine from Parker's shot. Don't know the extent of his wounds yet. Parker is gone." He frowned. "What are you doing here, Martin?"

"I'm the bearer of bad news. I wanted you to hear it from me first."

"Go on." Rick steeled himself for whatever would come. Hadn't he just preached faith to Angie?

"The boys at CSIS are pretty incensed by what happened last night, especially by your claim that Parker is dirty. They've mounted a full-scale investigation against you."

"Me?"

"Parker has some very powerful friends, and they are determined not a whit of scandal will blemish his name. Especially since it might rub off on them. Is there anything—anything at all—you can offer to prove that he's dirty?"

Rick closed his eyes, tried to think. "There was a picture, but he destroyed it. Without that to implicate him, or Syd's testimony about the warrant, I'm dead."

"That's what I was afraid of," Martin said.

One of the other men cleared his throat. "A hearing has been set for next week. They're going after you, Rick. I'd advise you to bring your lawyer because you're going to need all the help you can get."

"Suspended without pay?" Rick read the look in his boss's tired eyes and sagged under it. "Worse?"

"Much worse. Without something to prove you fulfilled the terms of the warrant, you could be looking at imprisonment."

The words were staggering.

"I'm sorry. I'll keep digging, of course. But there's only so much I can do."

"Yes, I understand."

"You're sure this person you saw is the same Michael Parker from CSIS?"

"Quite sure." He nodded. "Angie saw him too."

"Agent Grant once worked with you, didn't she, Rick?"

He nodded, heart sinking at the implication of those words.

"I don't think she's going to be much help. There's some question about her leaving Ottawa without authorization. Her superiors are not happy."

So Parker would take Angie down too. And there was nothing Rick could do but let her go back.

"Thank you for coming here, for warning me. I appreciate that, Martin."

Though the men left quickly, Rick waited till he had himself under control before going back to Angie. No way would he burden her with his problems. She had her own worries; she didn't need to know his. He needed to do something to distance himself from her, so she wouldn't be touched by the scandal that was going to mark him as a dirty cop, a cheat, and a liar.

He approached the bank of phones to call his best friend. "Hey, Kent. No news yet, I'm afraid. Syd's still in surgery."

"We're praying for all of you," Kent said.

"I knew you would be. Thanks." He took a deep breath, then made his request. "Tell Doug to get working. I think this is a case he can't win, but I'll appreciate any help he can give."

"Just a minute, he's here."

"I'm sorry I ruined your holiday," Rick said.

"Kent claims Camp Hope can outdo a ski hill any day of the week."

Rick smiled at Kent's quick defense of the camp he loved. As succinctly as possible he related what he'd just learned, then asked, "So what do you think?"

"I think you're going to be doing a lot of 'splaining, Ricky." But there was no mirth in Doug's voice. "This guy is quick, clever, and he's got his organization behind him."

"But we've got God." *Faith—I'm hanging on by my fingertips, Lord.*

"True. And nothing is impossible with Him, as Kelly just reminded me. Can you leave yet?"

"I'd rather not go till Syd is out of the woods," Rick told him.

"Okay, well, as soon as you can, hotfoot it back here. Don't go to Grant's house. It's a crime scene and it will be crawling with detectives. I'll get my research people looking into this Michael Parker's business."

"Thank you very much, Doug. There's just one other thing."

"Name it."

"I don't want Angie to know anything about this. As soon as her father is out of danger I know she'll want to get Kelly back to Ottawa. I want her to go on with her life, to forget about me and everything here. I want her out of it until this mess has blown over."

A long silence dragged out. Finally Doug asked, "You're sure that's what you want?"

"Almost certain sure," he muttered, glancing at the fiery, red gold head bent with weariness. "Bye."

Rick returned to Angie, sat beside her, and grasped her fingers in his. He held them that way as they waited.

Eventually his own reminder came back to haunt him: *"Nothing can ever separate us from his love. Death can't, and life can't. The angels can't, and the demons can't. Our fears for today, our worries about tomorrow, and even the powers of hell can't keep God's love away. Whether we are high above the sky or in the deepest ocean, nothing in all creation will ever be able to separate us from the love of God that is revealed in Christ Jesus our Lord."*

———⊱◆⊰———

"You can see your father now. But just for a few moments."

Angie followed the nurse down the hall, stopped beside the bed supporting the man she'd told herself she hated. Tubes, electrodes, all manner of devices monitored or assisted the steady rhythm of his breathing.

"Dad," she whispered, sitting on the edge of a chair, her hand reaching out to touch the mangled flesh of his hand. "I'm so sorry. For everything."

The machines whirred and beeped, but her father didn't open his eyes.

"I didn't mean for it to happen," she told him brokenly. "I never wanted you to be hurt." Tears ran down her cheeks, and pain flooded her heart.

"Why didn't you tell me?" she asked him, her soul aching to hear his gruff voice say her name just one more time. "Why didn't you ever say that you were protecting me, that you cared about me?" She gulped. "Why didn't you tell me that you loved me?"

*Did you* tell *him?*

The question shocked her. Angie thought back over the months and years. Had she ever told Syd she loved him? Even once in the last ten years, had she ever actually said it? The painful answer spoke for itself.

Never. Not once since she'd been old enough to understand what forgiveness really meant had she looked at him and seen past his bitterness and sour disposition to a man who needed to hear her say the words every bit as much as she needed to hear them from him.

The truth hit her hard. She'd treated God the same way she'd treated Syd—laid all the blame at His door, expected Him to fit her rules.

Because of her guilt.

For the first time since she'd done that awful thing, Angie faced the issue fair and square and saw the truth she'd ignored. The lack was not on God's part, but on hers. She'd done something wrong and instead of admitting it, she'd secreted that knowledge away in her heart.

And paid the price ever since. By blaming God for not forgiving her she squeezed out of the responsibility of admitting her sin, forgiving herself, and believing that she was free of it because God had said so.

So many times she'd felt dirty, unworthy of His grace. Of course she was unworthy! But that didn't mean God didn't forgive her, wouldn't take her shame, the ugliness of her sin and cover it with His grace and beauty.

If she let Him.

God's forgiveness wasn't based on her ability to be worthy. It was given because He loved her.

"Oh, God," she murmured, cupping her father's damaged hand against her cheek, "I'm sorry. I'm so sorry."

The man in the bed remained silent.

———➤◆◄———

Rick remained in the doorway watching Angie weep over her father. A full day had passed and still Syd hadn't wakened.

Her cheek pressed against the hand she clasped. So beautiful. So sad. He took one step forward, felt fingers grasp his arm.

Doug Henderson stood behind him. "Come on, you have to get changed."

"Why?" He refused to move, honed in on Angie's defenseless face as she waited.

"Things have moved ahead far quicker than I expected. It's 6:30. In three hours you have to stand before a hearing. I want to go over everything before it starts."

Slowly Rick turned to face him, all hope for the future draining out of him. "And then?"

Doug met his stare. "Unless you know more than you've told me and barring any miracles, they're going to charge you. You have to prepare yourself."

"Rick?" Angie stood behind him now, her eyes red-rimmed from crying. "What's wrong?"

He knew what he had to do and though it killed him to do it, Rick answered, "It's nothing to do with you, Angie. I'll handle this on my own. Go and sit with your father. He needs you now."

She flinched at the harshness of his voice.

Rick refused to back down. "I can't help you anymore. It's better if you stay away from me. Don't get mixed up in my battles."

"But—"

"There can't be anything between us," he told her, hating the flash of pain that filled her eyes. "I should have never said what I did. I know that now."

"But I wanted to tell you that—"

"No!" He grasped her arms, held her in a solid grip. "Don't say anything you'll regret later. Forget that I ever said anything, because

I realize now that I was wrong to think things between us could be different, that we could share a future. You don't see me that way, and it's too hard to pretend I don't care. So fine. Just let it end. All right?"

"End?" She glanced from him to Doug, who had backed away down the hall, shook her head. "What do you mean you were wrong? You said you loved me. You offered me a future. Didn't you mean it?"

"It was a mistake. I don't have a future. I have to concentrate on my own problems now. I've done my best to help you and Syd, but it's up to you to help him now. I don't have anything more to offer." He dropped his hands, let his eyes soak in her beauty for one long moment, then forced out the hard words. "Go back to CSIS, Ang. Take Kelly and finish your job. I wish you all the best. Good-bye."

Though his legs felt wooden, he forced himself to turn and walk toward Doug while everything he'd let himself dream of sharing with Angie Grant withered and died inside his heart.

"Rick?"

He froze at the soft word spoken in the only voice that could tear apart his insides. But he wouldn't turn around, because then he might never be able to set her free.

"I just wanted to tell you—I'll be praying for you."

*Praying? Angie?* His heart offered a song of praise that she'd managed that much, but he dared not look at her. So he said nothing. Merely nodded and resumed his long stride to the emergency entrance and out the door.

Whatever happened now was in God's hands.

# CHAPTER NINETEEN

Three days, three whole days she'd been away.

And though Angie had kept in touch with the hospital and knew that her father fluttered in and out of consciousness, she'd heard nothing about Rick. The detachment was no help. All Shauna would say was that Rick had taken leave for the next few weeks.

There was something wrong and Angie knew it, but no one was talking. Oh, Georgia and Kent answered her questions, but the answers were vague and unsatisfying and left her wondering what they weren't saying.

Not that she had a right to know anything about Rick. He'd made his decision clear by pushing her out of his life.

That had stung with a depth she'd never expected, and the pain of his rejection hadn't eased in the past three days. But she couldn't help asking herself what had been behind it. She had the time to think now. After all, she'd done her job. Kelly had testified against Carver and was now safely reunited with her father. Details were scarce, but Angie heard about unknown captors who'd kept him isolated until very recently when he'd suddenly been released. Kelly had been overjoyed at the reunion, and Angie was certain the child would soon forget their cross-country trek.

But she couldn't. Through the ordeal of returning to Ottawa, answering a host of questions about her time away, and filling out a mountain of reports—all along Angie had puzzled over Rick's strange behavior . . . until a suspicion dawned and grew.

He was in more trouble than he'd let on.

Now, as she pulled into the parking lot of the hospital, she chafed against the necessity of seeing her father first. Maybe she should seek out Rick—but no. It was time to clear the past. Only then could she look to the future. With God's help.

"Please give me the strength to do this," she whispered as she walked toward her father's room.

Sydney Grant looked small, defenseless, utterly helpless in the narrow bed. His pocked and scarred face seemed pitiful, less harsh in the bright wash of morning sun.

"Dad?" Angie stood by the bed, watching. *Please, God, let him be alert enough to hear, to understand. To forgive.* "Dad, can you hear me?"

He blinked through a groggy haze, as if he couldn't understand what she was saying. But the need to confess compelled her to keep speaking, to wait until Syd roused from his confused state so he would comprehend exactly what she confessed. Only then would she be free of this intolerable guilt.

A nurse stopped by. "He's weak but he'll come around. Just wait for him."

Angie waited.

Finally, just before one o'clock he blinked awake and, upon seeing her face, rasped her name.

"I'm here."

"You went away," he whispered, his eyes steady, full of questions.

"Yes. I had some things to do for Kelly. I came back because I need to tell you something." This was hard, so hard to expose the truth about herself.

Angie rose and paced to the door and back. She felt his scrutiny and knew she could no longer put off her confession. "I'm the one who turned you in, Dad. When you came back to the farm after the bank robbery, I gave the anonymous tip that brought the police. It's my fault you went to jail. I betrayed my own father."

Syd simply looked at her.

"I knew something was wrong when you came home that afternoon." Angie pushed on with her explanations though her throat felt tight, choked. "You were throwing clothes into that bag like a madman. I'd left something in the trunk, and I went to get it. That's when I saw the bag with the money. I figured out what you'd done, and I decided to get revenge for all the times you'd hurt me."

She sank onto the chair, bent her head. "I made the call, but that wasn't the worst of it." She dashed away the tears, faced him with the truth. "I moved the suitcase from the trunk to the backseat and opened it to make sure no one would miss it."

Angie swallowed, stared at him as the shame welled up inside. "I know now that you were trying to get me away from Parker, but I didn't know it then. I was angry that you hadn't gone to my graduation, and I wanted to make you pay, hurt you the way I thought you were hurting me. If I hadn't called the police, none of the rest of it would have happened. It's all my fault." She squeezed her eyes closed and waited for the recriminations.

"I know."

The words were so soft, so quiet, she was certain she'd misunderstood. "What?" She used the heel of her palm to clear her vision, stared at him. "What did you say?"

"I know, Angie." He smiled. "I figured it out while I was lying here. Don't be upset about that. I'm proud of you for doing it, for not letting me get away with stealing."

"You know?" She couldn't understand his meaning.

"Yes. I always figured Rick must have opened the trunk the day he arrested me. When Mikey testified that he saw the money on the backseat, I thought maybe Rick moved it or Mikey did. But Rick was adamant that he had followed the terms of the warrant, and I couldn't discount his implacability. So it couldn't have been him. I couldn't imagine Mikey seeing money and just leaving it behind, so I began to wonder who else was there."

"Me. I was. I betrayed you to the police. I moved the money. If it wasn't for me you would have been able to get away from Michael Parker. I'm the one who made it worse." She stopped as a soft sheen appeared under his lashes. "Oh, Dad, don't cry. I'm sorry."

She dropped her head into her hands and wept for the pain he'd endured because of her.

"Honey, you have nothing to be sorry for. I'm crying because I'm so proud of you. Your mother would have done the same thing, Angela." He reached out, touched her hair. "In a way, I think God used what you did to reach me. I'm not sure I would have ever turned back to Him if I hadn't come face-to-face with myself in that prison. I'm the one who should be asking forgiveness. I abused you terribly. Oh, not physically, maybe. But my words, my anger, leaving you like that—I should have explained. In retrospect I don't wonder that you hate me."

"I don't—" Angie stopped, suddenly aware that the hate was gone. Yes, the past with its pain still stung, probably always would. But the hate? It had disappeared the moment she admitted what she'd done and asked his forgiveness. "I don't hate you, Dad. I tried, but . . . I just can't."

"It's what I deserve. I was never the kind of father you needed. But I give thanks every day that somehow, in spite of me, God kept you safe. I had to go to jail to admit I couldn't handle things." His voice was weakening, so he struggled to get the words out. "I know now that I let Mikey Parker take over when I should have turned to God. My faith in Him was too weak, and I paid the price for trying to handle things on my own."

"I'm sorry, Dad. So sorry."

"So am I," he whispered, touching her cheek. "I've wasted a lot of years, Angie. I know you'll never forget, but can you ever forgive me?"

*"Forgive, and you will be forgiven."*

She leaned over to look into his eyes that were soft with . . . love? For her?

"If you can forgive me," she begged, letting the mask that had shielded her heart for all these years fall away for good.

"Nothing to forgive. You're my daughter; I love you." Syd squeezed her hand, but his grip was slack.

Angie could tell from his breathing that he was tired, that the talking had sapped his strength. When he licked his dry lips, she offered him one of the ice chips from a nearby glass.

"Thank you." He glanced around the room. "Where's Rick? I was certain he would be here with you."

"He was when we first brought you in. But—" she paused, cleared her throat—"I don't think he loves me, Dad. He said he did but then, after you were shot, he changed his mind. He told me to go back to CSIS."

Syd's head wavered from side to side. "Not right," he said, his voice husky.

The nurse walked in with a hypodermic but he held out a hand.

"Wait!" He looked at Angie. "Now I remember. Rick is in trouble. Because of me and because of you. They think he didn't follow the terms of the warrant. Plain sight."

Angie stared at him, her mind whirling. "Because the money wasn't in the trunk?"

His nod landed a weight upon her shoulders. She felt the blood drain from her face. "Oh no! All this time he's been trying to prove his innocence when I could have explained and settled everything. But if they think he didn't execute the warrant properly, that means he could be charged."

"Yes." Syd's eyes met hers as the nurse injected him. "You love him, Angela. He's a good man, a decent man. I think he loves you the way I loved Eve. Find him, set the record straight, then get on with the future. You've both wasted too much time."

"If I'd only known, I could have helped."

"Too many secrets," Syd mumbled.

"Way too many. That's why he told me to go away. Because he thought he'd be charged. He pretended he didn't love me anymore so I wouldn't get drawn into his fight." Angie leaned over, brushed her father's cheek with her fingertips. "Thank you."

"My pleasure." The words breathed out of him on a sigh.

"I have to go now, Dad. But I'll be back later. Okay?"

"Tell him the truth," Syd whispered just before his eyelids closed.

"From now on," she promised.

⟫◆⟪

"I believe in dealing in facts, Rick. And the fact is that this morning didn't go well. The afternoon isn't shaping up any better." Doug tapped his pencil on his file folder to cover his whisper. "Michael Parker is just too good. I wish we had something—anything—to offer as proof that you followed the rules."

"There isn't anything. Syd was very clear that the bag with the money was in the trunk. Without Mikey's testimony that he moved it, I can't prove that I didn't cheat. Parker wins again." Rick turned from his scrutiny of that polished man as Arden walked through the door. "What now?"

His coworker bent to whisper something in Doug's ear.

"I'll be back before the recess is over. Sit tight." Doug excused himself.

Rick watched him leave the room. Everyone else returned.

Finally Doug rushed back in and the proceedings began again.

"What's wrong?" Rick whispered.

Doug ignored him and rose. "I apologize for the confusion, but I have another witness, if it's all right."

"Who is this witness?"

"Agent Angela Grant, currently an operative with the Canadian Security Intelligence Service."

A murmur passed through the room. Rick noticed the corners of Parker's mouth tighten. Otherwise he gave nothing away.

"We will hear Ms. Grant's testimony."

Rick hung his head in despair. Why had she come? He didn't want her to run to his rescue by offering some kind of character witness. He didn't want her branded like him. A moment later he had his answer as Angie told the court that she'd moved the bag of money from the trunk to the backseat.

"I apologize to the court for this mistake. I had no idea that my actions so long ago would result in this confusion," she explained. "I was an angry eighteen-year-old trying to make her father pay for the pain he'd caused me. I called the police, then moved the bag with the money from the trunk to inside the car in hopes that someone would see it and arrest him. I wanted my father to pay for his crime. I wanted him to go away. Sergeant Mercer executed his warrant in good faith. He had no way of knowing I was involved."

Shocked by the words, Rick couldn't tear his eyes away from Angie. She'd never looked more glorious. Her auburn hair glistened in the light, and her eyes sparkled with some inner secret he couldn't decipher but echoed back to his heart in an arrow of joy.

The panel conferred for a moment.

"That's all very well, Ms. Grant. But you were a coworker of Sergeant Mercer's. How can we be sure that you haven't manufactured this story to cover his mistake?"

He saw Angie's surprise, felt his heart shrink at the tinge of chagrin that flooded her stunningly beautiful face.

"Manufactur—" She sputtered to a stop, spots of color dotting her cheeks. "I am a police officer. I've sworn to uphold the law. I wouldn't lie about anything, certainly nothing as important as this. I was there. I'm telling you the truth."

"You're saying that Mr. Parker, a distinguished military officer who's about to head up the very agency you work for, lied about what he saw?"

Rick knew the speaker was a representative of CSIS. He wondered if Angie did.

She shook her head, her eyes resting on the man who'd injured her father. "If Mr. Parker was there that day I did not see him. The only person who could confirm his presence on our land is my father, and I don't believe he's done that. I've already told you what I did. I removed the case containing the money from the trunk of the car and put it on the backseat. If Mr. Parker says he saw it in the trunk, then he saw it before I moved it. After that I phoned the police and told them that Syd Grant had stolen the money and that it was on the backseat of his car."

"That is the tip the police received that day." Doug reinforced her testimony with quiet strength.

With steely determination, Angie told them about the statues and the ring. "I further suggest to you that a man who would deliberately harm a coworker on an overseas mission in order to hide his own theft of valuable objects would certainly not be adverse to reworking the truth for his own purposes. Mr. Parker is the one who shot my father."

"For what reason?"

"Because my father had a picture of him, the man he knew as Mikey, wearing a ring he stole when he was in Iran."

"This is ludicrous," Parker responded. "Must I be subjected to these wild stories? Her father is a convicted criminal. You can hardly imagine that his daughter is any different."

"Is that why you arranged for CSIS to hire me?" Angie asked. "I saw my file and your initials approving my hire, sending me to protect the Blairs, ordering me to stay where I was even though I called many times for help and further instructions. You had to get me back here, didn't you? You needed that picture so there would be nothing left to incriminate you when you take that CSIS job next week."

"This is ridiculous!"

"Is it?" Doug pressed into the conversation. "Are they all lying about you, Mr. Parker? Mr. Grant, Sergeant Mercer, Agent Grant? Have they all concocted these stories just to get at you?"

"Yes!"

"Why?"

Parker pointed at Angie. "She's trying to get me because her father blames me for his injuries."

"But Ms. Grant knew nothing about that until she came back here, until you started threatening her." Doug passed out papers to each member of the board. "A bullet shot through Ms. Grant's living-room window came from a military assault rifle, Mr. Parker. The day before that incident, you took your rifle, of the same make using the same ammunition, through airport security. I have two security officers from the airport who will testify that you flashed your credentials and tried to intimidate them. They finally persuaded you to check the rifle in to the cargo area. Am I correct?"

"I was on a training mission."

"Here? Thousands of miles from your usual base? I'm unable to find any record of that."

"It was secret."

"Apparently to everyone but you." Doug smiled. "And what about shots fired at Sergeant Mercer's truck? Shots that could have injured a child in witness protection, a child you ordered Ms. Grant to protect. Those came from your rifle also, didn't they? In fact, you admitted to Agent Grant that you'd fired on her as a warning that if she didn't get the photo of the ring you stole and return it to you, you'd kill her."

"This is out—"

"Outrageous? Indeed it is." Doug shook his head. "Then of course there was the note you left behind. At the moment it's at a lab. I think they'll find several ties to you—paper, handwriting, fingerprints."

"I am the head of CSIS." Michael Parker's face grew tight with rage. "I have no need to go chasing junior agents across the country."

"You are not yet the head," Doug reminded him. "You have to pass the hearings. That would be difficult to do if someone saw you wearing stolen booty, wouldn't it?"

"I have nothing to hide."

"I think that once we start probing your affairs, we'll find a lot of

things you've covered up or glossed over to hide your dirty work."
Doug's scathing gaze raked across the harried man. "If the members
could grant us some time, we'd—"

"We appreciate that you'd like to dig up some dirt on Mr. Parker,
anything at all that could be misconstrued," the CSIS representative
sneered. "But the purpose of this hearing is to determine whether or
not Sergeant Mercer illegally executed a warrant. We've all seen the
public's distaste for crooked cops, and none of us wants to be painted
with the same brush. Certainly we're not here to smear a fine man
and decorated officer."

Doug tried to intervene but was silenced.

"Mr. Grant's affidavit clearly states that he placed the money in
the trunk. His daughter's rush to defend Sergeant Mercer, though
admirable, seems a little late, a little forced."

"I'm sure we'd all like time to consider what we've heard. You
are dismissed, Agent Grant." The chairman waited until Angie had
left the room. "Do you have any more testimony to offer, Mr.
Henderson?"

"No, sir."

"Then I'm afraid we will have to consider the case based on the
merit of its standing at this point. I see no need to prolong this. We
will meet again tomorrow morning at nine to give you our decision."

One by one, they filed from the room.

Rick glanced at Doug, saw what he feared confirmed on the
lawyer's face. "They don't believe her or me. I've lost it, haven't I?"

"Nothing is for certain until tomorrow morning, Rick."

"Yeah. Right." He tugged at his tie. "Maybe if Syd testified?"

"It would only be his word against Parker's, and Syd admitted that
he stole that money. The word of a bank robber?"

"I guess you're right." Rick rose. "I'm sorry I got you involved."

"I'm not sorry at all. I've got a case of perjury to defend. This has
given me some insights, even though it's not criminal court." Doug
slid his papers into his briefcase.

"Glad I could be of help," Rick said dryly as he trailed behind the lawyer out of the room. "If you wait long enough, it probably will go there."

Angie stood waiting in the hall. "I'm sorry I didn't explain earlier," she told them both. "But I had no idea that this was what your investigation was about. You should have told me, Rick."

"Like you told me it was you on the phone that afternoon or anytime since?" he muttered. He sighed, turned, and addressed Doug. "Sorry. You don't need to hear this. I'll meet you here tomorrow morning, unless you think there's something else we need to discuss."

"No, all we have left is to wait for their decision." Doug nodded at Angie. "Will I see you later also?"

"I'm not sure. But thank you for helping Rick."

"I'm just sorry your testimony didn't carry more weight. Parker's really quite clever. I have a private investigator digging into his affairs, but it would be better if his own people found discrepancies, though I don't know of anyone who could do that."

"I might." Angie chewed her bottom lip. "Maybe if I asked around—"

"Don't get more involved in this, Angie," Rick begged, praying she would hear him this time. "You could lose your job at CSIS, and I know how much you love it."

"Of course I like my work. But do you really think I'd put my job, my own happiness, above your future?" Angie asked him. "Is that how little you think of me?"

Rick had never seen Angie Grant quite so angry. He took two steps backward.

She thrust her chin up and stared him down. "I'm not someone you have to protect. Yes, I ran away from here, from the secrets I kept, from the shame of turning in my own father. But I've never abandoned someone who needed me. Unless you're saying this because you don't want me around."

"Angie—" Rick glanced at Doug, wishing he were anywhere else but here—"maybe it's better if you go."

Angie tried to pretend, but this time she couldn't mask the hurt in her eyes. "That's what you want? You'd prefer I didn't bother you anymore?"

He didn't answer.

She nodded. "Fine. I'm sorry I intruded, Rick. Good-bye."

There were a thousand things he could have—should have—said, thank you being one of them. But before anything could be spoken, Angie turned and almost ran out of the building.

"Well, Rick, I think you just lost an ally. Too bad. Friends are hard to come by." Doug spotted Abby Van Meter and hurried over to talk to her.

"Anything I can do?" Arden asked, stepping forward, following Rick's gaze toward the couple now tentatively smiling at each other.

"No, thanks." Rick inclined his head toward the lawyer and the widow. "It looks like that flame is still burning. They really seemed to get along last fall. I never understood what happened."

"I was thinking that about you. The woman you've been in love with for as long as I can remember just went racing out of here and you let her. Why?"

"She didn't understand."

"What? That you're too proud to accept her help? That the only part of a relationship you're good at is the giving part?" Arden's voice hardened. "Loving someone doesn't mean always being the tough guy, Rick. Sometimes the other person needs to be able to give too. I think Angie's carried a torch for you for years but figured she wasn't good enough. She could never let herself believe she deserved you."

"That was just infatuation."

Arden snorted. "Like you're infatuated with her?"

That gave him pause. "You really think Angie cared about me?" Rick could hardly let himself believe it.

"Cares. Yes, I do. Love like that—it doesn't come around that often." Arden matched Rick's step as they walked out of the building. "When it does, you should grab on with both hands."

"You really think—" Rick didn't dare finish the sentence.

"I do, but why not go to the source? Ask her. The truth shall set you free." Arden saluted him, then ambled away.

Rick stood on the sidewalk in the early evening breeze and watched the town scurry about its business while his mind tried to encompass the thought. Angie caring about *him*, not some fictitious romantic dream she'd concocted, not as a friend or a coworker. Not as a cop she had a crush on.

She'd worked with him, seen him in almost every situation and mood. She understood what made him tick. She didn't stew about the danger he faced because she knew all about it. She knew that at a moment's notice, everything in life could change.

So did he. In fact, it was about to change now. Angie would go back to Ottawa and CSIS. She'd leave here again because he was too afraid to believe that his prayers had been answered. She'd leave and nothing would be the same.

No way! There was a time to act. This was it.

Rick climbed into his truck and headed for Camp Hope. Michael Parker could do his worst, but Rick wasn't giving up, not before he learned exactly where he stood with Angela Valentine Grant.

# CHAPTER TWENTY

In the basement of the main house at Camp Hope, Angie stared at the stacks of albums she hadn't finished putting away. She had asked Georgia to let her stay one more night. Tomorrow she would see Syd and tell him good-bye before she headed back to Ottawa. Alone.

The albums were like the last chapter she needed to finish before she would be free of Camp Hope. But she would never be free of the memories here.

She assembled the remainder in piles of five-year blocks, then started placing them on the shelves while resisting the urge to peek inside. Maybe another time, when her heart wasn't quite so sore.

"I thought you'd be here."

Angie turned, stared into the beloved face. "Rick. I thought you wanted me to go."

The glow in his gentle eyes, the straight unyielding strength in his shoulders, the gritty determination in his jaw—it was all there, as solid and secure as ever. Only not for her.

Rick simply stood there, saying nothing.

Angie couldn't take the silence so she turned back to the shelves, to the work that kept her hands busy. The silence was too poignant.

She began to talk. "The day we arrived Kelly said this was a place where God lived. She was right."

He still said nothing.

"While I was sitting by my father's bedside, I realized exactly how near to me God has always been. Camp Hope is where I ran to when I needed a reminder of what my mother had taught me about Him and love. This is where I ran to pray when my life got too hard and I needed a friend. This is the place I learned about my past, about what had been. This is where I dreamed about what could be."

"Camp Hope has been a lot of things for a lot of people." Rick was standing directly behind her. "It's been like a refuge to me. I come here whenever I need a friend, human or otherwise. It's my sanctuary."

"That's good." She kept working, methodically placing one book after another on the shelf, surprised when he began handing them to her.

"Do you think it can be a place for us to start a future?" he asked.

Angie froze, unable to stop the book from tumbling out of her hand.

"Come home, Angie," Rick murmured next to her ear. "I want to live in that house with you. I want to share every day, plan every moment of the future. I want us to finish what your grandparents started, what your mom and dad couldn't do. I want to love you for the rest of my life. Is that something you're prepared to consider?"

Suddenly she was in his arms, snuggled against his warmth, his lips on hers. Angie laced her arms around his neck and kissed him back, reveling in the rush of joy that being in his arms brought.

"Consider? Are you kidding me?" she whispered when she could speak.

"No. I kidded myself for a while, until Arden made me remember that life gets dicey. Jobs come and go." When he looked down, she saw the love radiating from within him. "Loving you, that's permanent. If I get fired, I'll deal with it. If I have to be supported by you, I'll thank you. I just want us to be together forever in that house that sits right at the edge of Camp Hope."

"Oh, Rick." She laid her head on his heart, amazed by the pride he was willing to step on to be with her.

"That's why I started working on Barrons' Rest, Angie. I thought I could show you that your house could be more than a prison. That together we could make the past live again, and we could build dreams together."

"My prison was inside me," she told him. "All tied up with my guilt and my inability to accept that God had already forgiven me, that I had to forgive myself for betraying my father. That I was unworthy but loved."

"So loved." He brushed his fingertips over her hair. "And so beautiful."

"I thought you'd hate me for betraying him."

"I don't think it was only betrayal. I see it more as your attempt to rebuild your faith in him by making him do the right thing." He brushed the tumble of curls off her face. "But you haven't answered. Will you share the future with me, help me make Barrons' Rest a place where people can find rejuvenation and rest?"

It sounded so wonderful. Angie wanted to tell him yes.

Rick spoke first. "There's just one thing. I don't want a long-distance relationship. A few weekends here and there when you're not on a case isn't good enough. I love you. I want to be with you all the time. If the only way that can happen is for me to move to Ottawa, I'll do it gladly. We can find some other work, some place like Camp Hope to become involved in, a home like Barrons' Rest."

She stepped away from him. "Well, that would be silly." She shook her head at his frown, cupped his face in her hands, pressed a kiss against his lips. "Darling Rick, I believe I was led back here for a reason. Camp Hope is where I learned about my past. I choose it to press on toward my future. With you." She stood on tiptoe, met his gaze with an open heart, and felt the last secret doubts melt away.

"I want to come home, Rick. I'd hoped you might give me a referral to get back on the force, but if that doesn't work out, then I'll do something else. I'm leaving that up to God to sort out. After all, this is Camp Hope—Where nothing is impossible with God."

"Exactly. I think it's time I stopped worrying about my future and let Him show me the way. I'd still like to be a staff sergeant someday, but if it never happens, I'll still have you."

Angie tilted her head to one side. "Only if you marry me, Sergeant Mercer."

"Is that a proposal?" he asked, grinning. "Because if it is, I accept." He sealed that promise the best way possible.

Angie shifted, trying to get closer. But something stopped that. She glanced down. "We're being very disrespectful of Camp Hope's history." She bent to retrieve a book. The page had fallen open at a picture of some campers returning from a wranglers' breakfast. She could see her own house behind them, the camp barn to the left. "You'd better let me finish my job."

Rick's hand clamped around her wrist, preventing her from closing the book. "Wait. Angie, look!"

Her father was barely visible at the right of the picture, but his friend was. A tiny glint from the camera had captured his hand, especially his ring finger. "Is that—?"

"A ring. A very special ring." Rick set the book on the coffee table and bellowed for Kent. "We need a magnifying glass."

They all came rushing down—Georgia, Kent, Doug, Abby. Each one studied the picture.

"We can enhance it," Doug suggested. "We can prove that he took that ring, that he was wearing it long after Iran."

"But what about Dad?" Angie asked. "Won't Parker blame him?"

"He might try, but your father didn't profit. Parker has. According to the date on the album, this picture is only about eight years old, which means Parker still had the ring. It shouldn't be hard to find it."

"His secret has finally been revealed," Rick stated.

"As all secrets are. Just another example of the impossible made possible." Doug took the album upstairs. The others followed, spirits high.

Angie would have joined them, but Rick drew her back into his arms.

"Do you really love me, Angie?" he asked softly.

"I never thought of you as the kind of person to ask silly questions, Sergeant," she teased. "This is my answer." She strove to infuse every ounce of love she felt into her kiss.

# EPILOGUE

And so it happened that when the crocus pushed through the earth and the ground changed its snowy quilt to a sweet lush green blanket, newly promoted Staff Sergeant Rick Mercer married Constable Angie Grant in a delightful springtime wedding on the patio of their new home.

Everyone commented on the darling flower girl named Kelly with silver blonde hair, who was clearly devoted to the bride, the groom, and her dog. No one could miss the gorgeous, heart-shaped engagement ring the groom had surprised the bride with on her Valentine's birthday.

But the majority of talk was centered on the proud father who escorted his precious daughter to her groom, then stood watching them pledge their love with tears running down his scarred cheeks. No one who witnessed that doubted his love for his child.

The wedding reception, hosted by the Murdock sisters, took place in the dining hall at Camp Hope, where speculation ran rife about the bachelor possibilities of a certain groomsman who happened to be the Mercers' handsome lawyer friend.

Later that evening, after the bride's father hinted about a honeymoon in a warmer clime, the guests gathered outside to toss rice and wish the couple bon voyage as they drove away beneath the green canopy that encircled and protected Camp Hope.

In truth, Angie and Rick traveled only a short distance, to the house they'd worked so hard to make a home.

"Kent was right about the view from this patio," Rick said, wrapping his arms around his wife's waist as he stared into her face. "It's spectacular."

"He meant that view." Angie turned in his arms to watch the sun dip down over the horizon in a dazzling orange red glow.

"It's pretty good too," he agreed.

When the last reddish streaks had faded to black and the night insects began their chorus, Rick turned Angie to face him. "I promise to love you for as many days as we have together and beyond that, my darling wife.

"For this part of our journey together we'll be close to our friends, close to your father, close to Camp Hope. It really is a place of hope, you know. For today, for tomorrow, forever."

Angie stood on the tips of her toes and kissed him. "As long as neither of us keeps any more secrets," she whispered.

The agreement was sealed in love.

# A NOTE FROM THE AUTHOR

*Dear Reader,*

*I'm so delighted you chose to visit Camp Hope with me one more time. I pray the story touched your life in a way that causes you to want to know God better.*

*Whether you're searching for sanctuary, justice, or a way to be free of the shadows and secrets in your life, please know that our Father waits for you to turn to Him. In His arms you'll find love like you've never known, peace nothing else can offer, and hope that He renews each day. In His arms is the comfort you seek.*

*I look forward to hearing from you. My prayer is that you'll begin to discover just how much God loves you.*

*Blessings,*

*Lois*

## ABOUT THE AUTHOR

A former human-resources manager for a national chain, Lois now lives in a small Canadian town with her husband and two sons. After delving into the entrepreneurial realm, Lois settled down to full-time writing. It's a job she loves in an environment most would envy. The perks of working in her home office while the birds chirp outside her window, coffee breaks on the patio, and the chance to chat with fans around the world make this a career she wouldn't trade.

This prolific author of twenty inspirational romances for Steeple Hill has also penned a novella for Barbour. *Shadowed Secrets* is the sequel to *Forgotten Justice* and *Dangerous Sanctuary* in her romantic suspense series called Camp Hope. Lois enjoys making pottery, singing with a local group, and traveling, but her favorite activity is swimming.

You may contact Lois by writing to her in care of Tyndale House Author Relations, P.O. Box 80, Wheaton, IL 60189; or via her Web site at www.loisricher.uni.cc.

WELCOME TO

# HEARTQUEST

HEART
QUEST

Visit

**www.heartquest.com**

and get the inside scoop.

You'll find first chapters,

newsletters, contests,

author interviews, and more!

# Must-Reads!

**FORGOTTEN JUSTICE**
*The truth could destroy his
one chance at love. . . .*

**THE PEACEMAKER**
*Bullheaded Wynne Elliot has one
goal in mind: to shoot Cass Claxton
dead for leaving her at the altar and
running off with her money.*

Visit **www.heartquest.com** today!